ROBERT B. PARKER'S
KICKBACK

A SPENSER NOVEL

BY

ACE ATKINS

NO EXIT PRESS

First published in 2016
by No Exit Press,
an imprint of Oldcastle Books Ltd,
PO Box 394, Harpenden, Herts, AL5 1XJ, UK

noexit.co.uk

ISBN
978-1-84344-738-2 (print)
978-1-84344-739-9 (epub)
978-1-84344-740-5 (kindle)
978-1-84344-741-2 (pdf)

2 4 6 8 10 9 7 5 3 1

Typeset in 10.5pt Minion Pro
by Geethik Technologies Pvt Ltd., India
Printed and bound in Denmark by Norhaven

For more information about Crime Fiction go to @crimetimeuk

For Mel Farman,
A true friend to both authors

Maybe he shouldn't have gone out and celebrated. Maybe he should have stuck around for the vanilla ice cream after the lasagna victory meal. But what-ifs and should-haves didn't cut it the next morning as the gray dawn crept up at five a.m. over a row of clapboard houses with peeling blue and green paint. You could smell the Merrimack River rolling by.

The cops were there. They were talking to the old man with the gun.

The boy stood in the open, his pal Tim already in a squad car. Tim's old man's Coupe de Ville getting hooked up to a tow truck with spinning lights. His parents were going to freak.

Another cop was talking to the boy now, wanting to know how much they had to drink.

'I don't know,' he said. 'A beer. Maybe two.'

'That's illegal,' the cop said. 'You're only seventeen.'

'Yeah,' he said, not caring for a lecture, knowing he was screwed. 'No shit.'

The cop just shook his head. He was young, maybe five years older than the boy. The cop stood ramrod straight, had hair clipped close like he'd been in the military. He wrote down some notes, wanting to know the boy's parents' phone number.

'It's just my dad,' he said. 'I live with my dad.'

'Is your mom alive?'

'Yeah,' he said. 'But I don't talk to her. Listen, this is a big mistake. We weren't doing nothing. We were just fooling around and that crazy old guy comes busting out the garage door waving his pistol and saying he was going to blow our brains out.'

'Why were you in his garage?'

'We were lost,' the kid said. 'We ran out of gas.'

'Is the car stolen?'

'No, it's not stolen,' the kid said. 'It belongs to my friend. It was his grandfather's and then his father's. He rebuilt the engine. Now it's his. Kind of.'

'What do you mean "kind of his?"' the cop said.

'It's his,' the kid said. 'His old man lets him use it when he wants. He's gonna get the title on the Caddy when we graduate.'

'What school?'

'Blackburn,' he said. 'I go to Blackburn High. Am I getting charged with something? Because I don't see what we did. I mean, we're not the one with the gun.'

The cop looked over to a squad car and an older cop with stripes on his sleeve. The old man nodded to the younger. Out came the handcuffs.

'Shit,' the kid said. 'I knew it. I fucking knew it.'

The night was gone, slipping into a dull bluish-gray morning, roadwork light when he'd wake up and jog those five miles. Every day. Even Sunday. He wasn't an all-night-party kind of guy. But Tim had told his parents he was staying with him and he'd told his dad he'd be at Tim's. They didn't have anywhere to go after the party was over. There were girls and beer. Danielle had been there with that older guy and he wasn't about to leave first. Now the spinning blue lights.

'You're being charged with attempted burglary,' the cop said. 'You got some beer in the car. And we found a controlled substance.'

'Shit.' The girl from the party, the one Tim had made out with, had given them a few pills. They didn't know what they were, didn't even ask. Tim had tried to be cool, stick them in his pocket. Now they were drug dealers.

Yesterday morning, he'd stood on the podium with a gold medal around his neck for winning his weight class in Worcester. His dad had been proud. His coach. His grandmother had cooked a big Italian meal for them, even turning off the TV as they said grace. She'd made lasagna, a big salad to keep him healthy and in shape, ice cream since the next wrestling tournament was weeks away. It had been a perfect day. Damn near everything had clicked into place.

Now he was being pushed into the back of a squad car with Tim. He'd like to be mad at his friend, but this wasn't his fault. No one forced him into that garage to see if they could find a can of gas. Controlled substance? Now he'd be labeled a drug addict, too.

He tried to calm himself, think rationally. *You let your head get filled with a bunch of junk and you can't think straight.* What he did wasn't smart, but it wasn't the worst. He'd tell his dad the truth. He'd never lied to him. His dad knew some Blackburn cops and they'd straighten out the whole mess.

This was a mistake. A really bad mistake, but just a screwup. Nothing like this ever screwed up a person's whole life. A person does the right thing every day of his life and that has to mean something. A kid pushes himself to run faster, lift more, not ever quit. You build up some kind of points for that. Right?

'Can I have my phone back?' he said.

The cop didn't answer.

'Don't I get to make a call?'

'You can do that at juvie intake,' the cop said. The young cop wasn't looking at him as he slammed the door shut.

'What do we do now?' he said to Tim.

'Pray hard and fast,' Tim said. 'We're freakin' screwed.'

1

On the first day of February, the coldest day of the year so far, I took it as a very good omen that a woman I'd never met brought me a sandwich. I had my pair of steel-toed Red Wings kicked up on the corner of my desk, thawing out, when she arrived. My morning coffee and two corn muffins were a distant memory.

She laid down the sandwich wrapped in wax paper and asked if my name was Spenser.

'Depends on the sandwich.'

'A grinder from Coppa in the South End,' she said. 'Extra provolone and pickled cherry peppers.'

'Then my name is Spenser,' I said. 'With an *S* like the English poet.'

'Rita said you were easy.'

'If you mean Rita Fiore, she's not one to judge.'

'She also said you're tough.'

'True.'

'And hardheaded.'

'Also true,' I said. 'And did she say if you scratched behind my left ear my leg would shake?'

'No,' the woman said, squeezing into a client chair. 'But when I told her my problems, she said to go see Spenser.'

'And bring him a sandwich?'

'She said that would help.'

I shrugged and walked over to the Mr Coffee on top of my file cabinet, poured a cup, and offered her one. She declined. I mixed in a little sugar, set the spoon on the cabinet, and moved back to my desk. My peacoat and Brooklyn Dodgers cap hung neatly from my coat tree.

'You can go ahead and eat,' she said. 'Don't let it get cold.'

I unwrapped the sandwich, which was still miraculously warm, and took a bite. I nodded with appreciation. The woman had indeed made a friend. Outside, traffic bustled and zoomed along Berkeley and Boylston. It was still early, but dark and insular, with snow predicted all week. I had crossed winter days off the calendar until opening day for the Sox.

'My name is Sheila Yates,' she said. 'Three weeks ago, my son Dillon was taken from me by the state of Massachusetts. He was sentenced to nine months in a juvie facility out in the harbor.'

She motioned with her chin as if you could see the harbor from the Back Bay. I was still able to leap medium-size buildings in a single bound, but my X-ray vision was a bit iffy. Sheila was big and blond, with thick, overly styled hair, a lot of makeup, and gold jewelry. She wore a blue sweater and blue jeans under a heavy camel-colored coat. She also wore a lot of perfume, which in small quantities might have been pleasant.

'What did he do?' I said.

'Jack shit.'

'Okay,' I said. 'What was he charged with?'

'Terrorism, stalking, and making physical threats against a school administrator.'

I started to whistle, but my mouth was full. I chewed and swallowed and then took a sip of coffee.

'You want to know what he really did?'

I nodded.

'He set up a fake Twitter account for his vice principal,' she said. 'He's a funny kid. Although some might say he's a smart-ass.'

'I like him already.'

'Does any of this make sense to you?'

'What did your lawyer say?'

'Then?' Sheila said. 'We didn't have a lawyer. I couldn't make the hearing. I had to work or I'd get fired, so Dillon's grandfather took him. It's my mistake. I would have never signed that stupid piece of paper. It waived his right to an attorney.'

'Not good.'

'You bet your ass,' she said. 'Rita's now got a young attorney at her firm to help.'

'Did he make threatening remarks on Twitter?' I said.

'No way,' she said. 'It was all a big joke. He may have wrote something about the guy getting his privates stuck in an appliance. He did say the guy liked to garden in the nude.'

'In all fairness,' I said, 'pruning shears could be dangerous.'

'You get it,' Sheila said. 'It's a gag.'

'I've been doing this for a long time,' I said. 'And in those years it never ceases to amaze me the great wealth of people born without a sense of humor.'

Sheila took in a large breath, threw her hands up in the air, jewelry clanging, and said, 'Oh, thank God,' she said. 'So you'll help me?'

'What can I do?' I said. 'Sounds like Rita's firm is on it.'

'They are,' she said. 'But while they're filing papers and stuff, I want to know how this crap happened. Rita says it's one of the craziest things she's ever heard.'

'Where was he charged?'

'Blackburn.'

'Ah,' I said. 'The Riviera of the North.'

'Wasn't my choice to live there,' she said. 'I grew up in Newton. I took a job there after I split with Dillon's dad. You do what you can.'

I nodded. I reached over the sandwich for a yellow legal pad and wrote her name at the top left corner. I asked her for a phone number and an address. I asked her son's full legal name and his date of birth. She told me more about the charges and then a lot about the judge.

'Judge Scali,' she said. 'He's a class-A prick.'

'Now, that's a campaign slogan.'

'He's the Zero Tolerance for Minors guy,' she said. 'You know who I'm talking about now? He's all over the news and on the radio. He says what he does is tough love. Says parents that complain can deal with him now or go see their kids at Walpole later.'

'Never heard of him.'

'Well, he's a big freakin' deal in Blackburn,' she said. 'Everyone up there is afraid of him. They think his word is God. The DA, the public defender, the cops. No one will listen to me. That's when I called Rita. I used to work in the business office at Cone, Oakes. I don't have a law degree, but I know when I'm being jerked around.'

'How's Dillon?'

'They won't let me see him,' she said, reaching into her purse for a tissue. 'They won't let me talk to him but once every couple weeks. They say it's part of his rehabilitation out on Fortune Island. Rehabbing what? Being a wise guy? These people up there are nuts.' She started to cry but then just as quickly wiped her eyes and sat up.

I leaned back into my chair. I crossed my arms over my chest. 'I can't make any promises,' I said. 'But I can check into things. Maybe find out something to help your attorney for appeals.'

'Thank God,' she said. 'When can you start?'

I looked down at the day planner on my desk. I flipped through several empty pages. 'How about tomorrow?'

'Jesus, you mean it?' she said, standing, coming around the desk. As I stood, she reached to hug me. I didn't return the embrace, only patted her back a couple times. 'You know I probably can't afford your day rate, whatever it is. I saw how much some snoops charged the firm.'

'Outrageous.'

'But you'll help anyway?'

I nodded. She walked back to the client chair and grabbed her big purse. She did not sit. I looked down at my desk and saw my sandwich waiting, only one bite mark in place. The coffee had probably grown cold.

'Thank you,' she said. 'I haven't been able to sleep or eat since this happened. I blame my dad. I blame myself. The only person I don't blame is Dillon.'

'Doesn't sound like it's his fault.'

'He's a good kid,' she said. 'He doesn't deserve to be treated like this.'

'Nobody does.'

'Everyone in Blackburn says I'm an outsider,' she said. 'They tell me to let this all play out. Keep my mouth shut. Don't piss people off.'

'Let me piss 'em off,' I said.

'I heard you're good at that.'

'Yeah,' I said. 'I've had years of practice.'

2

Blackburn, Massachusetts, didn't appear on many tourist maps of New England. The old mill town, about thirty miles north of Boston on I-93, had lost any of its Norman Rockwell charm long ago. The huge brick mills stood like forgotten fortresses along the slow-moving black water of the Merrimack. The skies were gray. A light snow was falling. As I crossed over a rusting metal bridge, I saw ice chunks in the river. I made a mental note: only sixty-nine days until opening day.

I drove around a bit, cruising the downtown and Central Avenue toward the Victorian-era city hall. Most of the storefronts sat empty. I passed the police station, an all-night diner called The Owl, a Vietnamese grocery, and several corner bars. There was the high end of town with an upstart coffee shop and a ladies' boutique. There was a low end of town with Farman's Salvage and a scratch-and-dent furniture warehouse. I soon ended up in front of Blackburn High School and parked in a space reserved for the school resource officer.

Might as well start making friends now.

Blackburn High looked to have been built in the twenties, constructed of blondish brick and dull glass blocks. According to a sign, it was home to the Fighting Eagles. I checked in at the office, as thuggish middle-aged men were often frowned upon for wandering school corridors. And these days, schools were locked down after the first bell.

A dour-looking woman in an oversized T-shirt reading ACHIEVE! issued me a badge, unlocked the entrance, and gave me directions to where I was headed.

The school had that familiar scent of old books and disinfectants. Being in school always tightened my stomach. My best day in high school had been graduation.

I found Officer Lorenzo sitting at his desk, hunched over a computer and not looking up even after I knocked on his open door. He was a fat guy with a couple chins in need of a shave. He wore a baseball hat, too small for his big head, with an embroidered law enforcement star reading Blackburn Police Department. I waited in the doorway until he could summon the energy to look up at me. To call his appearance sloth-like was a true insult to the animal kingdom.

'Fill out the form,' he said. 'You can drop it at the front desk.'

He had yet to look up.

I didn't speak. Finally he lifted his eyes, refocusing.

'Yeah?'

'I'm not here for the form.'

'Aren't you a sub?'

'Do I look like a sub?'

'You look like me,' he said. 'A guy who loads trucks.'

'Well, I'm not here to award you officer of the year.'

'Ha, ha,' he said. 'Then what the hell do you want?'

I took a seat without being asked. His minuscule office was very sloppy, filled with stacks of newspapers, old copies of *Guns & Ammo,* and a shelf full of playbook binders. He'd fitted cardboard in the windows to keep out any light. He assessed me through smudged metal-frame glasses and shifted on his sizable rump.

I handed him a card across the desk. He took a very long time to read my name, occupation, and phone number. Cops in schools were still strange to me. But these days, it was the norm.

'Yeah?' he said.

'I work for Sheila Yates,' I said. 'Earlier this year, you arrested her son Dillon for setting up a Twitter profile for Vice Principal Waters. You charged him with stalking, making physical threats, and terrorism.'

'Goddamn right I did,' he said, crossing his meaty arms across his chest. 'That's all done with.'

15

'Not for Dillon,' I said. 'He's cooling his heels out on Fortune Island, which I gather isn't Boys Town.'

'Not my business,' he said. 'The kid was nuts. He's got mental problems.'

'How so?'

Officer Lorenzo leaned forward, took a sip from a plastic Coke bottle, and leaned back into his seat. His chair was under considerable duress and creaked loudly during the process. 'You clear this? Because you can't just walk in here and start asking me a lot of questions.'

'I checked in at the office,' I said. 'They told me all law enforcement matters were your turf.'

He smiled, eyeing me with new enthusiasm. The man in charge. The top dog. Still, I wanted to reach over and clean his glasses.

'You ever been a cop, Spenser?'

'Sure.'

'Then you know what kind of crap these kids are capable of,' he said. 'I back down an inch, show I'm weak, and they'll take advantage of it. I see them looking at me like I'm just some fat doofus. They think protecting this school is a joke. I start laughing with them and the next thing I know some kid like Dillon Yates is running down the halls with an AR-15.'

'Quite a step up from cracking jokes.'

'You can't give an inch,' Lorenzo said. 'Not a fucking inch.'

'No one wants to see a fat doofus in charge.'

'Damn right.'

I couldn't tell if he was doing Eastwood or Wayne. He seemed more along the lines of Roscoe Arbuckle. 'Okay,' I said. 'So tell me what concerned you about what he did.'

'Have you met Luke Waters?' he said.

I shook my head.

'He's a class guy,' he said. 'You know? Grew up in Blackburn and loves this town. He coaches the ninth-grade football team. Lives his life for these kids. This guy went from being respected to kids snickering behind his back because of that Yates kid. Last time he held an assembly he couldn't even get kids to sit still and listen. It broke his heart.'

'Wow.'

'What did Dillon's mom tell you? That these were just some smart-aleck remarks?'

'Pretty much.'

'The kid wrote some highly disturbing things on that tweeter thing,' he said. 'You know what I'm talking about? All the kids mess with that crap.'

'My fans run my account.'

'Well, I saw what he wrote. He kept on running down Vice President Waters. He wrote about crazy sexual shit and mutilations. We took it as a genuine threat.'

Lorenzo widened his eyes as if the vagueness was enough. I nodded a few times in mock understanding. 'For instance?'

'I don't have to discuss all this with you,' he said. 'Go talk with the chief. I'm a Blackburn police officer, and I did my duty to charge the kid. It was up to the judge to decide what to do.'

'Nine months is a bit excessive,' I said. 'For something written online.'

'Kid's sentencing isn't my department,' he said. 'You think I'm tough? You haven't met Judge Scali. He's the true ballbuster in this town.'

'I can't wait.'

'He doesn't care what you think, or the parents think, or any of the bleeding hearts,' he said. 'The judge was elected on Zero Tolerance and he means it. Since he's taken the bench, he's cut juvenile crime in half. He doesn't let shit slide like you people in Boston. He knows if he doesn't reach kids now, they're gonna be sticking a gun in someone's face tomorrow. It's tough love, but it works. I seen it happen.'

'Even if there's no crime committed?'

Lorenzo shook his head. 'You got sold a bill of goods, Boston,' he said. 'You got a couple parents around here who won't get with the program and they say life is unfair. I don't feel sorry for them in the least.'

'Can I see the report?'

'No,' he said.

'That's fine,' I said. 'I've got a release from his mother.'

'Good luck, then,' he said. 'Why'd you want to see me?'

'I wanted to meet the man who started all this.'

The fat man stood, showing he was much shorter than expected, which was perhaps the source of his irritability. He put his hands on his hips as if to show our conversation was over. He adjusted his BPD cap and tried in vain to suck in his gut. 'Don't expect a lot of cooperation in Blackburn,' he said. 'All your liberal crap doesn't fly here. It's a tough town to grow up in, and tough love is the only way we keep things safe. Understand now?'

I saluted him. He scowled back.

'How about you tell me this? Just what exactly did Dillon Yates write that got the vice principal so upset?'

'No way.'

'Doesn't matter,' I said. 'I can look it up. I just thought you'd stand behind your charge.'

'Goddamn right I do,' Lorenzo said, and reached up with his hand to rub both chins. 'What the hell. I'll tell you.'

I waited.

Lorenzo ran a finger under his nose and sniffed. He took a couple breaths. I tried to ease my quickening heart.

'He said Luke Waters got his dick stuck in a VCR.'

I stifled a laugh. Lorenzo didn't like it.

'You think that's fucking funny?' he said.

'I do,' I said. 'Man versus technology is always comedy gold.'

He glowered. It made me want to laugh even more.

On the way out, I winked at him and walked out into the hall, nearly knocking down a gawky girl fiddling with a locker. She looked embarrassed and smiled at me, pulling back a blackened streak from her otherwise white-blond hair.

I peered back into the open door, just in time to see Lorenzo tossing my business card in the trash.

3

The criminal courthouse was on Blackburn's highest hill, across from the city cemetery and a public housing complex. The building was old and stately, as it should be, with a lot of brass, marble, and dark oak inside. Cavernous, with the air quality of a museum or a summerhouse shut up for the winter. On the first floor, an art nouveau bronze statue of blind Lady Justice stood proud but tarnished, with courtrooms on both sides of an open staircase leading to the clerk's office. I bypassed a curving staircase for an elevator. I'd recently had surgery on my right knee.

A life's work of busting heads and kicking butts could be hard on the joints.

Upstairs, I found a frizzy-haired blondish woman not so hard at work at a computer. The building wasn't well heated or insulated. The frizzy-haired woman wore a blue overcoat and fingerless gloves at her desk. When I leaned in, I saw she was checking her Facebook account.

I gave her a high-wattage, dynamite smile and slid across a faxed release from Sheila Yates. She glanced up at me, somehow immune to my charms, and then down at the paper. I considered arching an eyebrow but I didn't want her falling out of her chair.

'What's that?' she said.

'A parental release.'

'For what?'

'For all police and court files related to one Dillon Yates.'

'Is he a minor?'

'Indeed he is.'

'Well, all juvenile records are sealed,' she said, with little remorse. Clicking away.

19

'Not to parents,' I said.

'Are you the parent?'

'I don't think so.'

'Law enforcement?'

'Not for a long while,' I said. 'I don't like to wake up early.'

'Sorry,' she said, with even less remorse. 'I really can't help you.'

I reached into my wallet and showed her that I'd been licensed by the Commonwealth as a private investigator. She glanced down at the license, unimpressed. I wondered what she'd have thought of my Napoleon Solo all-access badge. As she looked back at me, I arched the eyebrow. *Oh, what the hell.*

'Doesn't matter,' she said. 'The parent may view the file. But may not take the file with them or make copies.'

'The parent has signed the release,' I said. 'The release is now on your desk.'

'You can't just go and transfer parental rights.'

'I am not seeking to be the kid's parent,' I said. 'I am seeking access to the files to help with his court case.'

She looked at her screen, not switching over to a database, keeping it on her personal Facebook page. 'Has the case been adjudicated?'

'Yep.'

'Then how are you going to help?'

'Ever heard of an appeal?' I said.

She didn't answer, returning to her Facebook page, clicking away. I glanced down and saw her smile at a photo of a couple kittens in a basket of flowers.

'Always cute seeing tax dollars at work,' I said and left.

I ungracefully took the marble steps down to the lobby, past Lady Justice, my work boots echoing through the giant courthouse with each methodical step. The courthouse seemed empty, oddly quiet, and with all the personality of a mausoleum. I would have to return with some legal saberrattling from Cone, Oakes. Sometimes a threatening letter was better than a .357.

20

Back out into the spitting snow, I found a Blackburn PD patrol car had parked behind my Ford Explorer. A cop was examining my license tag and writing down the numbers. This town was just getting better and better.

The cemetery stretched out far and wide behind where we both stood. Last week's snow sat piled up high and dirty on the curbs.

I crossed the street, leaned against my SUV, and waited. The cop was a young, thin guy with the high-and-tight haircut of ex-military. If he hadn't been in the Army, he needed a refund from the barber. He wore wraparound sunglasses and one of those satiny blue cop jackets with a Sherpa collar. His prowl car idled, throwing out a lot of exhaust in the cold. When he finished writing down what he needed, he turned to spit.

I didn't offer to shake hands.

'Sir, were you at Blackburn High School this morning?' he said.

'Yep.'

'Why was that?'

'Signing up for Glee Club,' I said.

'A little old for that,' he said. 'Aren't you?' He stared at me with the black bug lenses of his sunglasses.

I smiled back and said, 'I do a mean Lady Gaga.'

'Vice Principal Waters said you were found roaming the halls,' he said. 'We take school security very seriously in Blackburn. Now, you want to tell me what you were doing?'

'I met with Officer Lorenzo about a legal matter. Why don't you call him?'

'That's not what we heard from Mr Waters.'

'Maybe Luke Waters is still sore after his encounter with the VCR.'

The young cop changed up his stance a little, called into dispatch from a mic he wore on his heavy jacket. The dispatcher came back with a rundown of my vehicle registration. I hoped my parking ticket collection didn't show up. I hadn't paid a ticket since the Flynn administration. The cop stared at me as he listened to dispatch.

'We could get you for trespassing,' he said. 'But I let you off with a warning.'

21

'Terrific,' I said. 'Thanks so much.'

'You think I'm kidding, sir?' he said, giving me his best hard look.

'No,' I said. 'But someone's giving you some bum information.'

He turned his head and spit again. He held the notebook in his hand and just stared at me. The patrol car continued to idle. I smiled at him. 'I'd stay clear of Blackburn, sir,' he said. 'Just please go on back to Boston.'

'I'm just a rambling boy who won't settle down,' I said. 'This just ain't my kind of town.'

The young cop didn't react, only turned and walked back to his prowlie, flipped it into drive, and drove off. I watched his taillights disappear over the hill.

Blackburn was going to be more fun than I thought.

4

When I got back to Boston, Susan met me at my apartment, standing in the doorway and holding an empty dog leash.

'Well, that looks interesting,' I said. 'Please be gentle.'

'Get your running shoes on, Fido,' she said. 'We've been waiting.'

Ten minutes later, we'd crossed Storrow Drive and were walking at a brisk pace along the Charles River. The river was frozen and covered in snowdrifts, looking barren. Few were so foolish as to be out exercising. But I was protected in my cold-weather gear, thermal underwear under navy sweatpants and a sweatshirt cut to the elbows with a watch cap. Susan wore black yoga pants and a gray Harvard sweatshirt under a ski jacket.

Pearl pulled Susan along, and we both strained to keep up. When it came to knee rehab, Susan made Henry Cimoli look like Florence Nightingale. But the knee had improved, the limp all but gone.

We followed the river, went over the Harvard Bridge, and took the path by the MIT boathouse and then went back to the river. The

Longfellow Bridge was still under renovation, tall wooden panels and chain-link fencing closing off the work. We cut through Beacon Hill and made our way down Charles and into the Public Garden, most of the green space hidden in mounds of snow.

'I miss the tulips,' she said. 'And anything green.'

'I miss the swan boats,' I said, 'baseball, and short skirts. Not necessarily in that order.'

Pearl's tongue lolled from her mouth. I tried to keep my tongue in place. I found it more dignified.

The night was full on, streetlamps blooming yellow light over snowbanks and skeletal trees. We made our way across Arlington, down Marlborough, and finally back up to my apartment. Once upstairs and inside, I opened the refrigerator and found a six-pack of Abita Turbodog. Susan and Pearl drank water.

'How'd it go in Blackburn, kiddo?' she said, leaning her fanny against my kitchen counter. She removed her hooded sweatshirt to reveal a snug-fitting black exercise top. As always, I felt a familiar surge zap through my chest. She noticed the staring and smiled, her teeth very even and white, her delicate face flushed from the cold wind.

'I was greeted with open arms,' I said. 'Everyone couldn't be more helpful. I pointed out the error of their ways and all charges against the kid were dismissed.'

'Uh-huh,' Susan said. 'They ran you out of town on a rail.'

'Not yet,' I said. 'But I heard they're prepping the rail.'

'Administrators seldom see the error of their ways,' she said. 'Why do you think I ditched the guidance-counselor gig?'

'Because you longed to be a shrink with a fancy Ph.D.?'

'I liked the kids,' she said. 'The administrators mostly sucked.'

I sat on a bar stool and stretched out my leg, pulling up the sweatpants to examine the new scar. 'I won't get much help,' I said. 'This judge who sentenced the kid is pretty popular among the yokels. They think he's keeping down the juvie crime.'

'Is he?'

'I don't know.'

'Maybe he's just an asshole?'

'That would be my guess.'

'You can't overturn a decision based on the guy being a jerk,' Susan said. 'I've worked with a lot of kids in that system. The judges have a free hand. You just hope they're fair.'

'My client believes there's something hinkier than just the judge being an a-hole,' I said. 'She thinks there's a conspiracy up there.'

'About what?'

'She doesn't know,' I said. 'She just knows a lot of kids are being railroaded through this system.'

'Are you being paid on this?'

I took a deep breath. 'My fee hasn't been discussed.'

'You did recently get a nice paycheck from Kinjo Heywood,' she said. 'You can afford to do one off the books.'

I stood and filled a pot with water to boil. I'd had red beans with andouille sausage simmering in a Crock-Pot all day. I added rice to the water when it boiled, then I started to chop green peppers and onions. My chopping was quick but masterly. I placed a baguette from the Flour Bakery in the oven.

I opened a second bottle of Abita, interspersing sips of beer with a glass of water. I pulled out some plates and opened a bottle of sauvignon blanc for Susan. I put an old Louis Jordan album on the turntable.

'While you slave over the stove, I'll freshen up,' she said.

'A truly modern relationship.'

'Would you rather me cook?'

'We each have our talents.'

Pearl trotted into the kitchen. 'And the baby's?' she said.

I tossed a hunk of baguette into the air. Pearl caught it.

'Kitchen detail,' I said.

'And mine?' Susan said.

'Besides helping the depressed, the neurotic, and the true wackos of Boston and Cambridge?'

'Yes.'

24

'How graphic would you like me to get?' I set down the knife, walked up close, and wrapped my arms around her small waist. Susan whispered things into my ear that would have made a fleet of sailors blush. I held her tighter.

We kissed as the rice simmered, and until I felt a buzzing in my pants. Susan laughed.

It buzzed again. Susan stepped back as I reached for my cell. She disappeared into my bedroom. I read through a text message and set the phone down.

'First day of school and I'm a big hit,' I said, yelling to the bedroom. 'Young girls already texting me.'

'Should I be jealous?' Susan said.

'Only if I take my letterman jacket out of mothballs.'

'Do you even own a letterman jacket?'

'Of course,' I said. 'She wants to meet tomorrow.'

'What's her name?'

'I'm not sure,' I said. 'She refers to Dillon as her BFF.'

'Maybe someone is trying to set you up.' I heard the shower start to run.

'Of course.' I sipped the beer and listened to Louis sing. 'But there's only one way to find out.'

He stayed fifteen days in Lawrence before two cops in a black van drove him to the Blackburn courthouse. They forced him to change into an orange jumpsuit, shackled his wrists, and led him up a back stairway and into a small courtroom with a tall ceiling. Every word and every move seemed to echo off the wooden walls. He was told to sit down in the front row and shut up. He turned to see his dad standing in the back row. His dad wore a suit. He didn't even know his dad had a suit.

Up on the bench was the judge, a short, Italian-looking guy with black hair and wearing a black robe. He didn't seem big or tough. The judge had on a Patriots Super Bowl cap and laughed it up with two bailiffs who wore guns. The judge spoke low, but something he said really set off the two men. They laughed hard.

He looked back to his dad. His dad caught his eye and nodded back.

Maybe he'd fixed the thing. Maybe his dad had called one of his cop pals and all this would go away. What he wanted more than anything was a shower and McDonald's. He'd had dreams last night about a double cheese and fries.

He looked down the row at the other kids brought in. He didn't see Tim, which was strange. Tim had been with him at Lawrence and then gone. He figured that they wanted to keep them separate, make sure they couldn't connect their stories like cops talked about on Law & Order.

The shackles and orange jumpsuit made the boy depressed and humiliated. He wanted his street clothes back.

The judge took off his Tats cap, showing a long strand of black hair plastered to his pale scalp. He nodded to a bailiff, who told everyone to rise. The room was very quiet and hot, smelling of a stale furnace. The judge flipped through some folders, his eyes never looking at all the faces crammed into the courtroom. Not nervous. Just seeming not to care. He wore the kind of glasses that had a purplish tint and would turn full dark in the sun.

The boy hunched his shoulders and looked down at his hands. He waited for his name to be called. He was a big kid, big for his age, but today he felt small.

It was Wednesday, and he'd already missed two weeks of school. He wondered what his friends would say. What his wrestling coach would say. This was senior year, and he couldn't have something like this in his file. Everything had to be perfect for a scholarship.

He never expected the room to be so crowded and so hot. He grew hungrier. More kids were led inside wearing orange jumpsuits, boys and girls. All of them with bound wrists. Some of the new kids' names were read before his. He figured it took nearly three hours before his name was called.

He stood, looked back to his dad. But his dad had disappeared.

He looked to the bench and the doorway he'd entered. His dad was gone.

The bailiff pushed him along until he stood before the judge. Judge Scali looked down from on high at the boy. He rubbed his face as he considered the papers in front of him.

'You go to Blackburn?' he said.

'Yes, sir,' the boy said.

'Did you come and hear me speak in the fall?' he said. 'Or were you skipping school?'

'I heard it,' the boy said. 'You came to our auditorium.'

'And what did I say?'

'Stay off drugs?' the boy said. Some kids snickered behind him and Scali shot them a mean glance.

'What else?'

'Stay out of trouble,' the boy said.

'Or what?'

'You didn't give second chances.'

The judge smiled. His glass lenses a deep purple. 'That's right,' he said. 'And so you rode around in a stolen car and then tried to rob an old man?'

'No, sir.'

Scali shook his head. He breathed deeply. He looked to a bailiff and shook his head like the boy made him sick. 'Are you telling me the police are lying?'

'No, sir.'

'I know the police in this town,' Scali said. 'I never even met you. You've been charged with car theft and attempted robbery. Do you understand your charges?'

The boy looked back behind him for his father. He searched each side of the courtroom but couldn't find him.

'Look at me,' Scali said. 'Listen to me.'

The boy nodded.

'I want you to listen good,' Scalia said. 'I'm going to give you a break here today.'

The boy felt like he could breathe. He nodded to the judge.

'You may not appreciate it now,' he said. 'But in ten years, you'll remember this day as the one that turned your life around.'

The boy's mouth was made of cotton. He couldn't swallow.

'I'm sentencing you to eighteen months at the MCC camp on Fortune Island,' he said.

The boy wanted to speak but the words wouldn't come. He felt the bailiff's big hands on his biceps, pulling him away from the bench.

'Next case,' Scali said, already forgetting him.

5

I was back in Blackburn bright and early the next morning. I bought some corn muffins and a regular coffee at Dunkin' and sat in my Explorer with the engine running and the heat on high. Downriver, the Merrimack's black water moved slow and sluggish under the thinnest sheen of ice. 'By June our brook would run out of song and speed,' I said, between bites of muffin.

Not much later, a girl walked in front of my SUV. She was tall and, like many tall teenage girls, slumped in a self-conscious way. She had a longish nose, not much chin, and stick-thin legs. She wore a puffy silver coat, blue jeans, and tall rubber boots. Her hair was a light blond with a black streak blowing across her face. When I got out, I recognized her from the hallway yesterday. I had nearly run over her.

She nodded at me. 'You work for Dillon's mom?'

'I do.'

'And you wanted to find out why that moron arrested him for nothing?'

'That's the idea.'

We stood in the shadow of the old mill, beside a city park with a snow-covered amphitheater. I asked her if she'd like to sit in my truck where it was warmer. Nothing like a middle-aged man trying to talk a teenager into his car. Even as the words came out of my mouth, I felt like a creeper. All I needed was to start keeping candy in my pocket.

'I'm already late for school.'

'I can drive you.'

'I'm okay,' she said. The girl held a battered purple backpack loose in her hand and hung there for a moment, seeming not to know what to say. She had a dark complexion with black eyes. The blond hair was probably fake but the streak was the original color. She shook a little in the cold wind.

'You fished my card from the trash?' I said.

29

'That asshole ran off to talk to Waters just as soon as you left.'

'He looked as though he needed the exercise.'

'Last year he broke into my best friend's locker and found a half-pint of gin,' she said. 'They arrested her and I haven't seen her since. She was sent to some camp for girls. They make them raise vegetables and sing songs.'

'A lot of that going around?'

She nodded. She looked around as if the trees had ears. She peered up into the empty windows of the endless mill that probably coaxed her ancestors over away from the potato famine. The girl shifted her feet and squinted at my face, hands deep into the pockets of her puffy coat. She pulled the long streak of black out of her eyes. I wondered how much it cost to have all but one streak dyed or if she'd done it herself. Probably herself.

'How many?'

'How many what?' she said.

'Kids are getting sent off?'

'I don't know,' she said. 'Maybe ten, twelve from my grade. I know there are a lot of others. No one wants to make a big deal about it. You're afraid to even open your mouth. You get labeled as a problem and they'll ship you off.'

'What about probation?'

'Haven't you heard?' she said. 'No second chances in Blackburn. You get arrested and you're done. Not just in school, but your whole life. You're a freakin' criminal.'

'What's your name?'

'I don't want to get in trouble.'

'You won't get in trouble,' I said. 'I just don't know what to call you.'

'Beth.'

'Beth what?'

'Beth Golnick.'

'Okay, Beth Golnick,' I said. 'You sure I can't give you a ride?'

She looked at her cell phone and then back at me. 'You could let me out at the gas station, down the street.'

'Sure,' I said. 'Wherever you like.'

We got into my Explorer and circled out of the lot. I adjusted the vent and the girl placed her hands in front of the blower. The wind had been sharp over the river. We drove along Central into the downtown and then turned toward the high school.

'Dillon was my friend,' she said. 'He didn't deserve this. He was just joking. He should have gotten detention, not sent to that prison.'

'Why do you think they sent him?'

'To scare us,' Beth said. 'They want to control our whole lives. They can't stand it that they can only tell us what to do at school. They want to watch everything we do at home, too.'

'Why don't the parents do something?'

'They're afraid,' Beth said. 'All the grown-ups around here have their own problems. They're scared to speak up. I mean, a lot of them are Cambodian or Vietnamese and don't even speak English. Some are from South America. My older brother, who's like six years older than me, said they had some real trouble with gangs and drugs when he was in school. He says it's different now. Better.'

'And now the school is abusing their power?'

'The school and the police.'

'They're together in this?'

'Yeah,' she said. 'Of course.'

'Can you give me the names of some kids who've been sent away?'

'I don't know.'

'Can you find out?' I said. 'It would help me to help Dillon.'

'Umm,' she said. 'I can ask around.'

I drove through Blackburn, keeping the girl talking, but it wasn't long until the school came into view. I spotted the gas station down the road and slowed beside the pumps. The gas station, like most things in the town, hadn't changed much in fifty years. The place advertised fuel with a red neon mule that said IT KICKS!

'You know,' she said. 'You're wasting your time.'

'How so?'

'Newspaper wrote something about all this last year,' she said.

31

'And?'

'And nothing,' she said. 'Shit happens. Nobody cares.'

'I care.'

'About Dillon, 'cause you're paid,' she said. 'What about the others?'

'One kid at a time.'

6

A big metal sign for *The Star* still advertised the newspaper from the top of the city's tallest building. But the building had long been condemned and *The Star* had relocated to a redbrick storefront several blocks away. An antique printing press sat dusty behind a plate-glass window surrounded by framed front pages of Extra editions: *Victory Over Japan, Man Walks on Moon, Nixon Quits,* and the October when the *Curse Was Reversed.*

I doubted the paper was printed anymore. If it was, it was probably the size of a Bazooka Joe comic. I walked inside to find anyone who was left.

The ceiling was high and the walls were exposed brick. There were maybe a dozen desks, all empty except for two. A young white man and an older black woman sat staring at laptops. The white kid hopped up and approached the front desk. He wore a wrinkled blue dress shirt and a loose black tie around his skinny neck. Hip.

'News?' I said.

He seemed disappointed that I didn't want to take out an ad. Maybe if all went well with this case I could open a branch office in Blackburn. The kid jerked a thumb over his shoulder. 'Over there,' he said.

The woman was heavyset but not fat, with a very short Afro and enormous gold hoop earrings. Her blouse was red and long-sleeved, with a keyhole cinch at the top. Black slacks and black boots. She looked to be in her late fifties or early sixties, with a bit of gray showing up in her hair. She wore canvas braces on her wrists and loosened them as she leaned back from her typing.

I smiled at her. She barely glanced up at me.

I told her I was an investigator from Boston. 'I understand you worked on a piece about Judge Scali last year.'

'*Mmhm,*' she said.

'I understand he's got quite a reputation,' I said.

'*Mmhm.*'

'Nice weather we're having.'

She looked over the top of her reading glasses and pulled off the wrist braces. She tilted her head, staring at me as if I'd come to the wrong place. I just smiled back. *Friendly old Spenser, community watchdog.*

'You don't remember me,' she said. 'Do you?'

'I don't,' I said. 'Should I?'

'Don't blame you,' she said. 'It's been a hell of a long time. But I sure as hell remember you, Spenser. You were looking for some fancy English book taken by some campus crazies about a million years ago.'

My face flushed. 'Iris?'

'None other, baby,' she said. 'Or you can call me the Last of the Mohicans. I wouldn't take a buyout, so I was forced up here and promoted to ME. I'm also a third of my entire staff.'

Some detective. A nameplate on her desk read IRIS MILFORD.

'How long has it been?' she said.

'Let's not think about it,' I said. 'Math makes my head hurt.'

'Mine, too,' she said. 'So tell me what you're doing up here.'

'A student was given jail time for pulling a prank at dear old Blackburn High,' I said. 'Kid's mother is my client. I'm being told this judge doesn't have much of a sense of humor.'

'Joe Scali?' she said. 'Shit. His face would fall off if he smiled.'

'Mean?'

'Yep.'

'Tough?'

33

'Yep.'

'Fair?' I said.

'Some folks aren't so sure,' she said. 'We wrote a four-part series last year on his record. He has sentenced more kids per capita than anywhere else in Mass.'

'How'd you find that out?'

'Would you believe another judge?' she said. 'He didn't like what he was hearing out of juvenile court and thought a little light needed to shine on the problem.'

'And Judge Scali apologized to all the kids.'

'Oh, yeah,' she said. 'You know it. Right after he dodged me for about two months. When I finally got him to sit down and talk, he spoke to me like I was some little girl who hadn't covered cops and courts longer than he's been on the bench. He said figures don't tell the whole story. He says that probation or house arrest has been proved to be worthless. Scali says he believes the only way to get the attention of these kids is to send them to these juvenile jails.'

'Even when they didn't commit a serious crime.'

'He blames the parents,' she said. 'Said we have a whole generation that doesn't know how to care for their kids. He said what he was doing was being father and judge.'

'God bless him.'

'Since he was put on the bench, kids doing jail time has gone up ten times in this county,' she said. 'Although they don't call it jail. What do they call it?'

'Placement?'

'Yeah, child-care placement.'

'Still jail,' I said.

She nodded. 'I asked him that,' she said. 'I asked if he ever thought about some of the kids he sentenced who hadn't committed a serious crime. And you know what he did? He just kind of stared at me. He's good at that shit, just staring, letting the question hang in the air like you shouldn't have been asking that.'

'I'm familiar with the type.'

'He said for every parent who complains to the courts or the newspaper, there are five kids and their parents who come to him and thank him,' she said. 'He says he turned a lot of lives around.'

'Has he?' I said.

'We found a few of those. Some petty criminals who got caught with drugs or shoplifting or whatever. We talked to them. Their parents say they changed their minds about Scali when their kids got home. But a year away from family and school isn't an ideal plan. Kids don't exactly flourish when separated from their parents.'

'Why don't the parents challenge the system?'

'If you hadn't noticed,' she said, 'ain't a lot of money in Blackburn. Lawyers cost money. And if you don't speak English, you tend to not try and buck the system.'

'How about that other judge, the one who tipped you. Can you give me an introduction?'

Iris shook her head. 'I wish I could,' she said. 'But he died last year. He had a heart attack. His wife and I still talk. She believes he died because of the stress over dealing with Scali. Apparently he took some real heat from Scali's buddies when he spoke up. The presiding judge demoted him.'

'Maybe I could speak to his wife?'

Iris nodded, reaching for a pen and her reporter's notebook. She scrolled through her computer screen and then jotted down a name and number. 'I don't know if she'll want to talk,' Iris said. 'I tried about three months ago, wanting to know if he left some files. She wouldn't even open the door.'

'How could she resist me?'

'Maybe she can't,' Iris said. 'But Scali sure as hell will. Closest you'll get to his court is standing outside those two closed doors.'

I stood and left my card.

'Nice to see you, Spenser,' she said. 'You gonna stick around Blackburn awhile?'

'Why not?'

'I have to say you'll definitely make this place a hell of a lot more interesting.'

'I doubt that would take much.'

7

Judge Price's widow lived in a two-story Colonial in the toniest section of Blackburn, a neighborhood along the park called Belleview. I figured it was tony because all the houses were painted, driveways were shoveled, and two passing drivers eyed me with suspicion. The house was a flat gray, with white trim and a bright red door. There were two fireplaces, neither emitting smoke, and a garage stretching from the left side of the home. An iron streetlamp wrapped in plastic holly lit a gray day as I walked past. All the driving and sitting had not been kind to my knee.

I stretched it as I walked to the door and knocked. And then knocked some more. A bundle of mail had been wedged under a brass door handle. I reached for my cell phone and tried the number. I heard the telephone ringing inside, but no one picked up. I made my way carefully along the walkway to the garage. A blue Honda was parked there alongside an empty space. Being a master detective, I figured no one was home.

I'd come back later. The problem was how to while away the hours in Blackburn. I could see if Officer Lorenzo wanted to discuss crime-busting techniques over coffee. I could see if Vice Principal Waters wanted to go shopping for home electronics. Or maybe I could make my way over to the Blackburn Mill history museum to ponder the good old eighteen-hour workdays and the benefits of child labor.

Instead, I called Sheila Yates at work and asked for names of other parents who had similar problems with Scali. She gave me five different names and three phone numbers.

The first on the list was a woman named Trinh Tran who ran an Asian grocery about four miles away in the Hastings Corner district.

The district was mainly a collection of one-level storefronts occupied by Asian businesses that branched off an old-fashioned tri-cornered building that sold liquor, cigarettes, and cell phones. There were a couple hair and nail salons, at least three Vietnamese restaurants, two bars, and another liquor store. I took note there was a sale on Boone's Farm strawberry wine. Trinh Tran owned Saigon Le, a combination pho house and grocery. Besides selling rice in twenty-pound sacks, live carp, basil leaves, and bok choy, Saigon Le acquiesced to Massachusetts culture by also selling Lotto tickets, forty-ounce beers, and stale donuts.

I found Trinh in a back office, cleaning up a storeroom. A back door hung loosely off the hinges and the cold wind shot hard into the room lined with shelves and stacks of boxes.

'Are you the police?' she said. She had little, if any, accent.

'When my hair grows out, I'm often confused with Jack Lord.'

'You have a cop face.' The accent was a little more pronounced, somewhere between Saigon and the South Shore.

'Weathered lines of integrity.'

As my eyes adjusted to the dim light, I noticed big sacks of rice had been cut open, spilling onto the stained concrete floor. Boxes had been slashed and emptied. 'This fifth time I've been robbed this year,' she said. 'They don't even use what they take. They take because they want to show they own me. They own all this business.'

'Gangs.'

'Doesn't everywhere have a gang?' she said. 'I have two nephews in the gang who probably did this.'

She got off her knees and looked to me. She was much smaller than I'd thought, in her black jeans with sparkly designs on the pockets and a very tight-fitting pink jacket. Her hair was very straight and very black and cut into a severe bob with sharp bangs above the brow.

'What a mess,' she said.

'Your son is Van?'

She nodded. Her face turned serious and she placed two small fists to her mouth. 'What's wrong? What'd he do?'

I told her about Sheila and Dillon Yates and meeting with the fun faculty at the high school, and all I knew about Judge Scali. All I knew about Scali could be written onto the ceiling of the Sistine Chapel on the head of a pin.

'This third time with him,' she said, holding up three fingers. 'Third time. He gets out of that place and next time it will be real jail.'

'What was he charged with?'

'The first time?'

'Yes.'

'Nothing,' she said. 'Not really. He got blamed for bringing marijuana cigarettes to school. Someone put it in his locker. He never did drugs. Not then.'

'And the second?'

'He left school early,' she said. 'He wanted to get home and to help me. They say he broke the school door. They said he was a vandal. He broke the door. We offered to pay. It was an accident.'

'I assume Scali wasn't in a forgiving mood.'

She shook her head. 'He called him a gangbanger,' she said. 'That's a lie. He spoke down to my son as if he didn't know English. Van was born here. English is his first language.'

'What did your attorney say?'

Trinh Tran stared at me, confused. She widened her eyes and shook her head. 'No attorney.'

'What about a public defender?' I said.

'Man at the court told us that teenagers don't need an attorney,' she said. 'He told us that was for adult court only.'

'Everyone gets an attorney,' I said. 'Even kids.'

She shook her head. 'Not in Blackburn.'

I rubbed my jaw. I did this often while I was thinking. I'd seen detectives do this often in movies. It's supposed to make you look smart and attentive. I repeated the gesture.

'Did an officer of the court tell you that?' I said. 'Were you told you could not have an attorney?'

'I signed a paper,' she said. 'They said everyone signed it.'

'But were you told it wasn't an option?'

She thought on it for a moment and then nodded. A brisk wind shot into the storage room. I walked over to the door and asked her if she had a screwdriver and a hammer. I wasn't exactly Bob Vila, and the job was ugly, but I helped get it back into the frame. It would close and she could lock it. I took a piece of scrap wood to replace part of the broken frame.

'Thank you,' she said, after I had finished.

We walked back through the market that smelled of exotic spices, ripe produce, and the pungent odor of the big fish tank. I contemplated buying an authentic wok for ten dollars. Trinh walked outside with me.

'I don't want trouble,' she said. 'I want my son back in school.'

'If Scali has denied lawyers for kids,' I said, 'he could be in a lot of trouble.'

'Nobody will talk against that man,' she said. 'No one knows what he does inside his court. How will you know?'

'I have an obsessive personality,' I said. 'Keep talking to enough people and the truth will shake out.'

'You're big,' she said. 'Shake hard.'

8

I spent the afternoon waiting out Blackburn's chief public defender. He didn't return to his office until nearly six o'clock, and by that time I'd gone through every issue of *American Lawyer, Entertainment Weekly,* and *Cape Cod* from the last three years. The pictures of sunsets, lobsters, and picket fences were stunning. The latest news on Angelina Jolie and Brad Pitt amazing. I was about to start from the top when a shabby man clutching a scuffed leather briefcase walked through the door.

Felix Bukowski wasn't pleased to have a visitor. He looked to have had a long day in court, but the closer I got, it smelled as if he'd had a long day at the tavern. He was short and thick, with an enormous head. He looked like one of those guys who needed everything custom made, from hats to pants. He looked to be a twenty-eight inseam with a thirty-eight waist. His hair was long and slick and matched his sparse gray beard. I couldn't tell if he was trying for the stubble look or just had forgotten to shave.

I followed him into his office, where he dumped his briefcase in a leather chair. He loosened an ugly flowered tie, took off his coat, and plumped down in a high-backed chair. 'Yeah?' he said, massaging his temples. 'How can I help you?'

I walked up close to his desk. 'You want to stick around here or can I buy you another drink?'

'Who the hell are you?'

I offered my hand and introduced myself.

'Private eye?' he said, making a gun from his thumb and forefinger. 'No shit.'

I was annoyed he'd stolen my patented gesture but let it go. 'How about a beer?'

'After today,' he said, 'how about a double Old Crow on the rocks?'

'I knew it,' I said. 'A true connoisseur. Let's go.'

We walked around the corner from the three-story brick office to a place called Jimmy's Pub. Jimmy's Pub looked the way a spot called Jimmy's Pub should look. It had beer signs in oval windows and a couple taps filled with the latest flavors of Sam Adams. The liquor selection was somewhat limited, ranging from bottom-shelf to under-the-counter. But we were in luck. They had Old Crow. I had a feeling Bukowski knew this.

I ordered a Sam Adams Winter Lager.

The attorney upended the whiskey and swallowed down half before lowering the glass and wiping his lips. A corner jukebox was playing the best of Sinatra. Felix tapped his fingers as he listened to 'Fly Me to the Moon.' I hoped on the next round he wouldn't be standing on the bar and belting out 'My Way.' I suffer enough for my clients.

'So are you going to tell me your case or not?'

'I work for the family of Dillon Yates.'

'Never heard of him.'

'Not surprised,' I said. 'You didn't represent him.'

'Then why are you here?'

A haggard woman missing two front teeth got up to slow-dance with a man in a flannel shirt and unlaced work boots. They could've taken a lesson or two from Arthur Murray.

Felix wistfully watched them.

'Trouble,' he said. 'I got four ex-wives.'

'I can't imagine.'

'Last one wouldn't shut up,' he said, motioning with his scruffy chin. 'I want something like that.'

'Missing teeth?'

'Magic,' he said. 'Ain't no magic left.'

I ordered another round for Felix Bukowski. He wore a big tan parka over his suit. The hood lay loose around his big head, making him look like Nanook of the North. I drank the Sam Adams Winter Lager, which was my favorite and almost made up for the company.

An old Asian man sat at the end of the bar watching television with the sound turned off. It was an infomercial about growing hair from a can.

'You do much work in juvenile courts?'

'Kiddie court ain't my thing.'

'But you do assign attorneys there?'

'If that's what they want.'

He sipped on the drink. The bartender leaned against the cash register and lit a cigarette. Christmas lights blinked on and off from over the jukebox. They looked like they went up a few Christmases ago and just kept blinking on forever. The two lovebirds had disappeared.

'I understand Judge Scali doesn't want attorneys in his courtroom.'

'Where'd you hear that?'

'From parents who got it from his bailiffs.'

41

Felix shuffled in his chair. His mouth twitched a little and he rubbed a fat finger under his nose. He shrugged. 'I don't know anything about that.'

'Have you heard about kids being denied counsel?'

'No.'

'But on average, do kids want some help from your office?'

'I mean, they get their own, and sometimes they ask for assistance,' he said. 'But if you're trying to say they were banned or something, that's nuts.'

I sipped my beer. The old Asian man was entranced by the full head of hair on the test subject. He was drinking a lime-green-colored liquid. I was betting they didn't serve absinthe at Jimmy's.

'I understand there's a waiver.'

'I thought you were a private eye on a case,' he said. 'Not a troublemaker.'

'I multitask.'

'Hmm,' he said as he hiccupped. 'I've been running this office for eleven years.'

'Congratulations.'

'I know people like to shit on public defenders,' he said. 'But I help the people. I do for people who can't hire hotshits from Boston.'

'Hotshits can sometimes be overrated.'

'You bet. But it doesn't really matter who you are or what firm you're from,' Felix said, making a considerable effort to turn on the bar stool and look me in the eye. 'You could have F. Lee Fucking Bailey in Scali's courtroom and still get time.'

'F. Lee Bailey is dead.'

'You know what I goddamn mean.'

I sipped my beer. I walked over to the jukebox and picked out a favorite by Wayne King. I returned to the seat and looked at Bukowski. 'What if it were you?' I said. 'If it were your kid. Would you be mad they didn't offer assistance?'

'I'm doing the best I can.'

'Does Scali play fair?'

42

'Who are you?'

'A harbinger of change.'

Bukowski raised his head back, took a deep swallow. He shook his head. 'No,' he said. 'He doesn't want us in there. I got enough shit to fight in this town without worrying about the kiddies.'

I laid down money for another drink and left Felix on the bar stool, head tucked deep into the parka, staring straight ahead at the row of booze. It had started to snow, the sidewalks covered in white. For maybe a good thirty seconds, Blackburn almost looked pretty.

9

Henry Cimoli had placed me on a strict upper-body routine while my knee healed up. He liked to remind me my legs weren't that great anyway. I told him he was crazy and intentionally wore a pair of navy gym shorts to make the point. I left my leg out straight while I cranked out several reps on the bench. The front of my gray workout tee was soaked in sweat. It had been a while since I had attacked the heavy bag.

'Let me know when you're done warming up,' Henry said.

'What makes you think I'm warming up?'

'I saw Hawk curl what you've got on that bar,' he said.

I slid an extra plate onto the bar and performed twelve reps to shut him up. When I racked the weight and sat upright on the bench, Henry stood nearby, unimpressed. 'Next time slower,' he said. 'And pause when the bar hits your chest. Don't bounce it. You'll get hurt that way.'

'I only get hurt when someone uses a tire iron on my legs,' I said.

'That's your own fault,' Henry said. 'You should've moved faster.'

'Is there no pity sitting in the clouds?'

'What the hell does that mean?' Henry said.

'Strike that,' I said. 'Imagining you on high takes too much effort.'

Henry stood about five-foot-five in lifts he denied he owned. But he was as loyal a friend as they made and tougher than a two-dollar

43

steak. I'd been working out in his gym since I'd been a wise-ass kid who thought he might be a contender. Those dreams, along with my profile, had been shattered by an aging heavyweight of some note. As of late, we'd both been working with a tough Native American named Zebulon Sixkill. Henry offered him boxing lessons and I was helping him get his investigator license. He had great potential.

'You heard from Z?' Henry said.

'I offered a letter of introduction to my people in Southern California.'

'Your people are damn good.'

'Yep,' I said. 'And they'll come through for Z. Whatever it is he needs.'

I walked over to a chin-up bar facing a plate-glass window. As I counted out ten reps and then went on to twelve, I looked out into the harbor. The water was black and choppy, and you couldn't see maybe a hundred feet beyond the pier. Everything was wrapped in a white haze. It felt good and warm to be inside. The snow fell into the water, dusted the docked sailboats, and covered pilings in gentle mounds. Sleet mixed in with the snow tapped at the window. I got some water. Henry stood next to me drinking coffee from a foam cup.

'What've you been doing, besides nothing?'

'I took a case in Blackburn.'

'Blackburn?' Henry said. 'Jesus. What are you doing in that shithole?'

'I'm not really sure.'

'Who's your client?'

'A woman named Sheila Yates,' I said. 'Her son was sent to kids' jail for making fun of an administrator.'

'Is that a crime?'

'Apparently it is in Blackburn.'

'Kids got nothing to do these days,' he said. 'When I was coming up, you had the streets or you had the gym.'

'Same for me,' I said. 'And Hawk.'

'Boys got all kinds of anger and energy,' Henry said. 'You got the body but you ain't got the brains. You got to find a place to focus it. If you don't, you end up in the can.'

'True.'

'You could've ended up in the can,' Henry said. 'Right? If it weren't for boxing and then the Army. Difference between you and Hawk was your uncle. Kept you safe after your old man passed.'

I nodded.

'And I did my best,' Henry said. 'Despite how you turned out. I take no credit for that.'

'Hawk had Bobby Nevins,' I said. 'Closest thing Hawk ever had to family.'

'I know for a fact Bobby kept on bailing Hawk out of the hoosegow.'

'Do people still say *hoosegow*?'

'Yeah,' Henry said. 'I just did.'

I slid my feet under the base of a weight bench and did three sets of sit-ups, fifty reps each. Henry stood sure-footed and gray-headed, lording over all his shiny stainless-steel machines. 'A little snow and it gives people an excuse,' Henry said. 'Look at this place. It's nearly empty.'

'The roads are about to freeze.'

'Roads are always freezing,' Henry said. 'If it ain't the snow, it's the rain. You can't run your life around the freakin' weather.'

'Have you no compassion for my poor nerves?'

'How does Susan put up with you?'

'The dog,' I said. 'We stay together for the dog.'

'Jesus,' Henry said, walking away.

They were in the van for what seemed like forever. There were no windows and no one told them where they were headed. It was just him and seven other boys. Four of them were black, two Asians, and another scared-shitless white kid. One of the black kids started to talk about the island before they even left Blackburn. He said he'd been to the island three times and it wasn't so rough. He said it got cold and the staff tried to fuck with your mind. But he said if you kept your head down and kept with the program you'd be cool.

The black kid had a paisley-shaped scar on one cheek and had kind of a far-off look in his eyes like he didn't believe a word he was saying. Nobody else talked. The two guards were separated from the kids by a wire screen. They listened to some sports talk radio, a show called Paulie & The Gooch, and didn't say much besides telling the kids to shut the fuck up twice so they could listen.

All of them were in orange. All of them had been cuffed and didn't have anything to do but look at the floor and try not to think about where they were going as the van raced along. The black kid told him his name was Perry but everyone called him Pooky. He was from the projects in Grove Hill. Pooky said he'd stolen a car just to get the hell out of town. The judge committed him to Fortune Island until he turned eighteen.

'When I get out,' he said, 'I'm getting the hell away from this damn place.'

The other white kid was Isaac, a chunky boy not even fourteen, who had stolen a copy of Grand Theft Auto from Target. The boy didn't talk much, trying to listen and learn a little bit more about the island. No one had told him a thing.

He'd seen his dad for only a second before they removed him from court. His dad was crying. His dad just kept on saying he was sorry but didn't say he knew what to do. For the first time, his father looked weak to him.

After a long while, the van slowed and the guards got out, slamming the doors. The boys looked at one another. No one spoke. You could hear the wind and sleet against the van doors. Finally the back door opened *and there was a bright artificial light. The two men who'd driven them this far telling them to get the hell out.*

'Move,' they said. 'Come on. Now.'

It was the first time the boy noticed they weren't cops but had uniforms with a patch that read MCC over an outline of Massachusetts. They told the boys to line up outside in the dark and cold. He could make out part of a parking lot and a dock in the streetlights. The guards marched them down a long path to a small dock, where an enclosed motorboat was waiting for them. They pushed the kids onboard, telling them to keep their feet inside because no one would be diving in after them.

'Sit down,' said an older man in a ball cap. 'Shut up. Don't start trouble for yourself before you even get here.'

The man looked to be in his forties and had a shaved head and a goatee. He wore a ski jacket and had a tattoo on his neck. The snow, sleet, and darkness made it hard to see past a few feet. The boy stared out the boat's window at the snow catching and melting on the windows, listening to the steady hum of the motor until it revved hard and they left the dock. The men's feet were hard and heavy around them. There was laughter and a lot of talk. Someone said something about those little fuckers. The man with the tattoo was at the wheel now, staring into nothing, the front of the boat lifting up and slamming back down.

The boy had never spent much time at sea. You could smell the cold salt air all around you.

He felt like he might puke.

He lifted his eyes, everything off-kilter. Pooky was across from him, shaking his head. 'Don't do it,' he said. 'Don't show you weak or it's all over.'

The boy just breathed and looked out the window, looking for something. In the distance came the swinging arc of brightness from a lighthouse.

'How bad is it?' the boy said.

'It ain't good.'

'What do they do to you?'

'Everything.'

10

A few days later, I sat across from Sheila Yates in a conference room at Cone, Oakes. We were very high up, and the view of the docks and the cold, breaking waves in the harbor was impressive. I almost wished I'd worn a tie, perhaps my J. Press blazer with gold buttons. Instead, I had on work clothes. Levi's, button-down Ball and Buck shirt, Red Wings, and my A-2 bomber jacket. I kept on the A-2 to shield my Smith & Wesson.

'I'm about to go nuts,' Sheila said. 'They take him out there. To that island, and there's no way to see him? This is crazy.'

'We'll get him out,' I said.

'How do you know?'

'Because we will,' I said. 'Scali has grown cocky and sloppy. The law is on our side.'

'That doesn't always mean jack.'

'Depends on who's cracking the whip.'

Just then a young woman walked into the office carrying a tall cup of Starbucks. She was thin, with a dimpled chin and big, sleepy hazel eyes under a ski hat. She trundled out of an enormous gray coat while she held a batch of papers in her teeth. She sat down at the head of the conference table, still in the ski hat marked with two crossed arrows, and shuffled the papers. I didn't want to be judgmental, but she looked all of twelve.

'Is Rita coming?' I said.

'Rita is in court today,' she said. 'I'm Megan Mullen. I'll be handling your case.'

'What are you, twelve?' Sheila said.

I stifled a smile. It was a good question.

'No, ma'am, I'm twenty-nine,' she said. 'There's no age discrimination at Harvard Law School. I passed the bar and everything.'

Sheila Yates raised her eyebrows at me. I smiled just a little. I didn't want Megan Mullen to notice, as she seemed to have small but sharp teeth. She pulled off the ski hat, unveiling a neat bun at the back of her head and two respectable-sized diamond earrings. She pushed up the sleeves on a navy V-neck sweater and settled in to read the papers before her.

I tapped my fingers. 'I'm Spenser, by the way.'

'I know who you are,' Megan said.

'Excellent.'

'Rita warned me.'

'Warned you?'

'She said you're a solid investigator and have done a lot for the firm.'

'And?'

'She said you'd make jokes about me being young.'

'But I've refrained.'

Megan looked up from the papers and gave me a wait-and-see glance. I waved an empty palm across the very long desk. We were up so high that a dense fog shifted below us like low-hanging clouds.

'I don't get this,' she said. 'Your son made a joke on Twitter and they arrested him?'

'I know,' Sheila said. 'Freakin' crazy.'

'On what charges?' she said.

'Keep reading,' I said. 'It gets freakin' crazier.'

Megan flipped through the file Sheila Yates and I had put together. This wasn't a murder case. The file was very thin. 'This is the most ridiculous thing I've ever seen.'

'So ridiculous my Dillon was hauled away in shackles and taken out into the harbor,' Sheila said. 'For rehabilitation, as if he were some kind of criminal. He doesn't drink. Doesn't do drugs. He once stole a pack of Doublemint gum when he was four. I made him take it back and pay for it. He's a great kid.'

'Some people can't take a joke,' I said.

Megan pushed the papers away from her as if they were a rotten meal. She made an *uggh* sound and crossed her arms over her very small chest. I bet if she stood on a box, she might come up to my

49

shoulders. She tilted her head at me, dropping those big, sleepy eyes like a hammer. 'Oh, I can take a joke,' she said. 'If it's funny.'

'Two lawyers and a priest walk into a bar,' I said.

Megan held up her hand. 'Just tell me what you learned in Blackburn.'

'You know Dillon's grandfather signed a waiver giving up his right to an attorney?' I said.

'I do,' she said. 'And we've filed an appeal. I just didn't know the circumstances behind his arrest.'

'For the record, I don't think the waiver even matters to them. The juvie judge doesn't like lawyers in his courtroom. Not to mention the public defender in Blackburn didn't seem too concerned. He said a lawyer wouldn't have made a difference. And he's got bigger problems than kiddie cases.'

'Like what?'

'Mainly draining a bottle of Old Crow.'

'So this isn't isolated?' Megan said.

'I think it's the Blackburn way.'

'They can't do that,' she said. 'A judge can't just make up his own procedure and rules.'

'Aha,' I said. 'You did go to Harvard Law.'

Megan dropped her chin at me and stared. I smiled. She waited for a moment and then smiled back. Friends after all. Any protégée of Rita Fiore's couldn't be immune to my charms. 'Disgusting,' Megan said. 'Completely disgusting.'

'How long will the appeal take?' Sheila said.

'We're working as fast as possible,' she said. 'Has no one complained about this judge before?'

'A fellow Blackburn judge,' I said. 'He got the local newspaper involved and they were able to prove Joe Scali had off-the-charts incarceration rates. The highest in the Commonwealth, with their annual budget being looted for keeping kids in private prisons.'

'And?' Megan said.

'And nothing ever came of it,' I said. 'The complaining judge died and Scali was able to explain things off as him being tough on juvie crime.'

'Surely there have been complaints to the Department of Youth Services and the bar?'

'One would think,' I said.

'Blackburn ain't normal,' Sheila said. 'People around there keep their heads down and mouths shut. They tell me that's the way it's always been.'

'I heard you're not too good at shutting your mouth,' Megan said, standing and offering her thin, small hand. I tried to look modest as I shook it.

'Tell Rita I'll win you over, too.'

'We'll see about that,' Megan said.

'You know, I have socks older than you.'

'Then I suggest you go shopping, Mr Spenser.'

I grinned and walked out of the law office with Sheila Yates. She clasped her hands together over her mouth, closing her eyes in prayer, the whole ride down to the first floor. 'What do you think?' she said. 'Is it going to work?'

'I think the kid will do nicely.'

'I want more than Dillon just out on appeal,' she said. 'I want Judge Scali to pay.'

'I'm working on it,' I said.

11

The Magic Bean was on Central Avenue in Blackburn, at the heart of what used to be a thriving business district. These days it hosted a lot of boarded-up storefronts, a Salvation Army thrift store, and the coffee shop. The Magic Bean sold hemp jewelry by the cash register, and local art from the brick walls, and two members of the staff had nose rings. One had blue hair. I felt a little less hip in my Levi's, steel-toed boots, and lack of nose jewelry. I'd put the nose ring on the list. Maybe someday.

I met my new BFF, Beth Golnick, there, along with two of her classmates who'd had run-ins with Scali. It wasn't even four o'clock and outside it was nearly black. But the shop was warm and pleasant, smelling of hot coffee and exotic teas. A good place to thaw out.

We seemed to be the only ones in the Magic Bean not staring at a screen. The room was packed with nervous and fidgety kids on their phones and devices. Both of Beth's classmates were boys, Jake Cotner and Ryan Bell. Jake had been a football player. He was broad-shouldered and muscular but not quite six feet. Ryan was tall, very thin, with nearly white blond hair. If he got a crew cut, he'd look a lot like Shell Scott.

'Why'd you go before Scali?' I said. 'Overdue library books?'

The kids laughed. *Oh, Spenser, friend of youth.*

'I got into a fight with my stepmother,' Ryan said. 'She's a total bitch.'

'She called the cops?'

'I told her she had no class and no business living with us,' Ryan said. 'I threw a steak at her. She screamed at me for an hour and then called the cops. She told them I was trying to kill her. *Jesus Christ.* She's only eight years older than me.'

'How long did you get?'

'Six months.'

I leaned forward, elbows on knees, and stared at Jake. Unlike me, Jake had worn his letterman's jacket. I didn't think I could pull it off without looking like a complete wacko.

'I was screwing around with some friends at one of the old warehouses,' Jake said. 'We were just breaking bottles and windows and shit. A cop caught us and Scali sent me away for nine months. I missed my senior year.'

'Are you in school now?' I said.

'Nah.' He shook his head and looked away. 'What's the point?'

Beth sat nearby in an oversized leather chair, feet off the ground, knees tucked up to her chin. Her hair band had been pulled up into a bun on top of her head with the black streak falling in a curlicue over one eye. She played with the strand, studying its color and then tucking it behind an ear.

'Did either of you have an attorney?' I said.

The boys looked at each other and then me, shaking their heads.

'Was an attorney offered?'

They shook their heads again.

'What did your parents say?'

'My dad told me it was good for me,' Ryan said. 'He said it would toughen me up. Said my stepmother was afraid to sleep at night. She's up all night because she's on pills and addicted to watching reality shows. He met the crazy woman on some kind of dating website. *Ick*.'

'I live with my mom,' Jake said. 'She tried to get me an attorney, but someone told her the judge would be harder on me if she did. You know, like he thought we were fighting the system? She was told for me to take what was given and say thank you. I didn't think it would be nine fucking months for breaking some windows.'

'Judge Roy Bean.'

'Who's that?' Beth said.

'A real a-hole,' I said. 'From the old days.'

'When you were a kid?' she said.

'Yeah,' I said. 'Exactly.'

The kids were impressed. I told them I'd like to talk to their parents, find out what the Blackburn court had told them about a kid's right to an attorney.

'What's it matter?' Ryan said. 'It's all a mess now. Nobody is going to go against Scali. This is just what people do here. People say you got to have a tough judge for a tough town. When he came to school and spoke to us, he said he was the reason we didn't have gangs around here.'

'You do have gangs,' I said.

'Yeah, I know,' Jake said. 'But not like the old days. People believe he's keeping them safe.'

'From kids breaking windows and throwing steaks at their stepmoms.'

The boys and Beth didn't know what to say. They stayed silent. The speakers overhead played a pop song that I barely recalled from thirty years ago and hoped to never hear again. I guessed now it was hip. This was the very reason I never threw away ties. 'So what's it like at the MCC?' I said.

'On the island?' Jake said. 'It freakin' sucked.'

'Sucked big-time,' Ryan said.

'Tell me about it,' I said.

'You got to live in bunks,' Ryan said. 'Five bunks. Ten boys to a room. They wake you up at five a.m. with an air horn. You know, like people bring to football games?'

'And then?'

'And then nothing,' Jake said. 'You get crummy food. You can go outside for an hour in the morning and at night. There's one TV that has shitty reception.'

'They don't have you weaving baskets or making license plates?'

'You're supposed to do schoolwork,' Ryan said. 'But that's a joke. You go to this big room where you fill out workbooks. No one can talk and then you turn them in when you're done. You never get them back. You never get a grade or anything. I started sketching in them to see if anyone would notice. I drew horses and dolphins and things like that. No one said a thing.'

'So you both left the island reformed and upright members of society?'

Beth snorted out a little coffee and then wiped her nose. Ryan got up from the sofa and went to join her in the big chair. He sat on her knee, her arm around his waist. She leaned her head onto his back the way a sister might. He smiled.

Jake excused himself and walked to the bathroom. I hadn't taken any notes. I'd write down a few things when I got back to my car. But I wanted this to be loose and informal. I wanted to talk to their parents. I still didn't know where I was headed or how it might help my client. Megan Mullen had appealed Dillon's case based on no counsel. We were playing the waiting game with legal channels while I continued to snoop. Maybe the snooping would help Dillon, or maybe it would just expose more ugliness.

'Are you really a private eye?' Ryan said.

'Yeah.'

'You like it?'

'Sure.'

'Why?'

'I have a big neon sign outside my office with a magnifying glass,' I said. 'And a sexy secretary who sits on my desk while I think.'

'No,' Beth said, looking doubtful. 'Really?'

'I don't like being told what to do,' I said. 'I like being my own boss.'

'I'd like that, too,' Ryan said. 'I just don't know what I want to do.'

'He can draw,' Beth said, rubbing circles on his back. 'He can draw really good. You see the artwork on the wall? He made those.'

I looked up and spotted his signature. For a teenager, they were very good. Charcoal etchings of bowls of fruit, trees, and vacant playgrounds. One of the sketches, I noted, as I stood up and walked closer, was of Beth. Her eyes were obscured, but it was the same nose and mouth, the same long strand of black. It was a nude. Beth's face flushed.

'It's okay,' she said. 'Ryan's not like that. I told him I didn't mind.'

'Oh.'

'She's not my type,' he said, rolling his eyes.

'You're gay,' I said.

'Very.'

'And was that a problem at MCC?'

'Yes,' he said.

'Can you tell me about that?'

He seemed to be very far away for a moment and then appeared as if he might cry. He didn't speak, only shook his head. 'Not now.'

Jake came back and said he had to get going. He looked to the door and around the coffee shop. Everyone was so intent on their phones, computers, and tablets that I didn't think our presence had even been noted.

'Where do you work?' I said.

'Warehouse,' he said. 'I move stone and tile. I take inventory. Drive a forklift.'

'Can't you go back to school?' I said.

'Now?' Jake said, shaking his head. 'Nah. I'm done. Screw those people. I need to get on with my life.'

'But that's not easy,' I said. 'Without the paper.'

'No,' he said. 'It's not.'

We all walked out into the dark together. My popularity was growing.

12

Susan and I were walking in Harvard Square on the way to Russell House Tavern. Susan had on a long black down coat and dark designer blue jeans tucked into a tall pair of Italian riding boots. She bought the boots on our recent trip to Paris and was fond of telling me the great deal they'd been. Nearly half-off at a boutique in the Saint-Germain.

'They remind me of the Brasserie Lipp,' I said.

'Everything about Paris reminds you of the Lipp.'

'The frankfurters with spicy mustard, the sauerkraut.'

'And don't forget the beer.'

'Don't be ridiculous,' I said. 'We'll always have the beer.'

Harvard Square bustled in and around the T station despite it being cold enough to freeze the banana off a brass monkey. A gray-bearded man in an Army coat and fingerless gloves played some Simon and Garfunkel on a battered guitar. Undergrads were hanging out outside the bars, smoking cigarettes and talking about things that Harvard undergrads discuss. Two inebriated girls were in an argument. One told the other that her judgment was skewed so heteronormative.

A homeless man in a ski hat smelling of Mad Dog 20/20 challenged passersby to a Bible trivia test for five bucks. Or at least that's what his sandwich board promised.

'Let me ask you a professional question.'

'No shrink talk after hours,' she said.

'This isn't about being a shrink,' I said. 'This is about your previous occupation.'

'Housewife or guidance counselor?'

'Guidance counselor.'

She linked her arm in mine. 'Fair enough. Fire away.'

'What are your thoughts about cops in schools?'

'When I was a counselor, we didn't have them,' she said. 'It's a relatively new idea, and while I understand the need, I don't like the message.'

'Meaning?'

'Some horrific things have happened in schools lately,' she said. 'But while the old model had the counselors or teachers or administrators looking for solutions to most problems, all those problems now seem to fall to the school resource officer, and they're ill-equipped to solve them. From what you've told me about Blackburn, and other things I've heard, it's gotten very much out of hand. They're cops. They have only one approach to a problem.'

'Cops make an arrest and the school's hands are clean.'

'Out of sight and out of mind.'

'Do you still have any old contacts who may know about the current climate in Blackburn?'

'I resent that my contacts are old.'

'*Old* is a relative term.'

'I can make some calls Monday.'

'Good,' I said. 'I'll buy you an extra order of the deviled eggs.'

'You were going to do that anyway.'

'How about a Bloody Mary?'

'This late?' she said. 'I'll take a gimlet. Ketel One. Fresh lime juice.'

'Of course,' I said. 'I may need a double myself.'

'That bad?'

'It's rotten as hell up there,' I said, both of us turning off the street and into the Russell House Tavern patio, tall mushroom heaters burning a bright orange, and ducking inside and down into the basement. 'The juvie courts don't have an issue with suspending the Constitution. And none of the locals, or even the public defender, wants to challenge it.'

Miracle of all miracles, we found a spot for two at the bar. I ordered a gimlet for Susan and a Harpoon Ale for myself. I tried to keep away from the hard stuff except on very bad days or for medicinal reasons. There was soft music playing and a lot of loud, but not unpleasant, conversation.

'It seems I'm dealing with a lot of trusting and naïve parents,' I said. 'Some of them are immigrants who are slow to question authority.'

'Are you sure their rights are being denied?'

'I spent a great portion of my day talking with parents,' I said. 'Some I found had the option of a release. My client had the option of a release. I found three others who said the release wasn't optional and they were told to sign.'

'Do you think that's the norm?'

'The good judge tries a lot of cases,' I said. 'All of them are confidential.'

'But even one case of a child being denied an attorney would be enough for an official inquiry?'

'One would think,' I said. 'Apparently another judge up there, a family court judge, filed a complaint that Scali was eating up his budget with all the kids he was putting away.'

'Then why not just talk to the judge?'

'I'd have to retain the services of Madame Blavatsky.'

'Dead.'

'As a doornail,' I said. 'Died last year. I tried to speak to his widow, but she seems to be out of town.'

The bartender, looking spiffy in a crisp white shirt and black vest, served our drinks. I liked the new trend of bartenders dressing like bartenders. The bar had a lot of handsome polished wood and marble counters. Single lights hung from the ceiling, filaments burning in vintage globes. We raised our glasses and clinked them together.

'If the kid gets off on a technicality,' she said, 'that won't be enough for you.'

'Or his mother. On principle.'

'I didn't think so.'

'Hard to open closed doors and secrecy,' I said.

'Unless you happen to have a size-twelve steel-toed boot.'

'You have a solid point.' I smiled and sipped some of the Harpoon. 'How'd you get so smart?'

'It doesn't take a Ph.D. to appreciate your unnatural persistence,' she said. 'Especially to those abusing power.'

'Toward kids.'

'The worst.'

13

I awoke early Monday morning, fixed myself two semi-poached eggs, some corned-beef hash, and rye toast lathered in Irish butter. Showered and closely shaved, I tugged on a pair of Levi's with a black cable-knit sweater, slipped a peacoat over the .38 on my hip, and drove north along I-93. At a quarter till nine, I knocked on the door of the late Judge Price. When the knocking didn't work, I tried the bell. If I ever dropped sleuthing, I would be a dynamite employee for Avon.

After the third attempt, the door opened and an older woman with perfect grayish-black hair and exact makeup stood facing me.

I introduced myself. I told her I was working a case related to her husband.

She stared at me. She did not smile or even register if she understood me. When I finished, her eyes lingered and then wandered down to my Red Wing boots. She nodded a couple times and said, 'All right then. I am Mary Price. You may come in for a moment, but I'm already running very late.'

I wiped my boots on a Christmas-themed welcome mat and walked into a still and dark house. The floors were wide-planked hardwoods. The walls were white and spare, with framed family photos and oil paintings of New England landscapes. She had a nice fire going in her family room, where she invited me to sit on a long brown leather couch. An old mantel clock over the hearth clicked off time in a steady and assured tick-tock.

'Would you like coffee?'

'I don't want to make you any later.'

'You said you wish to talk about Jim.'

'Yes.'

'Then my appointments can wait,' she said. 'If I acted rude, please excuse me. I wasn't expecting anyone.'

'No apology necessary.'

'You're the one who left the business card?'

'Yes, ma'am.'

'I was happy to invite you in,' she said. 'But if you call me "ma'am" again, I'll strike you with a fire poker.'

'Yikes.'

There was a hint of a smile. She wore a black turtleneck sweater and charcoal slacks. We were of different generations but I couldn't help but notice she was a very attractive woman. Thirty years ago, she must've been a knockout. I didn't know a nice way of saying that, so I kept my mouth shut and waited for her to return with the coffee.

She had her chair, high-backed and well used, close to the fire, with a woven blanket folded over the back and a book in the seat. After a few minutes, she returned with two cups of coffee on a silver serving tray and set them down on a table. The fire popped and the logs hissed.

She removed the book and sat. Her hair was long for a woman her age, with a portion pinned back and most lying on her shoulders. She had prominent cheekbones and gray eyes that watched me as I added a little sugar. I'd recently stopped with the cream. Every little bit counts.

'I work for a woman whose son was sentenced to a juvenile camp by Judge Scali,' I said. 'The sentencing was harsh and unfair. In the course of my work, I found out your late husband may have raised similar questions.'

'And where did you hear that?'

'From a woman named Iris Milford with *The Star*,' I said. 'She told me your husband had been a source for her before he died.'

She had not added any milk or sugar to her coffee. The steam curled and dissipated off the mug while the fire glowed and popped. 'I wish she hadn't told you that.'

'She wouldn't have, but knew it was important.'

'What did the young man do?'

'He made some jokes about his vice principal on the internet,' I said. 'They weren't exactly highbrow. But they weren't the kind of thing that needed the attention of a cop.'

She nodded, stared at me with her gray, hooded eyes, and bit the inside of her cheek. I downed some more coffee. I was pretty sure she was weighing the odds of shutting down altogether. The mantel clock ticked off more time.

'Joe Scali is an immoral, soulless bastard,' she said.

Hot damn. I tried not to show my excitement. I leaned forward on the sofa. The bright light from outside was blocked by a pair of heavy dark green curtains.

'As you know, Jim was appointed to family court,' she said. 'He held that position for more than twenty years.'

'And his connection with Joe Scali?'

'The whole mess started by a very honest, straightforward inquiry,' she said. 'Jim and Joe Scali shared the same budget. Three years ago, Jim was told he'd have to go to the county for more funding for his programs. He didn't care to go hat in hand.'

'What kind of programs?'

'His budget included counseling for parents who didn't want to lose their kids and for placement of kids into foster homes,' she said. 'He'd never had to ask for additional funding. This was all new. The next year, the same thing happened. Some administrators made innuendos about Jim's budget, which was laughable. These were all good and fair programs. Nothing had changed as far as the caseload.'

'Scali was eating it up.'

She nodded. 'Jim found out that Joe Scali's sentencing had increased tenfold.'

'Wow,' I said.

'One would think,' she said. 'But Joe Scali came along at the right time, in the time of school shootings, to become the Zero Tolerance Judge. You know he liked to be on cable news shows and loved to give speeches to students. He became immersed in cultivating his own celebrity.'

'A real rah-rah guy.'

'Jim made complaints about the ethics of what Scali was doing,' she said. 'He knew a lot of kids were being railroaded into a system where they had no business. Not to mention the children were being placed in new private facilities. Some might argue the private prisons were better for the kids, but the costs were astronomical.'

'To whom did he make the complaints?'

'The presiding district judge,' she said. 'You know Gavin Callahan?'

'No.'

'He's the top bastard,' she said. 'If you're looking for that kind of thing.'

'Top bastards are my business.'

'He and Joe Scali are lifelong friends,' he said. 'Callahan is the one who first appointed Joe Scali, although Scali hadn't been out of law school but a few years. This is a dirty town with a lot of dirty ways of doing business. No one even seemed to notice. Jim didn't make a fuss until someone was tampering with his budget. He liked to help people. He believed in his work.'

She swallowed and sat a bit straighter to compose herself. She stood up quickly, grabbed my nearly empty cup, and walked back to the kitchen. For lack of anything better, I stood and poked at the fire a bit, sending embers up into the chimney and into the frigid air.

When she came back into the room she brought a framed photograph of a smallish man with a lot of gray hair, wearing big black glasses and dressed in a black robe. It was an official-looking portrait taken among a lot of law books.

'Have you ever lost anyone, Mr Spenser?' she said. 'Someone you loved dearly and without whom you could not imagine your life going on?'

'No,' I said, not wishing to linger on the thought.

'I would imagine an amputation may be more pleasant,' she said. 'We have three boys. I have nine grandchildren. We weren't always happy, but the final few years were very happy. Jim took care of himself. He did not smoke and drank in moderation. He ran two miles, five days a week. He would not touch red meat, cheese, and processed food. What happened to him makes no sense.'

'He had a heart attack?'

'He was killed,' she said. 'It may have come from a natural cause, but Scali and Callahan couldn't be more pleased. As soon as Jim started asking questions, Callahan had him demoted to traffic court. It was a power play to make Jim quit. But Callahan underestimated Jim. He did not quit. He did not retire. He kept on the job. That should have been enough for them.'

The room was an enclosed pocket of silence with the draperies and the darkness and the crackling fire. I waited for her to finish.

'Callahan accused him of taking money in traffic court,' he said. 'He cited two thousand dollars. Can you imagine something so petty? It was almost laughable. We fought it. Jim became obsessed with the machinations in this rotten town. He told me he had something on Callahan and Scali that would vindicate him.'

'And did he?'

'I don't know,' she said. 'He went to work one morning, suffered a massive heart attack in chambers, and I never saw him again.'

'I'm very sorry.'

'I wish I could be of more help.'

'You've helped a great deal.'

We walked to the front door and out to the walkway. Everything was covered in a fine powder of snow, blinding white in the harsh morning light.

'There was a man in Boston he was speaking with,' she said. 'He was with some kind of state agency that oversaw budgets for family courts. I don't know his name or the agency.'

'Maybe I can find him.'

'These two are the worst,' she said. 'No one questions them. No one wants to know more. They'll ruin anyone who opposes them.'

I smiled. 'I don't scare easily.'

She smiled back. 'You don't appear to.'

14

I drove back to my office and spent the rest of the afternoon online, following the funding trail for the two judges and their programs. I learned that the old Office of Public Welfare was now defunct and had splintered into myriad state offices with fancy titles. Some of the work of Public Welfare, EBT cards and such, now went to the Department of Transitional Assistance, while the placement, care, and detention of kids went to the Department of Youth Services. All this sleuthing was exciting as hell. If only Bulldog Drummond had the internet.

It took two minutes to find a contact list for the DYS staff in Boston. I centered on administration and finance, the most likely to call an audit, and picked up the phone to start the cold calls.

Instead, I decided to visit the office in person. Perhaps my charisma and charm might open doors. It had absolutely nothing to do with the fact that I hadn't eaten and it was past three p.m. and the offices were on Washington near Chinatown. Hawk had introduced me to a place that made the best dumplings this side of Taipei.

I drove the short distance from Boylston past the Common, up to Tremont, and then crossed over to Washington. The offices were on the fifth floor of the old Washington-Essex Building where Duke Ellington once played the RKO theater. I recalled the same theater showing a lot of kung-fu movies and porn before the neighborhood got cleaned up. The neighborhood always made me think of April Kyle.

The fifth floor was a rat's maze of cubicles, with a receptionist stationed by the elevators. I had memorized a couple names from the DYS contact list. I dropped them. One was on vacation. Dave Nichols was on the phone. 'Do you have an appointment?' an attractive young black woman said.

'Would Mr Nichols handle audits?'

'It depends on the region,' she said. She had very big eyes and a wonderful mouth.

'Blackburn district, but this was two years ago,' I said.

'I believe that's him. Let me check.'

I removed my Brooklyn Dodgers cap and told her how much I appreciated the assistance.

I watched her steel herself against my charms and make a couple calls. 'Actually, that would have been John Blakeney.'

'Is he still with DYS?' I said, trying to imply I was in-the-know with my old pals.

'Let me check.'

Blakeney was two floors down with DTA. All the acronyms were starting to give me a headache. It seems that the old Department of Public Welfare hadn't really moved, only rejiggered their flow chart. I again took the elevator.

Blakeney was on the phone, a coworker told me. I waited in a very small, very hard red plastic chair by the elevator. I checked my phone for messages and stared straight ahead at a framed print of a young girl backed into a corner clutching a teddy bear. A hotline number was listed at the bottom.

A chalk-thin young man, completely bald on top with the sides of his head shaved, came up to me. He wore a green-striped dress shirt with a dark green tie. He had small eyes and a prominent nose. He seemed harried, telling me that he was, indeed, John Blakeney.

'Did you handle an audit of the Blackburn juvenile courts two years ago?'

He looked as if he'd just swallowed a whole lemon. I nearly pounded him on the back with the flat of my hand.

'Who are you?'

I handed him the card. It was the one without the skull and crossbones, to soften my approach.

'And who do you work for?'

He looked behind me. He looked over his shoulder. He asked if I would like to follow him back to his office. His office was actually just another cubicle, but I didn't argue. I sat down across from his desk in the cramped space. A lot of computer printouts of numbers had been tacked to the partition walls. He didn't speak. I wasn't sure if he was waiting for me to say anything.

'I work for the family of a kid railroaded by Judge Scali,' I said. 'I've heard he has the highest incarceration rate of minors in the state and you have the paper to prove it.'

Blakeney just stared at me, openmouthed. He wet his lips and picked up a pen and a paper.

'I'm no longer part of DYS,' he said, writing something down. 'You'll have to refer any inquires to my successor, Dave Nichols.'

He pushed across the paper: *I can't talk here.*

I tilted my head, having a brilliant idea for multitasking. I picked up his pen and wrote Gourmet Dumpling House. Beach Street. It was right around the corner. Two birds. One stone.

He looked to me and nodded.

'I'm sorry I can't be of more help,' he said.

'No problem,' I said, shaking his hand and walking out of the cubicle and back to the elevator. Only myself and Warner Oland could sleuth over a plate of scallion pancakes. I considered myself in elite company.

15

I sat at a window table at the Gourmet Dumpling House, working on my last soup dumpling, when John Blakeney walked in.

The scallion pancakes were gone, as was the order of sautéed beef with green peppers. I had just mastered holding a dumpling with chopsticks and then making a small hole to suck out the soup.

'My technique has really improved.'

'I've been here before,' Blakeney said.

'Have you tried the soup dumplings?'

'I don't think so.'

'You're missing out,' I said. 'It's what they do best.'

I offered to buy him lunch, or by now dinner, but he refused. We were the only ones left in the restaurant and I ordered another hot pot of tea. The tea was very good on a full stomach, and I had no illusions that I'd be hungry an hour later. Out on Beach Street, brightly colored neon signs advertised the rows of import/export shops, pho restaurants, and small groceries. It was snowing in microspecks, which blew around in a twirling wind. Blakeney took off a blue ski hat and his gloves.

He laid a thick file on the table. 'I would get fired for completing this audit.'

'Isn't this what you do?'

'It used to be. Now I track use of EBT cards. I have to make sure people aren't trying to counterfeit them or use them at liquor stores or strip clubs.'

'That sounds rewarding.'

'Yeah,' he said. 'I go home each day knowing I've made a difference. I'm so glad I got a master's.'

'The Blackburn audit caused the demotion?'

'They didn't call it a demotion,' he said. 'They called it a lateral move under the heading of Health and Human Services.'

'Got to love those lateral moves.'

'Yeah.' He reached for a napkin to dry his glasses. His ski hat was wet with melting snow.

'Who wanted you off the audit?'

'My supervisor, her supervisor, and it goes up from there,' he said. 'To be honest, Mr Spenser, I really don't know who wanted to shut down my inquiries. All I know is that they must be connected to some powerful people in state government.'

'Who?'

'Judge Callahan and his monkey, Scali.'

'Any official reason given?'

'No.'

'Did you find out much in the time you had?'

'You said it,' Blakeney said. 'Scali spends more money on sentencing kids to these facilities than anyone in the state.'

'Because he's Mr Zero Tolerance?'

'I'm not going to do your job for you,' he said. 'My job wasn't to find out the reasons. Only to find out how much money we were spending. You can interpret the reasons as you like.'

'But all of this started with Jim Price,' I said. 'That's how you got wind of this.'

He nodded. Both of his long hands rested on the file. He did not offer it to me, and I did not ask yet. The little specks of snow twirled and danced in the neon streetlights. Inside, several red-and-gold paper lanterns swung under the heating vents. An older Asian couple in heavy coats walked in the front door and spoke Chinese to the manager. He offered them a seat by the crab tank. I'd never been offered a seat by the crab tank. Had I been slighted?

'Judge Price and I became friends,' he said. 'This whole thing is what made him sick. When they demoted him, he kind of went nuts. All he could talk about was Scali and Callahan and their unholy alliance. He would call me in the middle of the night. We would meet in the city and in Blackburn for coffee. He had ideas. Conspiracy theories about what they were up to. Some were crazy. Some of them made sense.'

'Which ones?'

'I think Judge Scali's ego eclipsed any type of rational behavior,' he said. 'I think the job of the Commonwealth is to help children and families, not to further Scali's political and personal agenda.'

'What's his personal agenda?'

'Like I said, I'm not doing your job for you.'

'What about Callahan?' I said. 'What's his role?'

'To protect Scali,' he said. 'They've been friends since first grade. I don't know if you knew that or not. Judge Price knew everything about them. He said Callahan is the one who made some calls to Beacon Hill and had me reassigned. He's in tight with a lot of senators and congressmen. There's rumors he's pals with some Mob guys.'

'Like who?'

Blakeney patted the heavy stack of paper. 'I have absolutely no idea,' he said. 'Do I look like I know anyone in the Mob? All I know is that some people wanted this thing buried deep.'

'Even if you never finished?'

Blakeney smiled. He leaned back into his chair. He was quiet as the waiter returned to clear my empty plates. 'That's what they think,' he said. 'I spent weekends for three months finishing what I started.'

'Did Price ever know?'

Blakeney shook his head. 'Jim had died,' he said. 'He knew what they were doing wasn't right. I finished out of respect to him. I thought about giving it to a reporter, but they ask too many questions. I have a wife, three kids, and a mortgage. This job sucks. The people I work for do, too. But I have to pay the bills. Jobs aren't easy to find.'

'Besides being a private snoop, I have few marketable skills.'

'You really think you can do something with this, Spenser?'

'I'm going to try.'

'This isn't about Blackburn,' he said. 'This is about backroom Boston and old families and old favors. A shit ton of money. No one likes to be embarrassed. They'll come after you.'

'They always do,' I said. 'But I've dealt with worse.'

'They got rid of the judge, they got rid of me. They sure as hell will do what needs to get done with you. You won't see it coming.'

I touched the edge of the file as if it were a new and very exciting birthday present. Blakeney did not remove his hands, staring me in the eye. I stared back. I had a full stomach, an iron disposition, and a lot of time. Snow had started to fall in big flakes along Beach Street. It was very festive on the Asian neon signs. For a moment, it was hard to imagine we were in downtown Boston.

'I didn't give this to you,' he said.

'Nope.'

'I don't know you.'

'We never met,' I said.

He took his hands off the file, stood, and grabbed his hat and gloves. 'Good luck,' he said. 'But don't ever come to my place of work again. I'm through with all this.'

They made you shower and use some kind of soap to kill lice. The boy had never had lice in his life and the shampoo smelled like kerosene, burning his eyes. After the shower, he was given two sets of clothes. A faded-out black top and a faded-out green top. The pants were the same, both green. When he put them on, he looked like he was wearing hospital scrubs. He was told to wear socks with a pair of plastic shower shoes. When he asked about his real shoes, a guard told him this is what he wore inside. 'Outside,' he said, 'you get work boots.'

All the boys with facial hair were forced to shave. Everyone got haircuts whether they needed them or not. As a wrestler, the boy always kept his hair cut short. But when the guards got finished with him, he looked nearly bald.

The guards handed out heavy navy coats and walked them through the cold night to the bunkhouse. Some of the boys were sent into Building A, others were marched into Building B. The boy's name was called at C, cold air off the harbor freezing his face.

The building wasn't like a jail at all. It was one story and wide open. The whole place smelled like a hospital, a harsh chemical smell covering up something really bad. A black man in a guard's uniform told him to make his way to Group 4, where he'd get a bed.

Other boys dressed the same as him—black, white, Hispanic, and Asian—followed him with their eyes. Most just grouped around a flickering television watching an MMA match and yelling and screaming with each punch. He was handed clean linens for his bunk.

'What about my pillow?'

'Not now,' the guard said.

'What?' the boy said.

'You got to earn your pillow.'

The boy nodded, not understanding any of it. The guard left and the boy went to making his bed. He stowed the change of clothes in a footlocker, trying not to pay attention to the other kids watching. Some kid was lying heavy on the top of the bunk, then swung upside down to look at the boy as he made the bed.

'What's your name?' the kid said.

70

The boy told him.

'This place sucks balls.'

'No shit,' the boy said.

'You get any personal shit sent to you, keep it to yourself,' he said. 'Lock it away. Doesn't matter what it is. Someone will steal it. You stay here long enough and you get candy bars or dirty magazines, someone will kill you for it.'

'Come on.'

'Okay,' the kid said, and disappeared on the top bunk.

The windows had thick wire in the glass, bars covering every slot. The walls were white and the floors were gray. A toilet flushed in a bathroom way down the hall.

The kids in the television room yelled some more. A guard blew a whistle hard and told them to shut the hell up. The boy heard the wind coming across again and again like hard continuous slaps.

Out in the harbor, the winter wind was killer, blowing so hard he wondered if the little buildings could stand it. Like maybe all the buildings would crumble and fall into the harbor. When a real good gust would hit the windows, the lights would flicker on and off. For a moment, all the power went off and the boys from the MMA fight yelled and then started to laugh. Someone shot off an air horn. More yelling from the guards. A few flashlights scattered across the room. A generator kicked on.

The boy from the top bunk appeared again. 'So maybe they won't kill you,' the kid said. 'But they'll fight you for anything you got.'

'Great.'

'Can you fight?'

'Sure.'

'I can't,' the kid said. 'I'm screwed. I just make fun of them until they quit messing on me. The guards. The Roxbury crew. Maybe they'll be too tired tomorrow. Tomorrow is a workday. That horn will blow at five a.m., rain, sleet, or snow. It's kind of like sleep-away camp here. Except it sucks balls.'

'You said that already.'

'Thought you might need reminding,' the kid said.

The boy had his hands behind his head. He didn't look at the kid anymore, just stared at the bunk over him, the weight of the kid shifting and sagging through the mattress. The wind beat the hell out of the building some more like it had nothing better to do.

'Where you from?' the kid said. The two could not see each other.

'Blackburn.'

'No shit,' the kid said. 'Me, too. Wait. I don't know you.'

'Whatever,' the boy said. 'Who the hell are you?'

'Dillon,' the kid said. 'Dillon Yates.'

16

I drove back to my apartment and made a fire. I had bought a bundle of apple wood on a recent visit to Concord and used some small sticks for kindling. The fire was sweet and pleasant-smelling as I started to read through the files, leaving my Red Wings on the hearth to dry. Susan was having dinner with friends and so I made do with a block of feta, a half-pint of olives, and some Syrian flatbread from the East Lamjun Bakery. I set the food out on the coffee table on good plates, turned the Bruins match on mute, and opened my first Beck's of the evening. There was no rule that you couldn't enjoy yourself while you worked.

I made notes on a yellow legal pad as I read the report. The entire audit was about two hundred pages, most pages noting the expenditures from the Blackburn District family courts. Although not needed, Blakeney had left a summary of his findings. His name was nowhere to be found.

I got up and helped myself to a second Beck's. I stared out the window over my sink at Marlborough Street. It was sleeting a bit, needles passing through the yellow blossoms of streetlamps. The street was empty. Some of the parked cars had this afternoon's snow hiding their windshields.

I sipped some beer. I returned to my legal pad, making a few more notes. I continued to read. The Bruins were up by two goals. One of the players hip-checked another, starting a brawl. As if skating backward and precision with a stick weren't enough, you had to be able to use your fists.

I got back to reading and drinking beer. I was so talented at my job, I could do both at the same time. I could even digest what I'd been reading. If there was one continuous theme to the report, it was payments to a company called MCC. Massachusetts Child Care, as noted in the summary. Monies for juvenile transportation, meals, detention. A lot of money. I stopped counting after four million.

I knew from the Blackburn teens that Scali would send kids to either a reform camp in Haverhill or Fortune Island in the harbor. From the audit, I found out that Scali was definitely in favor of the island facility. Nearly the entire budget for boys was spent on Fortune Island. Girls were sent to the place in Haverhill. Both facilities were run by MCC. And after two seconds of detective work on my phone, I learned that MCC was not state-owned. It was a private prison run by a corporation.

I said 'aha' out loud and helped myself to a bit of flatbread topped with a wedge of feta and an olive. I drank some Beck's.

The folks at MCC would certainly want Scali to keep up his commitment to Zero Tolerance. The company was his go-to kids' jail. I didn't have a law degree, but I smelled the start of an ethics violation.

Sheila Yates thought something hinky was going on in Blackburn. She was right. I think we had more than enough evidence for the good folks at Cone, Oakes to win their appeal for her son. Scali had screwed up. He'd denied Dillon his right to an attorney for a ridiculous charge. From other parents and kids, I found out this wasn't an anomaly but his way of doing business. His breach of ethics in denying their rights to attorneys had helped MCC make a pile of cash.

If Dillon was released, I would write up a report and we could make a big stink with the state bar association. My client would be happy. Scali would have a lot to explain. And those behind his success would wring their hands.

I sipped some more beer. I had other cases to handle. Jobs that promised an actual payment. It had been months since the Heywood kidnapping. A lot of that fee had gone to flying to Paris with Susan. It cost a lot of money to eat well in the City of Lights.

An hour later, my phone rang.

'Oh, thank God you answered,' a young woman said.

'Most women say that.'

'It's Beth.'

'Oh,' I said. 'Hello, Beth.'

'I'm in jail,' she said. 'My mom won't answer her phone. I didn't know who else to call.'

'What happened?'

'I got pulled over,' she said. 'They found drugs in my car. It's not mine. I swear to Christ, Spenser. I swear.'

'Of course it's not,' I said. 'You're being punished.'

'For what?'

'For talking to me,' I said. 'For introducing your friends.'

'What do I do?' she said. 'Oh my God. My mom is going to completely freak the fuck out.'

'That sounds bad,' I said. 'Where are you?'

She told me. I turned off the hockey game, grabbed my coat and hat, and laced up my slightly dry but much warmer boots. I left my feast on the table and closed the doors to the fire. It had smelled so sweet.

17

Early the next morning, I sat in a booth across from Iris Milford at The Owl diner.

'That's pretty messed up,' Iris said.

'You bet.'

'Jamming up a kid for talking to you?' she said. 'When will she go before Scali?'

'Sometimes it can take a week or longer,' I said. 'That's too long to be in holding. I got her an attorney. It's my fault she's in the bind.'

Iris looked dynamite early that morning. Too dynamite for Blackburn and for The Owl. She'd hung up a black overcoat on a hook attached to the booth. She had on a slim-fitting black dress and black boots. A necklace made of faux Roman coins hung from her neck.

'I met Judge Price's wife.'

She asked me how that went. I told her.

75

'And this audit actually happened?' she said. 'Because that would be public record.'

'Yes and no.'

'How can it be both?'

'It happened after the auditor was relocated to a different department,' I said. 'He and Price had become friends. He wanted to see it through.'

'Did he file it?'

'No,' I said. 'But I have it.'

'Can I see it?'

'On one condition.'

'That I don't print anything until you've worked out all the details.'

'Wow,' I said. 'You've done this sort of thing before?'

Iris nodded. The waitress walked up to us and we ordered breakfast. I decided on the Greek omelet with wheat toast and an orange juice. The waitress refilled our coffees before she walked back to the kitchen.

'What did it say?'

'You ever heard of Massachusetts Child Care Inc.?'

'Of course,' she said. 'They got the contract when the old Fourth Street center closed. We did a whole series of articles about it. The place was more than a hundred years old. It was the original city jail and then became the juvie facility in the seventies. It was pretty awful. Place was falling apart. It had roaches and rats running around. Not the kind of place you wanted to put kids.'

'Did you cover the bidding process?'

'I don't know if there were other bids,' she said. 'A lot of people campaigned to have Fourth Street shut down. *The Star* was part of all that. We supported the closing and the state contracting with a licensed provider.'

I nodded.

'I know what you're thinking,' she said. 'But you didn't see this place. It was best for the community to find other options. This place was like something out of Dickens.'

I drank some coffee. The diner smelled of bacon cooking and coffee brewing. Silverware clattered, guys in coveralls told jokes, and old men talked about the weather.

'Do you know how much money the county has been paying MCC?'

'We were getting to that when Judge Price died,' she said. 'He thought the facility was costing too much. But we ran the numbers and did some interviews. MCC offered a fair rate for what they do.'

'How much?'

'I think it was like two hundred and fifty dollars a day per kid and about ninety thousand a year.'

'For two hundred and fifty a day, I could get them a good deal at the Taj.'

'Part of the cost involves schooling and rehabilitation.'

'Someone is getting rich.'

'Oh, hell, yes, it's wrong. All of it's wrong as hell. But so is this country's entire prison system. You want me to run down some numbers of young black males stuck in prisons across this country?'

I nodded. I drank some more coffee. A guy named Mel walked into the diner. Everyone seemed to know Mel and wished him a good morning. The short-order cook rang the bell several times in his honor.

'What do you know about MCC?' I said.

'Not much,' she said. 'It's a Boston company that runs correctional facilities throughout the state. Corporate prisons are a thing, in case you hadn't noticed.'

'You know who owns it?'

'I have all that information back at the newsroom,' she said. 'What are you getting at, Spenser?'

'I just would like to know who's profiting from Scali banging his gavel,' I said. 'Judge Price might have been onto something.'

'Jim Price was a sweet man,' she said. 'But he was a weird old white man. He saw conspiracies everywhere. He hated Scali's guts. He hated Callahan's even more.'

'His wife said that's what killed him,' I said. 'The stress.'

'I think she's right.'

The waitress brought out our breakfast. My omelet had spinach, tomatoes, and feta. The bacon on the side was a quarter-inch thick. Iris had some wheat toast and one scrambled egg. Heart healthy.

She pointed her fork at me to emphasize things as we spoke. 'I can run down the board of directors and that sort of thing,' she said. 'I think Scali is a hothead and a media hound. But it's a long jump to corrupt. Profiting from sending kids off. You'd have to prove a lot.'

'What kind of man denies attorneys in his courtroom?'

'Is that proven?'

'Nine out of ten teens I've met say so.'

Iris nodded. She ate some toast and picked at the egg the way Susan would. Maybe they weren't slow eaters, only trying to make the food go further. Up at the diner counter, Mel told a joke. When he hit the punch line, everyone laughed. Ol' Mel. What a card.

'I'll make copies of the audit,' I said. 'And send them to your office.'

'So that's what we're doing here?' she said. 'A little quid pro quo.'

'I only speak pig Latin.'

'Tit for tat.'

'More my speed.'

'Well, sure,' she said, taking the last bite of egg. 'I'm in. Just let me know before something explodes. Will you?'

I crossed my heart before eating more bacon.

'Feels good,' she said. 'Reminds me that I used to actually work for a real newspaper.'

'I feel bad for the kid.'

'Which one?' she said.

'Both of them,' I said. 'They wouldn't let me see Beth. She can't make bail until tomorrow.'

'You know who arrested her?'

'Same cop who rousted me after I left the high school.'

'Hmm.'

'I know,' I said. 'Small world.'

18

I met Megan Mullen at the Blackburn courthouse shortly after four o'clock.

I'd been waiting on a wooden bench on the first floor for the last hour, watching cops, plaintiffs, and legal eagles pass by. I liked courthouses. I'd spent a lot of time in them, both as a witness and as an investigator for the DA. This one was so old it still had a bank of phone booths by the restrooms. I half expected to see Clark Gable rush into one and tell his editor to go suck an egg.

Megan bounded down the marble steps. She carried a smart leather satchel. As she approached, she smiled, which I took to be a good sign.

'Your pal Beth will be out within the hour,' she said.

'I doubt she's my pal anymore,' I said. 'Being arrested puts a damper on one's relationship.'

'ADA didn't want to argue against the merits of keeping a first-time offender in school. I had to make some concessions, but ultimately they backed down.'

'Did you threaten them?' I said.

'Why not,' Megan said. 'Never hurts.'

'When all else fails.'

'Kick 'em in the balls.'

'I take it the ADA was a man.'

'Was that a sexist remark?' she said.

'And appropriate.'

Megan looked at least six months older today in a two-button black wool blazer over a knee-length black dress. She wore black-framed glasses, her brown hair stylish and loose across her shoulders. She took a seat next to me, clutching her satchel and glancing down at her phone.

'To be honest,' she said, scrolling through messages, 'it didn't take much to argue Beth's not a flight risk or a danger to others.'

'What were the charges?'

'Originally?' she said. 'They had her with possession with intent to sell. I got the intent dropped. She will have to go before Scali, but she can be at home until her court date.'

'What kind of drugs?'

'You ever heard of molly?'

'As in "Good Golly"?'

'As in the club drug.'

'I've been off the club scene lately,' I said. 'Since I quit the DJ gig.'

Megan eyed me with just a hint of suspicion. 'Just what does Rita see in you?'

I offered her my biceps and flexed. Megan looked at me and widened her eyes behind her smart glasses. She declined to squeeze. 'I don't like these people, Spenser,' she said. 'The clerk seemed completely ill-equipped to deal with a juvenile with counsel, as if having an attorney is unheard of.'

'You should meet the public defender,' I said. 'He's a real hoot after a few drinks.'

'From what you told me,' she said, 'ick.'

'Yep, Mr Ick. That's him.'

Two Blackburn uniform cops passed and eyed me with a bit of suspicion. Maybe the word had gotten out. Or maybe I'd just grown paranoid. They might have very well been jealous of my Dodgers cap or my vintage leather bomber jacket. Maybe they wanted to sit down and join us. Talk a little about Duke Snider and the '59 series.

'What sucks is how dismissive they are here,' she said. 'A senior partner had to call and ream out the DA.'

'Yowzer,' I said.

There was talk and laughter up on the marble landing, and as we both looked up, a short man with thin black hair and purple-tinted glasses descended the staircase. He wore civilian garb, a gray suit with wide lapels and padded shoulders, set off with a wide and bright silver tie. The last time I'd seen a suit like that was right before *Dynasty* went off the air.

Joe Scali walked with two men who looked to be cops. They wore street clothes and each displayed a shield and a gun on their belts. Scali did not break stride as he passed our little wooden bench. But the talk and laughter stopped and there was a slight beat of hesitation, a slight turn of his head, eye contact, and then he moved on.

'I'm ready for my close-up, Mr DeMille.'

'That's him?' Megan said.

'I know,' I said. 'I thought he'd be taller, too.'

'No, that's not it,' she said. 'I didn't think he'd be so—'

'Sharply dressed?'

'Oily.'

The few people milling about the halls were called back into one of the courtrooms. The ancient twin doors opened onto the street and Scali and his pals left the building. A cold wind shot through the entrance and down through the halls. I sunk my hands into my jacket. 'Thanks,' I said.

Megan smiled. 'I only wish I could do more for Dillon Yates.'

'You filed an appeal,' I said. 'Now we wait.'

'I do wish his mother had contacted us first,' she said. 'After working for the firm, she should have known better. He would have never been sentenced to that island.'

'You know much about Massachusetts Child Care?'

'No,' she said. 'Most of my clients are over eighteen.'

'They own Dillon's digs on Fortune Island,' I said. 'They get two hundred and fifty bucks a day to keep him there.'

'What can you do while we wait?' she said.

'Follow Scali around,' I said. 'See how the judicial set lives.'

I took off my Dodgers cap, rolled the bill, and set it back on my head.

'Good luck,' she said. We walked out of the old courthouse together and shook hands before going different ways.

19

A car, or even an SUV in my case, was only comfortable for so long. I once drove a '68 Chevy convertible with bucket seats. For a while I had a Subaru Outback with seats designed for Billy Barty. Sometimes I borrowed Susan's MG and later her Bronco. But I liked the Explorer. It was comfortable, innocuous in traffic. Good gas mileage for the size. It had seat warmers and Bluetooth technology. Sometimes when the tech gods were with me, I could talk dirty to Susan while keeping both hands on the wheel.

But my Ford was little match for Scali's gunmetal-gray Cadillac ELR. The car had jeweled brake lights, glowing with a lot of style at stoplights, and bright chrome wheels. I hung back as I followed him. I knew his address. I just wanted to see if he made any other stops on the way home.

I listened to an Artie Shaw CD as I drove through Blackburn.

He drove in the opposite direction of his Belleview home. He jetted along the Merrimack River to an exit off I-93 and parked in the lot of an International House of Pancakes. I knew that he'd seen my face. What a shame I'd miss a chance to dine at an IHOP. Maybe the old Bickford's cafeteria. But I drew the line at IHOP.

I waited inside my car with Artie. *When I'm calling you / Will you answer, too?*

Scali was gracious enough to take a seat by the picture window. He was seated alone, with a very large menu. About twenty minutes later, a beefy-looking gray-headed man in a tan overcoat joined him. Scali didn't stand or shake hands. The beefy man took a seat, and the waitress dropped off a menu. So many culinary choices, so little time. They both snapped their menus shut at about the same time. The sign outside advertised SIGNATURE FAVORITES. And the all-new Blue Cheese and Bacon Sirloin. Mario Batali, take note.

I checked my email. I checked my voicemail. I checked my profile for any stray hairs I missed while shaving. Late afternoon turned later. It got dark very early. It seemed even later in Blackburn. Susan would be finishing with her last client about now. She would be taking Pearl out for a long walk along Linnaean Street. Inventive cocktails were being poured in Harvard Square. Bistros along Newbury Street had opened for dinner. I had two dry-aged filets in my refrigerator.

I had three other cases to be stoked.

There was more dry apple wood in the cellar of my apartment building. And according to my phone, TCM was running *Monte Walsh*.

After an hour and sixteen minutes, Scali and the beefy man walked out together. Scali had on a long black overcoat and swiveled a toothpick in his mouth. The pancakes must've been something else.

The men separated with a handshake. I wrote down the tag number on the beefy man's big black Mercedes and gave Scali a two-minute start. I followed him back up the Merrimack and back into the center of town. There was something obsessively cold and dark about February in Massachusetts. The dull burn of streetlamps, the dirty snowbanks, the long, meandering stretch of a half-frozen river.

Scali's house was about a quarter-mile away from Judge Price's house in Belleview. Christmas decorations still adorned Scali's house. I thought about walking straight up to the door and regaling him with some carols. Any man who loved Christmas so much he wanted to celebrate it two months later couldn't be all bad. Multicolored lights ran up and down the V's of the roofline. A snowman made of LED lights glittered on the snow-covered lawn. I parked a few houses down the street. I removed my Dodgers cap, although I needed it, turned up the collar on my jacket, and went out for a stroll. This was in equal parts surveillance and a way of loosening my stiff knee.

I had already received two texts from Susan reminding me of my rehab. I walked for nearly a half-mile, trying to get a feel for the upper-middle-class neighborhood. I learned a lot of people liked to celebrate Christmas well into the next year. The houses were a mix of mid-century modern and neo-Colonial. I had my hands in my jacket pockets, my breath coming in clouds. I missed the jogging. I liked the rhythm and feel of pounding the pavement.

I turned back and walked past Scali's house. The curtains were closed and the Cadillac safely stowed away in his garage. The house was big, a three-story Colonial painted gray with white trim. A wrought-iron fence encircled the property. I gave up the idea of knocking on the door and singing carols and returned to my SUV. I plugged in the address to a realty website for an estimate of how much the good judge had paid for the house.

Being a master detective with a smartphone, I learned he'd bought the property only two years ago for $750,000. He paid about nine grand a year in property taxes. *Ouch*.

I didn't know how much a juvenile court judge made, but I could easily find out.

I waited for a couple minutes for Scali to run from the house and confess his sins. When this didn't happen, I started the Explorer and drove back to Boston. It was late, so I'd only cook one of the steaks and open a nice bottle of Cabernet.

I didn't even slow down when I passed the IHOP.

20

The next morning, I had huevos rancheros with a side of fresh fruit, OJ, and black coffee at the Paramount before driving out to the office of Massachusetts Child Care. The day was sunny and bright, with a hard white glint off the Common and the tips of snowbanks lining Boylston. I cut up to Soldiers Field Road and followed the Charles before crossing over the river and into Watertown, where I found MCC's offices on the entire third floor of a repurposed turn-of-the-century schoolhouse. The office had wide-plank wood floors, plaster walls, and transoms over the glass doors. There was soft light along a row of framed posters of happy children free of drugs, behavior problems, or crime. A sign on the door read making a difference for today's youth!

There were six glass doors along each side of the long corridor, old classrooms subdivided. A perky young black woman in a tailored suit asked if she might be of help.

'I'd like to speak to Mr Talos,' I said. After seeing Robert Talos Jr. share the hallowed booth at IHOP with Scali and running his license plate, I'd learned he was the big cheese at MCC. Putting two and two together, I'd come up with one.

'Do you have an appointment?' she said. 'Mr Talos is often out with business. May I ask what this is regarding?'

'You may,' I said. 'I have questions about MCC and a teenager in your care.'

Less than thirty seconds later, I was being introduced to Jane Corbin, parental communication specialist. Since I wasn't a parent, I worried we wouldn't be able to talk. Would a translator be necessary? I thought maybe I could win over Jane and then maybe get a handoff to Talos. 'My name is Knute Rockne. My son George is to be rehabilitated by MCC. I had a few questions.'

'Have a seat, Mr Rockne,' she said. 'Please. How might we be of help?'

Jane Corbin was short and plump, with a round face and reddish hair chopped to the shoulders. She wore a tweed skirt and a red V-neck cashmere sweater, a stylish scarf wrapped around her thick neck. I sat and tried to look worried. I screwed up my mouth and tried to imagine sitting through a movie based on a Nicholas Sparks novel. 'I don't really know where to begin.'

'Your son.'

'Yes,' I said. 'He's a good kid who's had a tough year.'

'It happens,' Jane said. She looked so sincere. So sincere that I thought she actually might be. She pursed her lips and nodded with great understanding.

'I guess I don't know what to expect,' I said. 'What exactly is it that you do here?'

She smiled. She'd answered this question many times before. She placed the flats of her hands together on the top of her desk. She licked her lips and said, 'First off, we are not a prison.'

'But one gets sentenced to spend time at MCC?'

'Yes,' she said. 'We are contracted by certain counties as alternatives to traditional juvenile jails.'

'Oh,' I said. 'Thank God.'

'This isn't just punishment,' she said. 'We have classes at all MCC facilities. Your son. What is his name again?'

'George,' I said. 'But we call him the Gipper.'

'Well, George can continue on with his schoolwork,' she said. 'His education will continue. We have a full staff of teachers who will help him earn class credit. And if he's looking toward college, we can even help him study for the ACT or SAT.'

I nodded. I tried to look interested and pleased. I thought of huevos rancheros with homemade salsa on top. I smiled. In my heart, my enthusiasm grew. Method acting.

'Most parents are worried about the stereotypes of juvie jails or work camps they've seen in movies,' she said. 'That's not the case here. We have classes and sports activities. Does your son play sports?'

'He's very good at football.'

'Wonderful,' she said. 'He'll have plenty of time outdoors. We also have nature activities, like hiking.'

'Should be lovely this time of year,' I said. 'It was almost twenty degrees yesterday.'

'The wind in the harbor isn't as bad as they say,' she said before emitting a funny little laugh. 'We make sure all the offenders—I mean teens—are well dressed for the nature walks.'

'Well, I know I'm feeling much better.'

She beamed. I tried to beam but wasn't very good at it. I tried to think of a lobster roll for lunch, but it wasn't working.

'Parents worry this is just punishment,' she said. 'But the whole philosophy of MCC is based on balance and restorative justice principles.'

'Which are?'

'We provide programs of supervision, care, and rehabilitation, with balanced attention to competency development, victim awareness and restoration, and community protection. George will receive structured, individualized treatment from a supervisor with no less than a master's degree. He will also receive individual counseling, group therapy, family therapy, and take part in psych educational groups, and life- and employability-skills groups.'

'Whoopee.'

'You don't seem pleased.'

'On the contrary,' I said. 'I'm thrilled. George has been so upset, he's bedridden. He might need a pep talk.'

'We have a multidisciplinary team approach to working with youth,' Jane said, smiling hard and tight. 'We work closely with contracted medical services and licensed psychologists. Our employees who have direct and regular contact with your child receive eighty hours of training before they are in the dorms with him.'

I whistled with awe. The whistle was convincing as hell.

'And if George isn't interested in college, we have life-skills classes, such as culinary arts, upholstery, Lego robotics, and lab volt work.'

'Lab volt?'

'Home electrical wiring and cable installation.'

'Wow.'

'So this isn't at all a bad thing, Mr Rockne,' she said. It's a—'

'Win-win?'

'Yes.'

'Somehow I knew you were going to say that.'

'When does George begin his time with us?' she said.

'Two weeks,' I said, taking a long breath and shaking my head. 'I have to say he's not thrilled. This fall was going to be his big year on the team.'

'He'll be fine,' she said, standing up, signaling a close to our nice chat. 'I assure you. The food is good. There is a nature club, a media club, and even a talent show in every season.'

'You make it sound almost like summer camp.'

'This isn't the old days,' she said. 'We're a team here, too. That's why what we do works better than anything the state can offer. We want to intervene with children before they turn eighteen. This is the crucial time to make it work for all of us.'

I smiled and stood also. 'Quite impressive,' I said.

She smiled. I smiled back. There was a long silence as we flexed our facial muscles.

'But is Mr Talos around?' I said. 'I feel like I should thank him in person. You know, for the forethought.'

'Mr Talos isn't here today,' she said, walking to the door and standing in the frame. I didn't move. 'But I'd be glad to pass along your kind words.'

'Who runs things in his absence?'

'Mr Talos runs a great many businesses,' she said. 'He just happens to be out this morning. But he is the individual in charge.'

'Perhaps I might stop by later?'

'I promise to pass on your thanks,' she said. 'And if you have any other questions about your child or our award-winning programs...'

I smiled and passed her in the narrow frame out into the hall of the old schoolhouse. The perky black woman and Jane Corbin exchanged hard looks. The hall was long and empty, every glass door shut, people going about their own business. Beside the art and the framed MCC posters, there was a lonely copy machine. The black woman then scowled at me. I smiled and turned back to Jane.

'Win-win,' I said.

Jane was no longer smiling. She looked doubtful of my story and swallowed a couple times. Her cheeks had a touch of red. I winked and showed myself out. As I turned to the elevator, both women watched me go. They were pros.

They knew a troublemaker when they saw one.

'Do you really want to get off this island?' Dillon Yates said.

'Hell, yes,' the boy said.

'Then you got to drink their Kool-Aid,' he said. 'You have to act like the MCC way is the real way. Say "yes, sir" and "no, sir" and get into all the speeches and pep talks they give. Sing their songs. Dance their dance. When you fill out the forms about your progress, quote shit they've said. You tell them that they've done something good and they'll take time off.'

'Is that what you do?'

'Are you freaking kidding?' Dillon said. 'This place is Looney Tunes. All they do is feed us, work us, and let us sleep and watch TV. The classes are a joke. The activities are a joke. The pep talks are downloaded off some kind of religious website. The people they hire are fuckups. They couldn't get work at a decent place. Two of the guards spent time at Walpole, for crissake.'

'Can't you tell somebody?'

'Like who?' Dillon said. 'The freakin governor? The guards like to watch us fight like we're dogs. Or see us fall on the rocks by the beach when we race. They think all the crap we get into is funny. The more dangerous it is, the funnier it is. Haven't you noticed they don't carry guns? They want to do something to you, they'll just beat the crap out of you. They'll report that you did it to yourself.'

The boys stood huddled together in the common area between the housing units. Snow powdered the dead grass and the basketball court was pocked with footprints. Two black kids shot some hoops. The boy liked Dillon. He was the only one who'd talked to him that much since he'd gotten to Fortune Island, telling him the unofficial rules.

1. Don't get caught smoking.
2. Don't ever go alone anywhere with just one guard. Always ask for at least two, so you'll have a witness.
3. Don't mess with the black kids. Or anyone from the South Shore or Revere. Just mind your own business.

4. *Don't volunteer for work. They'll have you picking up trash all day on the West Shore.*

5. *And stay the fuck away from Tony Ponessa.*

'Who's Tony Ponessa again?' the boy said.

Dillon Yates motioned with his chin at a gangly-looking kid with a shaved head standing alone by the edge of the open court. He was staring right at the boy and Dillon, his hands in his paper-thin coat. His face was thin and weasely. He had some kind of tattoo on his neck.

'What's the big deal?' the boy said.

'Ponessa is the mayor around here,' Dillon said. 'He's lived on this island since they built it five years ago. He killed his own brother back in Brockton. He likes to fight. He likes to start shit even if you don't. If he has it in for you, just turn away, act like he isn't there.'

'He's staring at me.'

'Because you're new,' Dillon said. 'When I got here a few weeks ago, we were out picking up beach trash and he came at me. I didn't even see it. He knocked me in the back of the head and started to fill my mouth with sand. He doesn't look like much. But he's strong.'

'I know how to fight,' the boy said. 'That shit doesn't bother me. I weigh more than him. I get him on the ground and the kid is done.'

'You can't win,' Dillon said. 'The guards like him. That's why he's always with Sergeant Fuckwad.'

'Who's he?'

'You see the muscly guy with the crew cut?' Dillon said. 'He's totally into saying "yes, sir" and doing pushups. He'll start talking to you about a career in the military. Just you wait.'

'He drove the boat out here,' the boy said. 'He watched me the whole time.'

'There's something wrong with that guy,' Dillon said. 'Something weird in his eyes like he's taking a leak on himself. He gives me the creeps.'

The boy nodded. Tony Ponessa had moved from the court, going over to talk to the two black kids shooting hoops. Ponessa stood flat-footed and easily sunk a shot. When the shot clanged through the hoop, he turned to stare at the boy. He wasn't smiling.

'I'm supposed to meet with the shrink today.'

'Have fun,' Dillon said. 'That guy is a true weirdo. Dr Feelgood. I think he's on drugs the way he talks. He wants you to look at pictures and tell him that you hate your mother and that you want to go and jump in the harbor.'

'He needs to know I'm not supposed to be here.'

'None of us are supposed to be here, man,' Dillon said. 'The only things that should be living on this island are seagulls and lizards. And Tony Ponessa. That kid's got serious head issues. Did I tell you he's into cutting himself?'

'What do you mean?'

'He likes to steal forks and shit and carve things on his arm,' Dillon said. 'Last week, he got some rubber bands and tied up his fingers until they turned black. The guard had to take him out of the line and over to the infirmary.'

'How come they don't send him away?' the boy said. 'To some kind of mental unit?'

'He hates himself but doesn't want to leave,' Dillon said. 'I think he wants to freakin' die out here or something. The guards love him. They bring him pizza and shit from the shore. They feel sorry for him or something.'

'Somebody will listen to me.'

Dillon smiled and shook his head. A cold wind shot off the harbor and cut down deep through the open space. 'I know my mother has tried,' he said. 'But she says it takes money to get people to listen. And we don't have much since my dad left.'

'How long until you go home?'

'Six more months until I get off this place,' Dillon said. 'But I'm never going back to Blackburn.'

'Why?'

'Because once you're tagged as a bad kid, the judge won't ever let you go,' he said. 'He'll find a way to get you back in until you're eighteen.'

'I hate that guy's guts.'

'I hate everything about him,' Dillon said. 'I see him in my sleep with those purple glasses looking at me. He doesn't care. Nobody listens. That's just the way things are.'

'My dad will straighten it out' the boy said. 'I didn't kill anyone. I didn't steal anything.'

The wind came up hard off the harbor and quieted the teens for a moment. The boy could make out a long line of black rocks that protected the shore and beach and this whole damn place from floating away.

21

I met Bill Barke at the Davio's on Arlington. He was already at the bar waiting for me, seated at the apex of the glass walls on the first floor. The bar was large and long, and within walking distance of my office. Before I sat down, I knew I'd get a lobster roll and a Harpoon draft.

Bill was about my age, with a thick head of graying hair and a mustache. He was a former college basketball player and stood a few inches taller than me. He wore glasses and a tailored suit. He was a self-made success who'd gone to a state school in Pennsylvania and had a good eye for solid character. I figured that's why he liked me. Or perhaps it was that I'd helped him out a few years ago when a couple of thugs were trying to shake down a Boston charity he supported. Either way, we'd become friends. Just this Christmas he'd sent me a fruit basket.

'So you want to know about Bobby Talos?' He had a firm hand-shake and a good, knowing smile.

'Any friend of Bobby's,' I said.

'I'm not his friend,' Bill said, smiling. 'How do I put this? Talos is a real horse's ass.'

'Any other part of the horse?'

'That part, too,' Bill said. 'Especially. He took over the board of a nonprofit I respect and ran it into the ground. He was more about the party than what they supported. In one year, the charity dropped below fifty percent of contributions while expenditures had tripled.'

'Nice.'

'How about you?' Barke said. 'How'd you cross paths with this son of a bitch?'

I told him about my client and Dillon Yates without mentioning the boy's name. Most of Bill's fundraising work revolved around children, and he sat on the board of Jumpstart, one of the best. He listened intently as I told him a little about the situation in Blackburn and what I knew about the facility on Fortune Island.

'Talos built this place?' Barke said. 'The island prison?'

'He didn't just build it,' I said. 'He owns it. Or his company, Minos Inc., does.'

'Private prisons,' Bill said. 'They get our kids if we don't get to them first.'

'Besides being a rich creep, what can you tell me?'

'Let's order first,' Bill said. 'It's best to discuss creeps on a full stomach. You hungry?'

'Is this a trick question?'

Bill grinned. He ordered us both lobster rolls with fries and two draft beers. We drank the beer as Bill collected his thoughts. 'I can make a few calls, but the overall consensus on Talos is that he does whatever needs to be done to get a project completed. With shopping malls, he has city council members, union bosses, and local thugs on speed dial.'

'That comes in handy.'

The lobster roll, even as judged by an advanced palate, was perfect. Emphasis on the lobster, not the mayo. The bread was spot-on.

'I knew his old man,' Bill said. 'He was a creep, too. But he was less flashy about it. Bobby keeps a one-hundred-thirty-foot IAG Electra in a slip at the Boston Harbor Hotel.'

'That's a boat?'

'That's a yacht,' Bill said. 'They're bigger and nicer than any boat. I went to a party he was having out there a couple years ago. I was trying to make nice, as I thought I could influence Talos into doing the right thing on a few issues. I was at the party all of ten minutes when I saw things I ain't never seen before.'

'Momma told you not to come.'

'You bet,' he said. 'Just use your imagination. It was like a big frat party for a bunch of old fat guys.'

'Did they wear togas?' I said.

'No,' he said. 'Thank God.'

'Do you know anyone who worked with him but has left the fold?' I said.

'No,' he said. 'But I can ask around. You think he's paying off this judge?'

'Yep.'

'That'll be tough to prove,' Bill said. 'I doubt they're meeting in the Common exchanging sacks of cash.'

'You'd be surprised how sloppy people get.'

I was already half finished with the lobster roll and the beer. I tried to pace myself; I wanted to prolong the experience.

'How's the knee?' Bill said.

'Better,' I said. 'How'd you know?'

'I've been working out at the Harbor Health Club,' Bill said. 'To hear Cimoli tell it, you're falling apart.'

'Ha,' I said. 'I'll be running again in a week. Henry's just jealous. It's a height thing.'

'Nobody gets out of this world without a little maintenance.'

I shrugged. I finished off the roll and drank the last of the beer.

'You want another?'

I shook my head. 'Yes, but no.'

I reached for my wallet and Bill put his hand out. 'On me, Spenser,' he said. 'It'll be nice for you to owe me for a change.'

'So noted.'

'Let me know what you hear about Talos,' he said. 'In a town of some authentic creeps, he's unique company to keep.'

22

When I returned to my office, I found three men waiting for me. They did not seem lost or in need of my sleuthing services. One was sitting in my chair with his feet up on my desk. Another had his back to the wall by my washbasin, and the other sat in a client chair, playing with his gun.

'You Spenser?' the man in my chair said.

'Jesus,' I said. 'You come in and lean on a guy, at least you could read the lettering on the door. No, I'm Ted Lipshitz, CPA. Spenser is two doors down. But be careful. He doesn't like illiterate dipshits putting their feet up on his desk.'

The man stood quick. *Thatta boy, Spenser.* Hurl the really tough insults.

He was a large man, as all leg breakers tend to be. He had a lean face and a square jaw. He had shaved his receding hair down to nearly nothing on his head and wore a black leather jacket, as did the other two guys in his crew.

'Nice jackets. Was Burlington having a sale?' I said. 'Two-for-one Naugahyde?'

'I'll cut to the chase,' the man said.

'Goody.'

I moved behind my desk and pushed in to a few inches of where he sat. He smiled, stood, and stepped back. The snug-fitting coat didn't do much to conceal the gun he wore on his left side. I sat at the desk, flicking my eyes at the other two. The man with the gun was really more of a kid, with a freckled white face and red hair that only a mother from County Cork could love.

The man leaning against the washbasin had gray curly hair and wore dark sunglasses. He looked like a guy I may have met once. The man didn't say anything. I edged forward, inching my hand under the desk, not far from the right-hand drawer.

'I'll spell it out to you,' the bald guy said.

'Let me know if you need help.'

'Keep on being a wiseass and they'll be cleaning you up off Berkeley Street with a mop.'

I nodded. 'How about you say it one more time, slower. And squint your eyes. You'll look tougher if you squint.'

The redheaded kid with the gun snickered. The bald man told him to shut the fuck up.

'Youth,' I said.

'Your services are terminated in Blackburn,' he said.

'Yikes.'

'Go ahead,' he said. 'Push it. You have no idea the kinda people you're pissing off.'

'That's where you're wrong,' I said. 'I have a pretty good idea of the people I'm pissing off. I have a list. Would you like me to write a note back to Mr Talos?'

Baldy looked at me, eyes narrowing. He was learning or just looked confused. Of course, he probably always looked confused. But I don't think he knew who I was talking about. I didn't think the guy was good enough to feign ignorance. He was too good at conveying the real thing.

'Jimmy.'

The redheaded kid stood holding the gun. The senior gentleman with the gray curly hair pushed himself off the wall. They walked toward my desk.

'I know you,' I said, snapping my fingers at the old guy. 'You were in the Mickey Mouse Club. You, Cubby, and Annette. Wow. Brings back some real memories.'

'I worked for Joe Broz,' he said. 'The man hated your fucking guts.'

'And now he's dead,' I said. 'Who said there's no such thing as karma?'

'He was a good man,' he said. 'Open your mouth again and I'll shoot you in the fucking nuts.'

'Hold on,' I said, reaching for my yellow legal pad and a pen. I did so with my left hand, using my right to open up the drawer. I awkwardly picked up the pen and reached into the drawer for my .357. 'First off, stay out of Blackburn. Second, don't open my mouth. Is there a third request?'

'Hey,' the redhead said. 'He's got it.'

'Shut the fuck up,' the bald man said.

The boy had a gun but he held it loose by his right leg. The gray-headed thug began to reach into his jacket. I grabbed the Magnum and pointed it dead center of the main guy. I began to whistle a sad rendition of the Mickey Mouse Club song. I let go of the pen with my left hand and began to wave. 'See you real soon.'

The big man with the shaved head swallowed. He stood there and breathed.

'You know me, Cubby,' I said. 'Tell him this isn't a bluff.'

'Nope,' the gray-headed man said.

'Stay out of Blackburn,' Baldy said.

I kept on whistling. '*Why*? Because we like you.'

'This guy is fucking nuts,' the redhead said. 'Old dude is nuts.'

'Drop the gun, kid,' I said. My eyes flicked over each one of them. The kid smiled but soon the smile dropped. He let go of the automatic. It clattered to the floor.

'Now, all of you walk out the door and go away,' I said. 'I'll need to fumigate the place after you're gone.'

The big man spit on my floor and tromped out. The gray-headed man smirked and winked at me before following. The kid stood like a deer in headlights, unsure whether to leave the gun or not. I leveled an unpleasant stare at him, gun in hand, as I heard the men's heavy footsteps move down the hall.

He said, 'Shit,' and turned and left.

When I spotted them on Berkeley getting into a large black SUV, I set the .357 on the table. I couldn't see the tag number and knew I wasn't fast enough to run down to my car and follow.

Besides, I knew they'd soon be back.

23

Susan and I went for another walk, this time in Cambridge. We had followed Mass Avenue from Linnaean Street, past the park and the Old Burying Grounds. A lot of the snow had melted in select spots, and you could see actual grass among the crooked tombstones. We crossed into Harvard Yard through the stately brick buildings and by the big bronze statue of John Harvard. It was dark, and the classroom and office lights made a checkerboard pattern in the dark.

Pearl did her business as soon as we walked under the iron gates, seeming to make sure not to desecrate the hallowed ground. We came out on Brattle Street and headed back from whence we came. On the return, I had the inspired idea to order a pizza with mushrooms and peppers.

I told Susan while we walked about what I'd learned about MCC and Minos Inc., and from Bill Barke. I mentioned a little about my run-in that afternoon with three men. I told her my funniest lines, but she didn't laugh.

'They brought guns into your office?'

'They weren't the first,' I said. 'Won't be the last.'

'But they threatened you.'

'Well,' I said. 'Yeah. It's what guys like that do.'

'And I'm sure you called the police?'

'Nope.'

'Why not?'

'Wouldn't do any good,' I said. 'I don't know who they are. And I didn't have much to offer the police.'

'You could call Quirk.'

'I use that contact sparingly.'

'When someone dies.'

'Always the best time for Quirk.'

We strolled for a little bit with Pearl. Pearl Two was about ninety-nine percent muscle, and had I decided to hook her up to a sled, we could've ridden in style to Susan's. But I kept her on a tight leash, trying to look dignified in an old sweatsuit and watch cap. Susan had on black leggings and jogging shoes, and a big black puffy coat over a sweatshirt. She wore a slouchy gray hat like nobody's business.

'When does Z get back?' she said.

'I'm not sure.'

'Of course, you could call Hawk.'

'The idea had crossed my mind,' I said. 'But I don't think a few knuckleheads merit reaching out to Hawk. He might make fun of me.'

'Is he in town?'

'Yep.'

'And when does the situation merit it?'

'If matters escalate.'

'What if they escalate without you knowing it?'

'These guys were semi-pro,' I said. 'One of them had been a garbage collector for Joe Broz.'

'Who do they work for now?'

'I don't know,' I said. 'Things aren't as clear as they used to be. You used to know who was who and what crew they ran with. If you were Italian or Irish or black, that gave you a little idea of the neighborhood. But color, race, ethnicity is of little consequence anymore.'

'Progress.'

'Yep,' I said. 'The hoods have finally integrated in Boston.'

'Whoopee,' Susan said.

'But if it were my guess, I hear there is a shake-up in the city. I think some of the men who shall remain nameless in Providence are setting up more branch offices in the North End.'

'Really?'

'That's the word,' I said. 'I heard it from a blind shoeshine man outside a Falafel King downtown.'

'That's solid.'

'You bet.'

We walked farther up Commonwealth. The sidewalks were clean of ice and snow, and for a moment I realized spring would be here soon.

'Why would some hoods from the North End be involved with a judge in Blackburn?'

'I haven't the foggiest.'

'What's your best guess?'

'I'll go with money,' I said. 'When in doubt, go with the money.'

'And how is the boy?'

'On the island,' I said. 'Megan Mullen thinks she can get the ruling overturned. But that'll take some time.'

'Could you go out and see him?' she said. 'See how he is?'

'I'd have to rent a boat and break into the facility,' I said. 'I tried to have a friendly sit-down with the company CEO, but he was away from the office. I was shuffled off to a happy plump woman who spoke in platitudes. All further calls to the CEO were unreturned.'

'Has his mother seen him?'

'No.'

'Can she speak to him?'

'They talk once a week,' I said. 'Phone calls are limited to fifteen minutes. They're also monitored.'

'So she has really no idea how he's doing?'

'Nope.'

'That must be horrible.'

'She's pretty upset,' I said. 'As you can imagine.'

We finally made it to Linnaean and walked up the steps of Susan's Victorian, where she lived and kept her practice. Pearl jumped up the steps as if ready to repeat the entire walk. I held on to the bannister and stretched out my leg. There was a neat little sign by the front door that noted SUSAN SILVERMAN. PSYCHOTHERAPIST.

'Do you ever get walk-in clients?' I said.

'You'd be surprised.'

'Do we have beer?'

'And wine and soon a pizza,' she said. 'What more could a good Jewish girl want for an evening?'

'Let's get changed and I'll show you.'

'My mother warned me about a goy like you,' she said. 'She said they only think of one thing.'

I leaned in and kissed her on the cheek as she unlocked the door. I whispered into her ear, 'Your mother was right.'

24

The next day, I hadn't been in Blackburn all of two hours when a cop pulled me over with his flashers. He asked me to step out of the car and put my hands on the roof.

I told him this technically wasn't a car. 'It's an SUV,' I said. 'It has four-wheel drive and everything.'

'Get the fuck out of the car, smart-ass, before I drag you out.'

'That would be interesting to see.'

'What?'

'I said I'd be thrilled if you'd try,' I said. 'You know, reach in, grab me by the arms, and see what happens? It'll be fun. You look like you could use a little workout this morning.'

He looked hard at me. I looked at him. I noted the name on his badge. *Murphy.* I took in the features of his round face and weak chin. A thin scar over his right eye. Small, vacant blue eyes and squat, wide nose. Short, oily blondish hair. I reached down to my smartphone and flipped through the apps as I kept eye contact. Looking at him wasn't very pleasant. It took great effort and fortitude. His breath smelled like the back alley of a seafood restaurant.

'You resisting?'

'You keep breathing on me and I'll write out a confession.'

'Get out of the vehicle now.'

'Are you arresting me?' I said.

'You bet your ass,' Officer Murphy said.

'Just for the hell of it, what's the charge?'

'You people make me sick.'

'Educated?'

'Pederast,' he said. 'Bopping little girls. Probably keep porno shit on your computer. Now get out of the car.'

There was a lot of blood rushing into my face and I felt a jolt of adrenaline zap my chest.

I wanted to hit him very hard and very fast in the big bazoo. The cop had his hand on his sidearm and stepped back so I could open the door. I touched my smartphone to start recording as I got out.

'I think you have me confused with your old priest.'

He stared harder at me. I resisted the urge to shudder.

My window was down as I closed the door. Several cars zoomed past on Central Avenue. Across the street was a used-tire business, and you could hear the quick zapping of the air gun on the lug nuts. I started to yell over to the men working in the open bay but decided that would be cowardly. Besides, I wasn't a local. Only special visitors to Blackburn get harassed.

He touched my shoulder, very light, and I spun very fast. He jumped back and pulled his gun. 'Wow.'

'You want trouble,' he said, 'you got it, big guy.'

'Big guy?' I said. 'Wow. You improvise that? Or have you been practicing that in the shower. Along with other things.'

'Turn around,' he said. 'Hands behind your back. And shut up.'

He touched the mic on his lapel. He let dispatch know he'd gotten the guy and would need another unit to transport. It made me feel very important.

'Are you going to tell me the charge? Or would that ruin the surprise?'

'Attempted lewd and lascivious act with a minor.'

'This minor have a name? Or was this with all the minors in Blackburn?'

'Beth Golnick.'

'She tell you this?'

'Her mother filed a report this morning,' he said. 'You got the girl into your car, or fucking SUV, right by the old mill. You told the girl you wanted her to service you.'

Yeah, I very much wanted to punch the man in the bazoo. But it was a joke to him, and to me, and the more I tried to fight him, the more I'd make his day. Judging from the food stains across his uniform, I didn't believe he had a hell of a lot of things going for him. A second unit arrived and the cop I'd met at the courthouse got out.

The young guy with the military cut had on the same dark sunglasses. He stood cocky and sure, popping gum as he looked at me. His face had so many pits in it, it resembled pictures I'd seen of the moon.

'Thank God you're here,' I said. 'Officer Murphy and I were having a misunderstanding. I just know you're here to straighten it out.'

'Shut the fuck up,' he said. 'Put the cuffs on him, Murphy. If he keeps talking, put a sock in his mouth.'

"O, speak to me no more; these words like daggers enter in my ears."

'What?' Murphy said.

'It's a slick way of telling someone to keep quiet.'

They would arrest me no matter what I tried. I could kick both of them in the teeth, but they were dirty cops with guns drawn. When the dust settled, I'd be dead, and their version of the truth would win. I crossed my arms over my chest. It wasn't much, but it was something. More cars zoomed past. The guys at the tire place hadn't so much as turned their heads, finding threadbare tires a lot more interesting.

'Hands on top of the vehicle,' the pitted-faced cop said. 'I got to frisk you before I cuff you.'

I shook my head and placed my hands on my Explorer. 'Do me a favor?'

'What's that?' the pitted-faced cop said. Murphy had sidled up to him and was giving the old stink eye.

'Be gentle,' I said. 'I bruise easy.'

The young cop sighed and pulled the .38 I wore on my right hip. He handed it over to Murphy. Murphy called a wrecker for my Explorer and then I was chauffeured to the Blackburn Police Department.

25

They had me wait a great long while in a cinder-block room with a long table and four folding chairs. They'd taken away my phone, my

.38, and my pen. I didn't even have the pleasure of scrawling *Officer Murphy Sux* on top of the desk. My wrists were still cuffed.

So I sat there and waited. I paced a little bit, but the room was short and the pacing didn't last long. I rolled my head around on my shoulders to loosen my neck. I thought about all the kids who'd probably waited in this same room. Dillon Yates, Van Tran, Jake Cotner, Ryan Bell, and Beth Golnick, who I thought wanted my help. I had little confidence there was any truth to anything the cops said. I imagined the city erecting a sign with a new town slogan: BLACKBURN, WHERE LIES ARE A WAY OF LIFE.

I wondered how Dillon was making out on Fortune Island.

I wondered if the Sox would return to the lovable bums of old.

I wondered if Bobby Talos would invite me to one of his yacht parties.

An hour later, Murphy opened the door and a man I assumed to be the chief walked into the room. He had receding gray hair and a wide florid face with bright blue eyes. He wore a blue uniform with four stars on each of his epaulets, an American-flag patch on one shoulder, and a patch that said CHIEF ARMSTRONG on the other. He sat down across from me without a word. He slipped on a pair of half-glasses he wore loose around his neck and read through a stapled report. His lips did not move as he read, which I took as a sign of middling intelligence.

When he finished, he carefully slid the paper to the middle of the desk. 'What do you have to say for yourself, Spenser?'

'I'm a friend to dogs and bartenders everywhere,' I said. 'Turn-offs are corruption and cops abusing their position. Especially for dirty judges.'

'Those are some big-time accusations,' Chief Armstrong said. 'A lot to hear from a guy we caught cruising around with a sixteen-year-old girl.'

'I don't start leering until they're twenty-one,' I said. 'Beth Golnick reached out to me. I met her regarding a case I'm working on.'

'I bet that piece of paper you carry around impresses these kids,' Armstrong said. 'I understand you offered to let her polish your pistol.'

'I don't mind waiting around for two hours in this craphole,' I said. 'But there's a quota to the bullshit I can hear in one day.'

'You weren't making advances to Miss Golnick?' Armstrong said. He craned his head over his left shoulder to grin at Officer Murphy. Murphy's big cheeks brightened with pleasure.

'Nope.'

'She appeared with her mother this morning,' Armstrong said. 'The little girl was in tears. She said you told her you were a cop and needed her help to find out secrets about Judge Scali.'

'Jeez, you guys have it all figured out,' I said. 'I think this is the part when you look at me over the top of your glasses and wait for me to quiver a bit. After you think I'm scared, good and scared, you kick me loose and tell me not to come back to these parts again.'

'No, sir,' Armstrong said. 'You're being charged with an attempted lewd act.'

'Don't forget *lascivious*,' I said. 'You leave out the *lascivious* and the meaning of it all is shot to hell.'

Armstrong thumbed his nose. What was left of his hair was swept back in a large mound, exposing a lot of real estate on his forehead. He blinked at me a few times and pursed his lips. He thumped his fingers and then looked at me again.

'Who's your client?' he said. 'If you even have one.'

'You already know that,' I said. 'You're in cahoots with Officer Lorenzo.'

'What?'

'Cahoots,' I said.

'Are you trying to blackmail Judge Scali?'

I didn't think that one deserved a response. I waited. Armstrong pushed the half-glasses farther up on his nose, read the report to himself again for emphasis, and then took off the glasses and looked up at me. 'This will ruin your reputation,' he said. 'No one will want to hire a guy with charges like this against him.'

'People have made up a lot of stories about me before,' I said. 'It all works out.'

'I guess we'll see,' he said, standing. I hadn't moved. I sat very still and relaxed, keeping both Murphy and Armstrong in vision in case they tried anything.

Murphy reached into his pocket and handed over a digital recorder to the chief. The chief set it in the center of the table and pressed play. I recognized Beth Golnick's voice immediately. She spoke calmly and without much emotion about our meeting last week. Some of it was true. Much of it wasn't. A woman was asking her questions.

A: *He offered to give me a ride to school.*

Q: What did you say?
A: *I said no. But he kept asking. He said he didn't want the local cops to see us in public.*

Q: Did he force you?
A: *At first, no. He was quiet while we drove.*

Q: When did he first touch you?
A: *When we stopped near the school. He told me I was pretty. He touched my leg.*

Q: And what did he say?
A: *He asked me to do something for him.*

I held up my hand. 'Enough,' I said. 'Not that I don't enjoy the Lux Radio Theatre. Nicely done. I imagine this is what you had in mind when you arrested her in the first place. Really grand job. I have to hand it to you.'

Armstrong leaned back into his seat. He did not smile. The heater cut in overhead and even more hot air filled the small room.

'Judge would look favorably on a confession,' he said. 'You think this sounds good on tape? Wait until we get her in front of a jury.'

'Would this be Judge Callahan?' I said.

'You bet.'

107

'What are the chances?'

'I don't know your agenda, Spenser, or who hired you to try and shake down some good men, but you can't act like this up here.'

'Is it the judges or the solicitation?'

'Both.'

'A double play.'

'Call it what you like,' Armstrong said, showing a lot of effort getting out of his seat. He left the recorder and the report on the table and walked out past Murphy.

'Come on, sunshine,' he said. 'Let's get you processed.'

'Do I get to call my attorney, or has the Constitution been suspended in Blackburn for adults, too?'

'You can call who you like,' he said. 'But it'd be a shame if you didn't make your first appearance in the morning. You just might get to stay with us a few days. You know?'

I stood and winked at him. 'Murphy, I think this is the beginning of a beautiful friendship,' I said.

'Shut the fuck up.'

'Or perhaps not.'

Tony Ponessa came for the boy late that afternoon. The guards had the kids on the west beach picking up garbage among the rocks and sand. They had sticks with nails in them to poke the trash, and when a stick didn't work, the guards told them to use their hands. It was disgusting stuff: old soda cans, burger wrappers, and a few condoms. The stuff people put in the harbor was enough to make him never want to eat seafood again. He had a half-filled black plastic bag when he felt the long arm around his neck and a nail in his side. Ponessa put his mouth close to the boy's ear and told him to get down on his knees and kneel to him.

The boy shot a hard elbow back into Ponessa's ribs. He heard the boy make an ooof sound and stumble back. The other boys on the cold beach, fifteen of them, started yelling and waving their sticks. None of the guards said a word. Ponessa had his stick in his hand and swiped it at him, the nail snagging the boy's pants, and then tried to jab it into him.

The shoreline was rocky and tricky to walk across. Old stones and broken pieces of concrete jabbed upward. The skies were gray and growing darker. A few ragged seagulls flew in loopy patterns over the little islands, landing in the tall grass up on the bulldozed dunes.

'Come on,' Ponessa said. 'Come on. Get on your knees. And I won't stick you.'

The boy waited for him to lunge again as they circled. Behind him, the crew-cut guard watched with a big smile on his face. Ponessa made a couple quick pokes and then went hard for it, stabbing at the boys center. The boy stepped aside and grabbed the stick. He got a good two hands on it, like you would hold a bat, and twisted it from Ponessa. He tossed it far into the harbor as Ponessa jumped on him.

All the boys had formed a circle around them, closing them at the center, black and white and Asian, and yelling for them to please, for the love of God, kill each other.

Ponessa made a lot of noise when he fought. He called the boy a lot of names and threw sloppy, hard punches into his kidneys. The boy knew he'd have to get him to the ground, spinning quickly and snatching

Ponessa's head to pull him into a head-lock. He twisted the kid's neck, pulling all of Ponessa's weight forward, and tossed him hard into the sand with a hard thud.

Now all the boys were screaming, going crazy. The mayor was down. The mayor was down.

Ponessa went for the boy's eyes, clawing and screaming. The boy was breathing hard as he pulled in Ponessa's neck tighter, walking with his feet, finding purchase and pinning both the kid's shoulders to the wet sand. With his free hand, he pummeled Ponessa good several times until the blood was flowing free from his nose. Ponessa was yelling that he couldn't breathe and making gaspy little-girl noises.

The boy felt good and started to let up on Ponessa's neck when a thick forearm reached around his own and pulled him up and off the sand and breaking surf. The crew-cut guard spun to face him and smacked the boy hard across the mouth. He pushed the boy hard with the flats of his hands, knocking him back time and again until the boy lost his balance and fell forward.

'Get the stick,' the guard said.

The waves were ice-cold and breaking hard off the concrete and rocks. Even if he knew where to find the stick, he didn't want to get in the water.

The guard stepped up closer and looked down at him. He kicked the boy hard in the ribs, knocking all the breath from his lungs, and told him to get to his knees. 'Start diving and don't come up without no fucking stick.'

'I'll drown,' the boy said.

The guard picked the boy up by the back of the neck and walked him out knee-deep into the freezing water.

26

Not making good on their promise, the Blackburn PD didn't wait a week but instead sent me over to the courthouse the next morning. I had not shaved, showered, or changed my clothes. I was lucky. They gave me an orange jumpsuit to wear. Rita Fiore, who sat across from me in a client conference room, didn't seem impressed.

'Orange is not your color,' she said.

'I thought it brought out my blue eyes.'

'Charging you with an indecent proposal is the dumbest thing I've ever heard,' Rita said. 'Jesus, you won't even make one toward me. The judge will toss this out quick.'

'Did I forget to mention Callahan and Scali are buddies?'

'Which one is Scali again?'

'The one who sentenced Sheila Yates's kid to hard time for poking fun at his vice principal.'

'Okay, you're screwed.'

'Such a fancy legal term.'

'Seriously, you're screwed,' Rita said. 'But let me see what I can do. Even judges have limits to what kind of bail they can set.'

'He'll go for the max.'

'Can't you pay it?'

'I'll have to sell my Sandy Koufax and Ernie Banks,' I said.

'And then what?'

'Maybe the Harmon Killebrew rookie card,' I said.

'Don't run to Sotheby's yet,' she said. 'Let's see what he says. All of this is just to scare you.'

'My hands won't quit trembling.'

'I bet.'

'I don't think they've thought any of this out.'

'Who's this girl again?' she said. 'Megan says you knew her.'

'I thought I did,' I said. 'Maybe I still do.'

'You think she's being coerced?'

111

'She came to me for help,' I said. 'Her name is Beth Golnick. She's been introducing me to some teens who've gone before Scali. As you know, some cops planted drugs on her. And then yesterday the cops played a tape for me where she accuses me of asking for sex.'

'Wonderful,' Rita said.

'I think she's been threatened, or at least strongly coerced.'

'Well, I can't cross-examine her today,' Rita said. 'Today is only about getting you sprung and out of that ridiculous suit.'

'How would you rather see me?'

Rita appraised me, tapping her chin with her forefinger. 'In nothing but a nice red ribbon.'

'I'll borrow one of Susan's.'

'Susan will never have to know.'

'But I'd know.'

Rita crossed her legs, sat up straighter, and grinned at me. Like Susan, she had a very wicked grin. We had known each other a very long time and in the small space it was a great comfort she'd come to help. I reached for her hand and squeezed.

'I sure know how to pick em,' she said.

The guard opened the door and let her out. I was led back to the court with the other prisoners. Rita found a spot in the courtroom. I got to sit on a long, hard bench waiting for Callahan. He did not seem to be in any hurry, looking down from on high, shuffling through the docket. He was a pig-faced Irishman with a high-pink complexion and white hair swept back from his forehead. He had a thick, bloated neck and looked to be wearing a size-XXL black robe. He held a big cup of coffee on the bench with him and took an audible slurp between his pronouncements. At the moment, he was talking to a skinny young woman who'd been busted for possession of heroin.

'Not my problem,' he said. 'The court ordered you to rehab and you left early. How long has it been since your last appearance?'

The skinny woman mumbled something I could not hear.

'Two weeks?' Callahan said before slurping his coffee. 'Well, Jiminy Cricket on a stick. What? *Okay. Okay.* Sorry, sweetheart. Off you go.'

Bond was set for ten thousand bucks. The woman cried very loudly. Callahan slurped some coffee and launched into a coughing fit. Four cases later, my name was called. Rita joined me at the lectern. Callahan had not glanced up once, reading the charges and then taking a long pause. The lectern had a microphone. Perhaps some 'Volare'?

The bailiff told the courtroom I'd been charged with sexual misconduct with a minor. *Perhaps not.* I looked to Rita and Rita back to me. She spent the next four minutes telling the judge that I was actually a pretty swell guy.

Callahan stared down at me and smiled. The smile was quick, but it was there. He slurped his coffee a final time and set bail at a quarter million.

Under her breath, Rita accused Callahan of being intimate with his mother.

'I'm sorry,' she said. 'This is ridiculous.'

'I know.'

'You want me to call Susan?'

'She knew what would happen.'

'And what's she going to do?'

'It's been taken care of.'

27

Hawk met me in the lobby of the city jail. Back in street clothes, I was in need of a hot shower and something edible. We did not speak while we walked from the jail and down the steps to the parking lot. It was a dark morning and snowing. Snowplows were out scraping clean the potholed streets of Blackburn.

Hawk hit the locks on his Jaguar and I slid into the passenger seat. The car smelled of new leather and civilization. He had his stereo on low. I recognized the guttural voice of Howlin' Wolf from the original Chess sessions. He sang a song called 'Smokestack Lightning.'

'They sure want to fuck you hard, babe.'

'Yep.'

'Coming at you from all sides,' he said. 'The creeps and the law. Got to believe you hit a raw nerve.'

'Would you believe this all started because a kid said his vice principal liked to garden in the nude?'

'What's wrong with that?'

'The man didn't have a sense of humor.'

'And what happened to the kid?'

'Cooling his heels in a juvie facility out on Fortune Island.'

'I was nine years old first time I was arrested,' Hawk said. 'Stealing a bottle of whiskey for my uncle.'

'What happened?'

'A big fat white cop whipped my ass with his gun belt,' he said. 'Second time was much worse. Didn't get out of that place for nearly a year. Those guards sho' did love to watch us niggers kill each other.'

We drove out of the downtown, following a snowplow, until Hawk passed, and led us away and over the old metal bridge. He wore a long navy coat and a snug-fitting cashmere cap to match. His sunglasses had the Chanel insignia at the hinges. Big snowflakes hit the windshield before the wipers knocked them away.

'How much do I owe you?'

'Chump change,' Hawk said. 'Unless you're guilty.'

'Got to cost something.'

'I invest wisely.'

'Might take some time,' I said.

'You know where it's all coming from?'

'I do.'

'But the bitch of it is in the proving.'

'Yep.'

Hawk turned south onto I-93 and we drove back toward Boston. Not long into the drive, Hawk stopped off at Dempsey's at Medford. I ordered Irish eggs Benedict, home fries, and a pot of coffee as fast as anyone could.

Hawk had Texas French toast and fresh squeezed orange juice. 'Susan said you had three sluggers stop by your office.'

I shrugged and cut off a bit of hash. The food was so good I could feel it in my toes. I wiggled them inside my boots as I chewed.

'You know who paid their bill?'

I shook my head. It was rude to talk with your mouth full.

'Any idea?'

I swallowed. 'One of them recognized me,' I said. 'Said he used to work for Broz.'

'And the other two?'

I described the older guy, Baldy, and the redheaded kid. Hawk cut up his French toast like a surgeon. An attractive waitress in a form-fitting uniform stopped by to refill our cups. Hawk thanked her and smiled as the wolf must've at Little Red Riding Hood.

'What sharp teeth you have,' I said.

Hawk smiled bigger. He ate a little more and then wiped his mouth with his napkin. 'The older gentleman is Arty Leblanc,' he said.

'Arty Leblanc?'

'Yeah,' Hawk said. 'Sound nicer than he is.'

'How bad?'

'Stupid and bad,' Hawk said. 'He once gave a man an enema with a garden hose 'cause he late on his vig.'

'Inventive,' I said. The Irish eggs Benedict was excellent. I speared a bit of bread with a runny poached egg and a little hash. 'How's the Texas French toast?'

'Giddyup.'

'You had a run-in with Leblanc?'

'Worked two jobs with him,' Hawk said. 'Never will again.'

'Can you find out who holds his leash?'

Hawk took another bite and thoughtfully chewed. Outside the plate-glass windows, the snow scattered and twirled in the bluing of the late morning. I hadn't been in jail long but felt an ease in my back and shoulders with the freedom.

'I know a guy who can help,' he said. 'But you won't like it.'

I drank some more coffee and started into the last of the Benedict.

'Like what?'

'The man in the know.'

'Ming the Merciless?'

'Only with more hair and a better suit.'

'Vinnie Morris.'

'Yep,' Hawk said. 'Vinnie will know who Leblanc working for. You think he's still pissed at you?'

28

Since he'd split with Gino Fish, Vinnie Morris had kept an office on the second floor of a bowling alley on the Concord Turnpike. When we walked in, a fat guy wearing a Hawaiian shirt and shiny shoes nodded us to an open staircase. I'd been there before. The alley hadn't changed its décor since the Beatles appeared on *Ed Sullivan*. The upstairs promised an exciting lounge with nightly entertainment. Now it was a storage area filled floor-to-ceiling with boxes. I didn't know what was inside the boxes, nor would I ask.

Vinnie waited for us at the landing.

He didn't look pleased to see me. We'd had a falling-out the year before over a hidden interest in a casino slated for Revere. He nodded to me. I nodded back. Civil.

Vinnie looked good. He'd given up the baggy tracksuits for his preppy look of old. His salt-and-pepper hair had been expertly trimmed. He wore a three-piece gray suit and black tie that made him look more Beacon Hill than North End. A smile crept on his face as he tossed a half-dollar into the air and nodded.

'I thought George Raft was dead,' I said.

'Heard you were dead, too,' Vinnie said. 'Some Puerto Rican gangbangers after you.'

'Cape Verdean,' I said.

'Whatever,' Vinnie said. 'Hello, Hawk.'

'Vinnie.'

They shook hands. Vinnie didn't offer to shake my hand. He turned his back and walked to an old-fashioned U-shaped bar. Stools had been put up upside down. The beer taps didn't have handles. Neon signs for cheap beer flickered with delight.

'What time is the show?' I said.

'Up here?' Vinnie said.

'Yeah.'

'Nineteen sixty-five.'

'So noted.'

Vinnie reached up and pulled down three bar stools and righted them on the floor. The only light upstairs shone from the strategically placed neon beer signs. There was a painted mural on the far wall of a ball hitting a strike, pins flying in the air.

'I guess you ain't here to talk about the old days.'

Hawk and I sat. Hawk on my right. Vinnie on my left.

'Arty Leblanc,' Hawk said.

'Oh, shit.'

'Is that a nickname or an alias?' I said.

'What the fuck are you guys doing with Arty Leblanc? He's a freakin' head case. Did you hear about the garden-hose thing?'

'His reputation has preceded him,' I said.

'Stuck it right up this guy's keister and turned up the water pressure,' Vinnie said. 'He's nuts.'

'So he's not your employee?' I said.

'Employee?' he said. 'What kind of business am I running? The menswear department at Sears?'

'Not in that suit,' Hawk said.

'You like it?' Vinnie said, looking down at his sleeve, admiring the fabric.

Hawk shrugged. 'Needs a better tie,' he said. 'To make it pop.'

Vinnie walked behind the bar and uncorked a bottle of grappa. He pulled out three small glasses and lined them on top of the dusty bar.

117

'Feeling nostalgic?' I said.

Vinnie shrugged. 'It's a gesture,' he said. 'Remember when that meant something?'

I nodded. Vinnie poured. He raised his glass. We did the same.

'Doesn't mean we're good,' Vinnie said, giving me the eye. 'Unnerstand?'

'Arty,' I said. 'Leblanc.'

Vinnie drank down the grappa. I sipped mine. It tasted like licorice-infused rocket fuel. I drank half and attempted to smile. Hawk downed the whole glass and set it down with a thud.

'He make a run at you?' Vinnie said.

'He made a request,' I said.

'Arty Leblanc doesn't make no requests,' he said. 'He insists.'

'I showed him and his two pals my .357 and insisted they leave.'

Vinnie nodded. The old lounge had a wide and sprawling dance floor made of parquet tiles. The tiles were old and scuffed and in need of a good waxing. I rested my elbows along the old bar. Someone had started a game downstairs. You could hear the roll of the ball and the explosion of pins. There was a nice rhythm to it all.

'You know the DeMarco family?' Vinnie said.

I nodded. Hawk did not respond. He stood completely still, relaxed, as he rolled the shot glass between the fingers of his right hand.

'They're taking on new territory,' he said. 'They've overrun Gino, squeezing out Fast Eddie Lee. They're in tight with Providence.'

'The old gang is getting back together.'

'Everything was busted up before Joe Broz disappeared,' Vinnie said. 'It's not the same. But it's a lot of the same people. Or their kids. You know.'

I nodded.

'You ever heard of a judge named Joe Scali?' I said.

Vinnie shook his head.

'Callahan?' I said.

Vinnie shook his head some more.

'Bobby Talos?' I said.

Vinnie didn't shake his head this time. He reached for the bottle, poured out a little more grappa. *God help him.* He sipped it slowly. The ball rolled again downstairs. More pins were knocked down and scattered.

'He on the same team?' I said.

'Don't know,' Vinnie said. 'Depends on the money. I've done business with him before. Mainly just to make sure things run smooth.'

'No union issues.'

Vinnie sipped some of the grappa. His eyes were hooded and withdrawn. Hawk picked up the bottle and examined the label.

'Nice to know if the DeMarcos are in with Bobby Talos,' I said.

'I bet.'

'It would help me,' I said.

Vinnie shrugged again.

'I'd consider it a favor,' I said.

Vinnie didn't speak. He examined the color of the grappa refracting in the neon light. It looked to be the most interesting liquid on the planet.

Hawk stared at Vinnie. And Vinnie looked to Hawk and then back to me. He shook his head with disappointment.

'Goddamn, Vinnie,' Hawk said. 'History is a bitch.'

Vinnie put down the glass. He righted his tie. He looked to both of us and shook his head some more. 'For crissake,' he said. 'I'd really like it if you didn't get me killed.'

29

Two days later, Iris Milford showed up at my office. She looked bright and pretty, holding a smile that hid some terrific secret.

'You look like a woman who knows things.'

'You have no idea.'

'Perhaps some things you'd like to share?'

'Just the secrets of the world, baby.'

'In that case, take a seat.'

I'd just returned from a lunchtime workout at the Harbor Health Club. I was properly tired, four miles on the treadmill at a nice clip and a few rounds on the heavy bag and shadowboxing. The knee was coming along. My right punch was like the kick of a frisky mule.

'You're not too busy?' she said.

'Gisele is stopping by later for fashion tips,' I said. 'Later, I plan to rearrange the bullets in my gun.'

'Thought it best to drive to the city,' she said. 'Of course, I look for any excuse to leave Blackburn.'

'Have they put up the wanted posters yet?'

'Of you?'

'Yeah.'

'Just a few,' she said. 'You look better in person.'

'Hard to capture the nose,' I said, touching the flattened end.

'Looks like too many people captured that nose.'

I winked at her and pulled a clients' chair from the wall. She sat and I returned to my desk. After the time off, my legs felt like Jell-O.

'I had to write about your arrest,' she said. 'I'm sorry.'

'You had to do your job.'

'I quoted several people who called the claims outrageous,' she said. 'You have a lot of friends in high places. A lot of cops. Even more called after the arrest.'

'You don't know where you truly stand until you're accused of propositioning a teenybopper.'

'They've gone way too far.'

'I think that started a while back.'

'How's the boy?' she said. 'Dillon?'

'Still on Fortune Island,' I said. 'It's out of Scali's hands now. He'll be free in a few days.'

'How about the girl, Beth Golnick?'

'I tried to call her, but her cell number is no good. Wasn't too keen at stopping by her house unannounced.'

'You do know her mother works in the courthouse?'

'Nope.'

'Probate,' she said. 'Along with the bogus drug arrest to scare her, they probably scared her mom to get to her. Ain't easy being a single woman in Blackburn. Jobs are hard to find. Lots of connected families and friends.'

I nodded. 'Did you at least use a good photo of me?'

She tossed down a small scanned mug shot. It wasn't pretty. 'Figure you might want to hold on to this,' she said. 'You know. One day we'll all laugh.'

'Tell me when that day comes.'

Iris shook her head. She crossed her legs, a stylish boot swinging back and forth. She wore a white cashmere sweater under a high-necked black coat. Bracelet-sized gold hoops dangled in her ears. She peered around my office, checking out my place of work with a reporter's eye. Her eyes lingered on framed pictures on the wall.

'Vermeer,' she said. 'Always wanted to go to Amsterdam.'

'It's nice,' I said. 'But a friend bought them at an exhibit at the Fine Arts Museum.'

'One day.'

'When the kids are grown?'

'Shit,' she said. 'I got grown kids and grandbabies. And I got a sorry-ass pension and a sadder retirement.'

'At least you love your work.'

'Some days,' she said. 'When you make things right.'

'Doesn't last long,' I said.

'Never does,' she said. 'Only live for the moment. Order is an illusion.'

'Who said that?'

'Probably some dead white man.'

I smiled at her. She smiled back. Our first meeting at the university seemed eons ago. 'Would you like some coffee?'

She shook her head and reached into a large black leather purse for a reporter's notebook. She took her time flipping to the right page before glancing up at me. 'You mentioned the judges were living beyond their means?'

'Yep.'

'So I took that as a clue,' she said. 'I checked out the property records of how much they paid for their homes.'

'So did I,' I said.

'Nice digs,' she said. 'Almost a mil for Scali. Two-point-five mil for Callahan.'

I leaned back into my chair and set my feet onto the edge of the desk. The features section for the *Globe* lay spread out where I'd left it. *Arlo & Janis*. 'Perhaps they have family money?'

'Maybe,' Iris said. 'Each house in the name of their wives.'

'Maybe it's a statement.'

'Or maybe they're hiding something,' she said. 'So I checked into both of them. Victoria Scali and Barbara Callahan own a travel agency in the city. With another office in Tampa.'

'Okay,' I said. 'So the wives are more successful than the men.'

'Do you want me to explain my second husband?'

'Do I want you to?'

'Nope,' she said. 'Last I heard, the son of a bitch was living in Costa Rica.'

'Maybe the women are a tax dodge?'

'The business is small,' she said. 'But they keep an office in a high-rise off Atlantic.'

She read off the address and the name of the business. Being a trained detective, I wrote both down. 'Okay,' I said.

'I guess it doesn't mean much.'

'Or maybe it means everything,' I said.

'How do we know?'

'I'll work some investigatory magic,' I said, feigning my Liberace movements on the keyboard. Or more likely Dave McKenna.

'And if that doesn't work?'

I nodded. 'Keep pushing till I piss someone off.'

'You're coming back to Blackburn,' she said. 'Aren't you?'

'Wild horses couldn't deter me.'

'It ain't the wild horses I'm worried about,' she said. 'It's the Blackburn PD and Scali's goons.'

'If something happens to me, do you promise to write a glowing obit?'

'If only the paper had the space.'

'Are you okay?' Dillon said.

'I'm fine,' the boy said.

'You don't look fine,' Dillon said. 'And you were talking to yourself when you were asleep.'

'I'm cold is all,' he said. 'I just can't quit shaking.'

The boy lay curled under the single sheet, teeth chattering. Dillon had come down from the top hunk and pulled up a chair. He'd remembered seeing Dillon after he went to the infirmary and walked back to the pod. No one spoke to him but Dillon. He heard some of them whispering about what had happened to Tony Ponessa. A lot of them talking revenge.

'You whipped that guy's butt,' Dillon said.

'He started it,' the boy said.

'And you finished it, too,' Dillon said. 'Nobody thought that was going to happen.'

The boy felt his teeth chattering as he curled tighter into a ball. Dillon disappeared onto the top bunk and brought down a blanket and a pillow. The boy hadn't earned either yet.

'Take it.'

'I'm okay.'

'I don't need it,' Dillon said. 'I'm not the one sick.'

'I'm not sick.'

'Is that what they told you?' Dillon said. They were the only two in the bunk room, all the other boys down on the first floor of the open pod watching TV. He could hear the tinny sounds of the television and the murmur of kids talking. 'They're bullshit.'

'I'm okay.'

'That son of a bitch made you swim out in the harbor, for fuck's sake,' Dillon said. 'What did you think was going to happen? Your damn skin had turned blue when they finally pulled you out. You nearly choked out on that cold water.'

'Yeah?' the boy said, laughing. 'But I got the stick.' The laugh turned into a cough.

Dillon stood and reached out, feeling the boy's head. When the boy looked up at Dillon's face he wasn't pleased with what he saw. Dillon was now yelling for the guards, telling them they needed to get in here, now.

'What are you doing?' he said. 'Jesus, you're going to get me killed.'

'They don't want to treat you because they'd have to admit what they've done. Guard!'

'I'm okay,' the boy said, shaking.

'Get the fuck in here,' Dillon said, yelling. 'Guard!'

'I'm fine,' the boy said, wrapping himself in the warm blanket as tight as he could. If only he could get warm.

30

I met Jake Cotner the next afternoon inside the Blackburn cotton mill museum. I paid my six-buck admission and walked inside the weave room, the old looms shaking, long ropy belts turning spindles hung from the ceiling. I couldn't tell if they were actually making stretches of fabric or if the mechanizations were for show. Either way, the machines made a lot of noise and radiated an impressive pulse of energy. The mill room stretched out as far and wide as a gridiron. A couple of old-timers in overalls roamed the floors, checking the belts and century-old machines. I looked for Lyddie, but it must've been her day off.

Cotner wore the same letterman's jacket as before with his jeans and work boots. The jeans had been cuffed a couple inches. I didn't know kids did that anymore, but the look suited him, as did the buzz cut. He was standing at the protective rail, watching the machines hammering in the big open space. I walked up next to him. In all the noise, I'd surprised him, and he flinched a bit when I touched his back.

'Jesus Christ,' he said.

'Nope,' I said. 'Just Spenser.'

'Mr Spenser.'

'Just Spenser.'

'Can we make this fast?' he said. 'I can't get in any trouble. I didn't mind meeting with you the other day, but now, you know, with all that crap with Beth. You know. Well, I just don't want to get arrested or something.'

'Have you spoken to Beth?' I said.

He shook his head.

'Cops talk to you?'

He shook his head.

One of the old guys was on a ladder, threading the belt back through a spindle. He looked like he'd done this maybe a thousand times before and could rework the loom in his sleep. He had on thick glasses and a red bandana tied around his neck. He used the bandana to wipe the back of his neck like prospectors in old Westerns.

'How about Ryan?' I said. 'Did he find her?'

'Yeah,' he said. 'He said Beth was leaving town. Her mom made her. She has family down in Plymouth. I think she's going to switch schools and everything. What the hell happened?'

'What do you think?'

'I think the cops made a deal with Beth to make her drug charges go away.'

I nodded. The old man stepped off the ladder and flipped a switch, and the weaver started working again. At closer inspection, I could see that the loom was real, actually fashioning a broad piece of white cloth. Outside the towering industrial windows were three other identical brick mills. The whole town of Blackburn was built on the idea of industry, nestled by the river, with man-made canals dug throughout the town, intersecting and powering the mill. I took off my hat and dried off the melted snow.

'You're a smart kid,' I said.

'Doesn't get me much at my job.'

'You could go back to school.'

'When?' he said. 'My old man kicked me out.'

'There are ways.'

'I'm nineteen years old,' he said. 'I got six thousand dollars of credit card debt and I'm a month late on my rent for me and my girlfriend. I ain't going back to school.'

'When I dropped out of college, I joined the Army.'

'My dad would love it if I joined the Army,' he said. 'But I don't really like people shooting at me.'

'That is a downside,' I said.

'Did you like the Army?'

'Not really,' I said. 'But some of it I enjoyed very much.'

'You think the cops are going to arrest me?' he said. 'They came after Beth and then you.'

126

'You think she told them about you and Ryan?'

'That's why Ryan wanted to talk to her,' he said. 'He was worried about the same thing. But she swore to God she didn't say anything about her introducing us to you. As far as they know, she just talked about problems with some kid named Yates.'

'Dillon Yates.'

'That's him,' he said. 'You know him?'

'He's the reason I'm here,' I said. 'Scali sentenced him like he sentenced you and Ryan. And it looks like a whole lot of other kids in Blackburn.'

'He's a total dick.'

'That's a given,' I said. 'But he's become a wealthy one at that.'

We walked down the empty row blocked off with rails to a hallway and then turned up a flight of steps. You had to go up the steps to get off the floor and then through the museum to get out of the building. I was pretty sure you had to exit out of the gift shop after being dazzled with the romance of the Industrial Revolution. I wondered if they had a pinup calendar of the mill girls of the 1890s.

'I'm sorry,' he said. 'Beth shouldn't have done that.'

'I don't think she had a choice.'

'Sure she did.'

'She's seventeen,' I said. 'And adults were pulling her in to say that either she tells the story they want her to tell or else she's going to prison.'

'I hate this place,' he said. 'It's become the crappiest city in the state.'

'I think it was destined to be that way.'

'Yeah?'

We stood alone in the middle of wide displays of black-and-white photos of workers standing by their looms. Women who'd come from Canada to work night and day in the mills, eat at the mills, live at the mills. 'Probably always been pretty crappy,' I said.

'What are you going to do?'

'I don't know,' I said. 'I kind of figure this stuff out as I go along.'

'What if they put you in prison?'

I laughed. 'That won't happen.'

'How do you know?' he said. 'They can do whatever they like. You go against them and you'll end up in Walpole. My uncle is in Walpole now. But he should be. He killed a guy.'

I shook my head. 'But I didn't do anything wrong.'

'You think that freakin' matters?'

'Scali and Callahan and these cops pick on kids because they can't fight back,' I said. 'They target kids from families without money. Or families who don't even speak English. They're cowards. Besides, unlike most kids, I have a very good attorney.'

Jake nodded. We walked through the historical displays of fabric, wooden spindles, and mannequins wearing very uncomfortable-looking uniforms of old. A light sleet tapped on the floor-to-ceiling windows. Outside, Hawk was waiting for me in a nice warm car he stole for the day.

'Jeez,' he said. 'For your sake, I hope your attorney is tough.'

'The judges better start wearing cups under their robes,' I said. 'She knows right where to hit them.'

31

'You get this thing figured out, babe?' Hawk said.

'Oh, sure,' I said. 'Now we can head back to Boston and have dinner at Rialto. I hear Jody has a special with scallops tonight.'

'Haw.'

'Or we can kick around Blackburn a bit,' I said. 'See what's shaking.'

'Might get both of us in the clink.'

'That's why we are incognito,' I said. 'Forward thinking to steal this luxury vehicle.'

'I didn't steal it,' he said. 'Borrowed it from one of my neighbors.'

'I always knew that was the way it worked on Beacon Hill,' I said. 'Just take the closest car. Wouldn't want anyone inconvenienced.'

'May have a fresh car, but we do stand out.'

'Hard to be this handsome.'

'And be this big and black,' Hawk said. 'If you hadn't noticed, I kind of put the black in Blackburn.'

I smiled. Hawk started the car. It was a nice car, leather seats, push-button ignition. The engine ran so quiet, I couldn't even tell it was running. Hawk's taste was exquisite. He wore black leather gloves and a matching cap. I had on my trusted Navy peacoat and Dodgers cap. The day was cold and gray, and about perfect for a field trip to an old mill town.

'I'll tell you what,' I said. 'Both judges are in court. Let's drive up to Lawrence and I'll buy you lunch.'

'How you make my heart pitter-patter,' Hawk said. 'Lunch in Lawrence.'

'Better than sticking around here,' I said. 'And then we'll head back and see what's going on with Callahan and Scali.'

'You don't think the cops on the lookout for you?' he said. 'Probably watching both houses in case you show up.'

'Maybe,' I said. 'Or perhaps they believe they've taught me a lesson.'

'Don't they know your forehead is four inches thick?'

'Trade secret,' I said, knocking on my brow.

We drove up to Lawrence, had a nice lunch, and returned to Blackburn by late afternoon. We followed Scali home. We drove past the Callahan place. I checked out Beth Golnick's place, but no one was home. We drove back to Boston.

The next morning there was a hard snow. We headed back to Blackburn.

Again, nothing.

The third day was indeed a charm. Hawk had grown tired of our routine, no more pleased with sojourns to Lawrence than he'd been spending the day in Blackburn. We followed Scali as he left the courthouse, and this time he did not return home. He crossed the half-frozen Merrimack and took I-93 south. Hawk hung a few cars back. Hawk could follow a car down a back highway in Arizona without anyone noticing. And in traffic, he could really work his hidden art. On the third day, we had a third car. This one was a Lexus.

'You ever think about stealing a Hyundai?'

'Nope,' he said.

'You people really do like flashy cars.'

'Almost stole me a pink Cadillac,' Hawk said. 'We could drive around Blackburn blaring some Curtis Mayfield from the speakers.'

'Anytime.'

'Okay,' Hawk said. 'Where's Scali headed now?'

Scali braked to a quick stop and took an illegal and very sloppy U-turn. But I guess when you're a local and crooked judge, you can make a few traffic infractions. He headed back a block or two north on I-93 and pulled into the parking lot of the IHOP.

'Aha,' I said.

'Been here before?'

'Yep.'

'You eat here?'

'God, no,' I said.

'Good,' Hawk said. ' 'Cause there's a limit to the shit I'll do for you.'

Hawk found a parking spot with a good vantage point in a neighboring parking lot. He killed the lights but kept the engine and the heater running. The radio was tuned to a local jazz station. Mingus and his Pork Pie Hat.

'Now what?'

'We see who shows up,' I said.

'You private detectives sho' do have some powerful smarts.'

A few minutes later, the honorable Judge Callahan showed up in a Lincoln and met up at the table with Scali. And twenty minutes later, a thick, beefy guy in a zipped leather jacket and jeans hopped out of a tow truck and walked inside to take a seat at the table. He looked to be in his forties and had a disreputable nose and close-cropped black hair.

'You know him?' Hawk said.

'Nope.'

'I do.'

'Jackie DeMarco?'

'None other, babe.'

The men read off their menus, snapped them shut, and all laughed together at the table. 'Pals,' I said, turning on the windshield wipers to clear away the ice.

'Warms a man's heart,' Hawk said.

32

I met Sheila Yates and Megan Mullen the next day at Peet's Coffee & Tea in Harvard Square. We sat inside, huddled around a small table in the very back. I drank coffee with only a little sugar and abstained from the scones and muffins they sold. As I sipped the nearly black coffee and watched others devouring sugary pastries, I marveled at my restraint. Had we been at Kane's in Saugus, all bets would be off.

'They're going to let your son go,' Megan said.

Megan Mullen removed her ski hat and set her leather satchel on the floor. A lot of people were crammed into the space. It was eighteen degrees outside. The windows were all frosted and a lot of snow and ice had been tracked inside.

Sheila put a hand to her mouth and made a little squeal. Her hair was bright and big that morning. As always, she wore quite a bit of perfume. Several bracelets jangled from her wrist.

'And they will expunge the charge,' Megan said. 'That was a condition of our appeal.'

'I can't thank you enough,' Sheila said. 'When?'

'Next Friday,' Megan said. 'Dillon will be taken off the island and out-processed at the Blackburn juvenile detention center.'

'Oh my God,' she said. 'Thank you. Thank you both.'

She reached out and squeezed my arm. I instinctively flexed a bit.

I couldn't help but show off. Megan didn't speak while she added a couple packets of fake sugar to her coffee and stirred. She stared down at the coffee. 'Of course, there's more to it.'

'Let me guess,' I said. 'They want me out of Blackburn by sundown.'

'Did you speak to Rita already?'

I nodded.

'So you know what's on the table,' she said. 'The DA is obviously aware you're working on Dillon's case. That's why they also agreed to drop charges against you. On the condition you won't return to the city.'

'And I'd grown so fond of it.'

'No one ever mentioned a taped interview with Miss Golnick,' Megan said. 'I'm betting she recanted her story. But since I got her out of jail, neither she nor her parents will answer my phone calls.'

'How grateful is that?'

'At least she didn't accuse me of a crime.' Megan reached for her satchel and turned to Sheila Yates. She pulled out a single piece of paper and handed it over to her. 'They faxed this over this morning. It's a lot of fancy wording saying you will not pursue a civil complaint against the Blackburn Courts or Middlesex County. Someone is telling the cops to make this all go away.'

'Fat chance,' Sheila said, not reading the paper and handing it back.

'If you don't sign it, they won't release Dillon.'

'And my continuing to poke around would violate the terms of Dillon's release,' I said.

'Not stated,' Megan said. 'But heavily implied.'

'Can't get me for being a pervert,' I said. 'But they can threaten to punish my client.'

A long line had formed at the cash register. A middle-aged woman in a knitted red hat was having a hard time deciding between coffee and tea. She was asking the cashier which ones she'd prefer. Those behind her were growing agitated. I had ten to one that the woman was on the tenure track in Harvard's English department.

'When I get my son back, I'm leaving,' Sheila Yates said. 'I can find another job. I can't run the risk of them arresting him again. And to release him with threats? I don't like this. I don't like this a bit.'

'I'm not very good at being told what to do.'

'I plan on sending them our own waiver,' Megan said, sipping coffee, her hazel eyes very big but not quite innocent over the rim of the cup. 'Where the terms are more definite and applying only to a civil suit. If that's what you want.'

Sheila Yates turned to me. She rested her hand on mine and looked me in the eye. 'You,' she said. 'You give 'em hell. I'm taking Dillon so far away from here they won't ever find him. As soon as he's off that fucking island, bust these crooks up. Okay? You do that for me?'

I smiled. She patted my hand.

'What's wrong with these people?' Sheila said. 'Jesus. They're either greedy or lazy or just plain stupid.'

'All that's needed for evil to triumph—' I said.

'Is some dirty, sneaky bastards,' Sheila said.

'Nobody ever said it better.'

33

'Okay,' Vinnie said. 'There's this guy. A lawyer. His name is Ziggy Swatek.'

'You're kidding me.'

'You think I'd make up a fucking name like that?'

'I guess you're right,' I said. 'Nobody in their right mind would.'

'You were asking me about the DeMarcos and this developer named Talos,' he said. 'So Zig is kind of like their...'

'Common denominator.'

'Exactly,' Vinnie said. 'They all work together, too.'

We stood at the railing overlooking the bowling lanes. Vinnie had a cigarette hanging from his lips, despite several signs around the premises forbidding smoking. Several lanes away, two old men in tracksuits took turns knocking the hell out of the pins. I had stopped counting after six strikes in a row. Vinnie eyed me for a moment and blew out some smoke.

'He's a real shitbag,' Vinnie said.

'Give it to me straight,' I said. 'Don't pull any punches.'

'Man doesn't have any style,' Vinnie said. 'He has a picture of himself on his legal website. He's standing by a Harley and he's wearing a leather vest with no shirt.'

'Not a good look.'

'No,' Vinnie said. 'And he don't even have the arms for it.'

'I don't think anyone can pull off a leather vest.'

'I don't like these people,' he said. 'None of them. Ten years ago, old man DeMarco tried to have Gino whacked just for being queer.'

'I imagine he had some territory to gain as well.'

'Yeah,' Vinnie said. 'That, too. But mainly he couldn't cut up a piece of the pie with a guy like Gino. Behind his back, he called Gino all kind of names and said he was an embarrassment to the city's Italian community.'

'But robbing, stealing, and killing is good for the image?'

Vinnie shrugged. He blew out some more smoke. I'd forgotten how much I disliked being around it. I took off my ball cap and waved away the smoke. Vinnie smiled.

'Nobody can say the old man wasn't stand-up,' he said. 'He did a twenty-year stretch. Never opened his mouth.'

'And he died a free man.'

'So this guy, fucking Ziggy, now looks out for the old lady who's like a hundred years old and the two sons.'

'Let me guess, they went into the arts?'

'Yeah,' Vinnie said. 'The art of making money.'

'Any specialty?'

'Doesn't matter—girls, drugs, plasma TVs from China,' he said. 'They run a tow-truck company in Eastie. By the airport. The older one is in charge, Jackie.'

'What's he look like?' I said.

Vinnie described him. I nodded.

'You've seen him?'

'Last night,' I said. 'In the company of two Blackburn judges.'

'Maybe they needed their car towed?'

I shook my head. 'So what's Zig to Jackie DeMarco and his brother?'

134

'I don't know,' Vinnie said. 'He's a professional bag man. He ain't Perry Mason.'

We stood leaning over the railing watching the two old geezers bowl. One of the men wore a warm-up jacket that read LOWELL CHIEFS. The other said LYNNFIELD MEN'S SOFTBALL. Beer bottles littered the table where they kept score.

'So that's not much,' I said. 'Zig does work for a Boston developer and some local gangsters. Can't really fault him for that.'

'Alleged,' Vinnie said. 'Alleged gangsters. None of the DeMarco boys have been indicted.'

'Momma must be proud.'

Vinnie walked over to a table by the lanes and crushed the cigarette into an ashtray. He had on a blue cashmere blazer and gray slacks. His tailored blue shirt was open at the neck, where he wore a thick gold chain that spoiled the preppy ensemble.

'Only thing else I know is Ziggy does most of his business in Florida,' he said. 'He helps get some folks settled down there and into business.'

'You know where?' I said.

'Tampa Bay.'

'Tampa Bay is a body of water,' I said. 'Is he in Tampa or St. Pete?'

Vinnie shrugged. 'Why don't you look it up?' he said. 'You being a fucking detective and all.'

'The two judges' wives do business in that area,' I said. 'They own a travel agency and some rental property.'

'Fly down,' he said. 'Go get a tan and drink some beer.'

'And detect.'

'Yeah,' he said. 'That, too.'

'You want to come?' I said.

Vinnie shook his head. 'No,' he said. 'Not anymore. I got business to attend.'

'I'll ask Hawk.'

'He doesn't need a tan.'

'I'll tell him you said that.'

Vinnie grinned and pointed his chin at the two old men down the lanes. 'You ever think it'll be like that for us?' he said.

'I don't bowl,' I said.

'Yeah?'

'Or play golf.'

'I don't mean that,' Vinnie said. 'I mean retire. Take it easy. Get out of the life.'

'I live the life I love.'

'And you love the life you live,' Vinnie said. 'Yeah. I know that old number.'

I winked at him, started to whistle the tune, and walked out of the bowling alley. It was snowing while I called to make reservations to Tampa.

34

Two days later, Hawk and I arrived at Tampa International and took a monorail to the terminal. Our luggage and guns were waiting for us in baggage claim. The guns had been safely locked away for travel, forms filled out to say they were unloaded, the ammo sealed in boxes. The conveyers spit out the bags first. Hawk traveled with a Louis Vuitton hard-case that probably cost more than my SUV.

'You get that in Chinatown?' I said. 'Almost looks real.'

'Haw,' Hawk said, lifting up the case and flicking up the telescopic handle.

My travel bag was black nylon and made by Rawlings, with a tag on it like a catcher's mitt.

We rented a Ford Expedition, nice and roomy for men of a certain size. Guns and luggage were stowed away and the hatch shut with a tap of a button. It was bright, sunny, and in the low eighties as we hit the exit ramp, Hawk in his designer sunglasses, designer jeans, black T-shirt, and a gray scarf.

I was dressed for work. Jeans, blue pocket tee, and New Balance running shoes. I stowed my leather jacket away as soon as we landed.

'Where to?' Hawk said.

'How about we just reconnoiter.'

'How about some lunch before that reconnoiter begins?'

'We are of like mind.'

I followed signs over the Howard Franklin Bridge to St. Petersburg. The judges' wives owned rental properties north of St. Pete, where they also listed their travel agency. The sun was shining so big and bold that it made me squint as we hovered over the water. I put on my sunglasses to adjust my Boston vision and followed I-275 past the city and curved toward a sign that read BEACHES.

I let the windows down and Hawk inhaled deeply. I followed the signs until I hit the Gulf of Mexico. We stopped in a little community called Pass-A-Grille and parked in front of a gray gable-front restaurant I'd been told of called The Hurricane.

We sat at a picnic table under a big umbrella. It didn't take too long before I was enjoying the sunshine and drinking Sam Adams on tap. Some habits were hard to break. Hawk asked for a top-shelf margarita.

'You think a grouper sandwich taste like cod?' Hawk said.

'Grouper isn't as fishy and tastes sweeter,' I said. 'How about a fried grouper sandwich and some fries?'

Hawk nodded. He sipped the margarita.

'I have addresses close to here,' I said. 'I'd like to see how a couple of judges from Blackburn, Mass., live on the coast.'

'Looks just like Nantucket with palm trees.'

'Less picket fences.'

'No lighthouses.'

I finished my beer and ordered another. Hawk sipped his margarita. 'Main thing I want to know is about this local lawyer and the DeMarcos,' I said. 'Be nice to find out what a nice Boston family has cooking.'

'Reason you brought me.'

'Some might object to me asking questions.'

'Or maybe they open the door wide,' Hawk said. 'I can kick back at the hotel and entertain ladies in bikinis.'

'What if we're out of season for ladies in bikinis?'

'They'll show up,' Hawk said. 'Always do.'

I nodded. The grouper sandwiches arrived and they did indeed taste better than cod and even haddock. But it still wasn't as good as a lobster roll. Hawk ate with mannered grace, touching the edge of his lips with a napkin.

'Better not get tartar sauce on that scarf.'

'I'll send you the bill.'

'As agreed, all expenses paid.'

The wind was warm and smelled of salt. I finished my sandwich and the beer. We both sat in silence for a long while listening to the surf and enjoying the sense of thawing out. A well-proportioned woman in a small red bikini rode a bike past the restaurant. Hawk did not ogle, but gave a simple nod. 'What'd I tell you?'

Back in the rental, we followed the highway north along the coast to a small community called Dunedin about ten miles away. We kept the windows down and the sunroof pulled back. The main street was long and pleasant, one-story brick storefronts of boutiques, art galleries, and mom-and-pop restaurants. The address I had for the travel agency was right off Main, the business called Destinations Inc. Catchy.

I had checked out their website before we left Boston. I had called the business from there and got an answering service. When we pulled up into a small strip mall, we found an empty office space. A paper sign in the window read DESTINATIONS INC., with the same number I had called. Peering into the window, I could see only a single black desk, no chairs, nothing hanging on the wall.

'This what you detectives call a clue?' Hawk said.

'Maybe they're not into aesthetics.'

'Or maybe this be what we thugs call a shell,' Hawk said.

'Damn, you're good.'

'Now what?' Hawk said. 'Check on the bad guys?'

'Hard to know who is who,' I said. 'How about we check in to the hotel and get changed. Nobody looks tough wearing a scarf.'

'Babe, I could wear a pink dress and it wouldn't matter.'

'I shudder to think,' I said.

They gave him medicine that made him sleep. The boy had dreams, weird dreams, that took him home and back with his forgotten mother. He thought about his dad with his back turned. Danielle was there watching, but not speaking. He remembered waking up shaking and a big black woman bringing him more pills. She walked him to the bathroom and then back. And after a few hours, or a few days, he woke up. The mattress was wet with sweat. He was having another dream and he awoke with his breath caught in his throat.

He sat up.

And there was the guard. The one Dillon called Robocop. He stood at the end of the boy's bed holding the stick with the nail in the end. He'd been watching the boy sleep.

There was something unnatural about the man. He was wiry thin but corded with muscle. He had a skeletal face with the eyes that burned a weird, almost neon, blue. He palmed the stick in his hand. A long twisted row of black-and-blue tattoos snaked from under his T-shirt down one arm.

'What do you want?'

The man didn't answer him. He tightened his jaw, eye twitching.

'What?' the boy said. The words felt weird and tight coming from his cotton mouth. These might've been the first words he'd spoken in days, and everything felt hollow and weird. His mind was still half in a dream and his arms shook just holding himself upright. He felt like he'd just run a marathon.

'Don't you ever make me look bad again.'

'Excuse me?'

'In front of the other boys,' he said. 'Don't do it. When I saw you on the boat, I knew you'd be trouble. I seen a lot of you come and go off this island. It's up to me who stays. You go when I say it.'

The boy tried to remember the man's real name. All he could think of was Robocop. He hadn't seen the man without sunglasses since that first night on the boat. The way the man had stared, appraised him, made him feel uncomfortable then. His mind rushed with thoughts of explaining that Tony Ponessa had jumped him. That this wasn't his fault. He'd meant no disrespect. But he stopped himself. He looked at the man. Maybe he did mean some disrespect. This man just wanted to break him.

'You could have killed Tony.'

The boy nodded.

'He's special here,' he said. 'You're nobody.'

It was early in the morning. A soft light bled through the blinds in the sterile room. Someone had brought him a clean uniform and left it on a hard folding chair. The man continued to stare. The boy waited for him to hit him with the stick. Or yank him from bed.

Instead, the man tossed the stick to the linoleum floor.

'Get it.'

'Excuse me?'

'I said, "Get it".'

When the boy shook his head, the man lunged for him, gripping the back of the boy's neck, like you would a puppy, and pulled him from the bed. He fell to his weak legs, but then was up. It was no different than wrestling. You get tossed down, you get up. It was all automatic.

'Did I say, "Get up"?'

You couldn't win. The boy stared at him.

'Get dressed,' Robocop said.

The boy crossed his arms tightly over his chest to stop shaking. Outside he heard yelling and a group of boys running through the morning count off. They yelled out their number aligned on the broken basketball court.

'You're nobody,' the man said. 'Nobody cares if you ever make it back home.'

The man picked up the clothes and threw them at the boy. He watched as the boy took off some white threadbare pajamas. Robocop licked his lips, his Adam's apple bopping up and down. He ran a hand over his forehead as if he'd been the one with the fever.

The man spit on the ground. 'Follow me.'

35

We checked into the Vinoy in St. Petersburg, changed into lighter attire, and drove back over the bay to Tampa and a bar district called Ybor City. The Florida secretary of state's office noted Scali and Callahan's wives also having an interest in a place called Dixie Amusements. It was nearing night by the time we pulled up in front of the address on Seventh Avenue. There was a lot of pulsing dance music and women wearing next to nothing strolling along the street. The address for Dixie Amusements turned out to be a bar called Bikini Wings.

'Charming,' Hawk said.

'Marketing geniuses at work.'

'Shall we?' Hawk said.

'After you.'

Bikini Wings was, as advertised, a bar that had beer and hot wings served by waitresses in bikinis. They only wore the bikini top and hot pants below. Perhaps pants is where the health inspectors drew the line. The bar was a long, open space in an old store-front, with the original terrazzo floor indicating it had once been a bank. We ordered a couple of beers at the bar and looked around the place.

'Inspiring to watch a master at work.'

A very short Latina in a black top and with many tattoos down one arm set down two Sam Adams. I liked to stick with one type of beer for the evening. Must be loyalty.

The light was low and I counted eight customers in a space that could have held a hundred. I glanced down at the laminated menu, protected from the hot sauce, and noticed they served over fifty different flavors of wings. Buffalo to Szechuan.

'You find this in the Zagat guide?'

'Yeah,' I said. 'Off the rating chart.'

Hawk glanced down at the menu. 'Must be those Hawaiian wings,' he said. 'Inventive.'

Ceiling fans spun overhead. There were Sam Adams beer signs and mirrors behind the bar and framed jerseys for the Celtics, Red Sox, and Patriots on the wall. Hawk noticed me staring and pointed out the Pats jersey for Kinjo Heywood.

'Lot of Boston down South,' he said.

I nodded.

He sipped his beer. Hawk had changed into a white linen suit with a navy dress shirt. He wore a gold rope chain, not unlike the magnetic charms of ballplayers, with an authentic Roman coin as a pendant. Underneath the coat, he sported a .44 Magnum with a blue finish. The coat fit well, but loose, and the bulge was not noticeable.

In a booth across from us, a group of five guffawing men in cheap suits tossed chicken-wing bones into the center of the table. They were drunk and loud and would whistle for the two women in bikini tops to bring them another round or order another specialty off the menu. Salesmen out for an evening on the town. One of them offered the waitress a hundred-dollar bill to take her top off.

Hawk drank a bit more beer. The fans twirled overhead. I didn't even know he was listening. 'I could make the shot backward,' he said. 'Over my shoulder.'

'May cause a disturbance,' I said.

'Thought our job was to make ourselves known in these parts,' Hawk said.

'To the right people,' I said. 'I hate for us to waste our professional abilities on random creeps.'

'You mind if I glower?' Hawk said.

'Be my guest,' I said.

Hawk turned to the table. He wore sunglasses, but the direction of his gaze was obvious.

The table grew very quiet. The men huddled over their beers and looked up at the television monitors. Hawk turned back around and sipped his beer.

'Bravo.'

'Smart boys,' Hawk said.

'What's a nice Boston bar doing in a place like this?' I said.

'Why don't we ask?' Hawk said.

I glanced back to the kitchen and saw two men walk out from the swinging door. One was big and square-jawed, with a shaved head and a Vandyke beard. The other was pudgy and redheaded. The big guy wore a black tank top to show off the muscles and tattoos on his arm. He had the look of a juicer. The pudgy kid was taller and had the same leather coat he'd worn the other day when they broke into my office.

'Don't think we'll need to,' I said.

'Those the boys who showed up at your office?'

I nodded.

'Hot damn,' Hawk said. 'Where's Arty?'

The gray-headed guy came through the front door. He nodded at the two boys walking in from the kitchen, stopped to cup his hand to light a cigarette, and then glanced up at the bar. He did a double take just like you see in the movies. A cigarette hung loose in his mouth as he stared and then shook his head.

Arty had on a Sox golf shirt, pleated khakis, and boat shoes. He looked like he sold insurance for a living.

We didn't move. I gave him a two-finger wave and he walked over.

'Jesus,' he said.

'Arty,' Hawk said. 'What are the chances?'

'Hawk,' he said.

'Nice place, Arty,' I said. 'You come up with the concept yourself?'

'Fucking Vinnie,' he said. 'I heard fucking Vinnie Morris was asking around about me. That son of a bitch.'

'Vinnie didn't tell us,' I said. 'We came for the owners. Two nice women from Blackburn, wives of esteemed judges. I thought this was connected to a travel agency?'

'Figured we might book a ticket on a cruise,' Hawk said. 'Play some shuffleboard and shit.'

'We got a lot of partners,' Arty said, placing his left hand in his pocket and his right on the cigarette. As he exhaled, he squinted at us through the smoke. 'So the fuck what?'

'Interesting, is all,' I said.

Arty inhaled the last bit of cigarette, the fans scattering away the smoke. The young Latina with the tattoos asked if we'd like another round.

'They were just going,' Arty said.

Hawk began to whistle the theme to *High Noon*.

36

The bikini girl smiled, looked to Arty Leblanc, who was not smiling, and then quickly walked back toward the kitchen. The bald thug and the redheaded kid joined Leblanc and tried their very best to look tough. The bald thug wasn't bad. The kid was terrible. He looked about as menacing as Howdy Doody dancing on a buckboard.

'Anyone ever tell you that you look like Howdy Doody?' I said.

He snorted. 'Who the fuck is that?'

'He's fucking with you,' Baldy said. 'He's saying you're young and don't know shit. Howdy Doody was a fucking puppet on TV a hundred years ago.'

'He was actually a marionette,' I said. 'Marionettes are played by strings. Puppets are controlled by someone shoving their hand up their keister to make them do things.'

'You saying I'm a fucking puppet?' Baldy said.

'I don't know,' I said. 'From this angle, I can't see Jackie DeMarco's right hand.'

Hawk smiled. He had turned on the bar stool and his feet were firmly planted on the ground, but I had never even seen him move. His right hand touched his belt slightly below where he kept the .44 Magnum.

'This is a class place,' Arty said. 'How about we all talk outside? You know, like gentlemen.'

Two more men walked in through the front door. They were dressed about as well as Arty Leblanc. Cheap pleated khakis and

144

golf shirts. The men's faces glowed from being out in the sun all day. They were telling jokes and stumbled slow and fast into the situation. 'What's up, Arty?'

Arty eyed me. Baldy stepped up closer. His nose was maybe six inches from mine. If my nose wasn't so flat, it could have invaded my personal space. 'These men were just leaving.'

I picked up my beer. It was half full. Or half empty. I swirled golden liquid around in the light.

'Let me finish up,' I said.

'Just leave,' Arty said. 'Your tab is paid. Just don't make us have to punch your ticket.'

'Yikes.'

The jolly businessmen walked quickly out in a cloister, like a school of fish out the front door. Three of the waitresses huddled near the kitchen door at the end of the bar. They didn't seem scared. They were smiling and whispering to one another.

'You know why I hate golf?' Hawk said.

'Too many assholes play it?' I said.

'Exactly.'

Baldy pulled his coat back to show a shiny new automatic. Arty, unarmed on the links, smiled. He had a lot of gold fillings. As Hawk stood, Howdy Doody swallowed a couple times.

'Why you harassing these people?' Arty said. 'What's the matter with some folks from Boston making some bucks down here? What are you, the IRS?'

'Tell me about Jackie DeMarco and Bobby Talos.'

'I don't know no one named Talos,' Arty said.

'Come on, Spenser,' Hawk said. 'Shall we dispense with the pleasantries? Arty doesn't know. He's too low on the food chain.'

'What'd you say, spade?'

I took in a long breath. I stood, planted my feet firmly, and judged the distance between me and Baldy.

'What's my name, son?' Hawk said.

Arty Leblanc snickered.

145

Hawk moved close enough to him that he bumped chests. 'What's my name?'

'I know you, Hawk,' he said. 'You're one badass spade.'

Hawk hit Arty Leblanc so hard and fast under his chin, I heard the pop before I saw a thing. A neat, clean undercut turned out Arty Leblanc's lights and he slumped to the floor. One of the other golfers dropped down to catch him as Baldy came for me, throwing a hard left at my face. I twisted and covered up my face, and his knuckle connected with my forearm. I pivoted back and shot two hard rights at his temple. The first one connected hard and knocked him back. The second one connected with the top of his head as he dipped his chin. Howdy Doody ran for Hawk and Hawk grabbed him by the front of the shirt and threw him over the bar. The two golfers attended to Arty, wanting no part of the action. One of the bikini girls shrieked. Another called for Richie to knock me on my ass. Richie. For some reason the bald guy didn't look like a Richie. He looked like his name would be Animal or Bronco.

I hit him again, connecting with a left. He hit me again with a right. Hawk was leaning against the bar, jacket pulled back, .44 exposed, drinking his beer.

Richie and I circled. He was breathing hard. His body was shaped like a barrel, equal parts stomach and chest. A little blood was spilling off his lip. He felt it and wiped it away with his right hand. He smiled, trying to circle in close. I moved a little to the left and stepped in hard and fast with a couple jabs, then a right hook and another right hook. It rattled him, and he dropped the boxing and rushed for me. I sidestepped him and hit an elbow to his throat. That slowed him down a great deal. As he lurched forward, I got two uppercuts nice and clean into his big, bloated gut. He couldn't breathe, and in a panic reached into his coat, where I caught his fingers on a revolver and ripped it from his hands.

'Let him go,' I heard someone say.

'Uh-oh,' Hawk said. 'It's Howdy Doody time.'

Howdy Doody had a shotgun up in his arms and pointed it at me and then to Hawk. Hawk hadn't moved. He picked up the beer again and finished it off.

'Say, Art?' Hawk said. 'That tab still paid?'

Arty was unconscious. He wasn't moving from the floor.

'Guess so,' Hawk said.

My breathing wasn't as good and I could feel a bad give in my newly assembled knee. I nodded to Hawk. Hawk nodded back. One of the girls was shaking. The fun was over. She was calling the cops.

I pushed past Richie and the trio of golfers on the floor. The red-headed kid had a wild look in his eye that I didn't like.

Hawk and I walked out together onto Seventh Avenue and strolled back to where we'd parked our car. The globes of the old-fashioned streetlamps were burning bright, the sky pink and blue. Women wearing next to nothing walked past us, talking on cell phones and chatting and laughing. Boys in tank tops and baggy jeans followed them into the dance clubs and bars. We passed a big plate-glass window where old men were rolling cigars for tourists.

'Got what you wanted,' Hawk said. 'DeMarcos know we here. And I didn't even have to mess up my suit.'

'Might need a press.'

'How about that Richie?'

'I think I wounded his pride.'

'How about that knee?'

'Might have wounded that, too,' I said.

'Lets get something to eat,' Hawk said. 'Whipping up on white boys sho' gives us darkies a powerful thirst.'

37

We had a four-hour dinner at an old steakhouse in Tampa called Bern's. Hawk downed two bottles of Iron Horse champagne and the next morning showed no ill effects. He was dressed and ready in the lobby as I emerged from the elevator, reading the business section of the *Tampa Bay Times*. He had already gone for a five-mile jog and had breakfast. I was moving a bit slower, having ordered room service and called Susan.

We drove north along Highway 19, the morning sun high and bright, to Dunedin, where the final two addresses were. Both were in a development called Esperanza Marina on an inlet off the Gulf of Mexico. It wasn't until we got there that we realized it was, in true Florida style, a gated community. I stopped at the gate and a woman in a white golf shirt emerged from the guard shack. She held a clipboard, which seemed to indicate some serious duties. A pleasant smell of salt air blew off a warm, sticky wind.

'Hello, sirs,' she said after I'd rolled down my window and she'd looked inside. 'Names, please?'

'We've come to look at some property,' I said. There were several realty signs staked around a nearby palm tree. The gate was big, wrought-iron, and impressive.

'Which address?'

I looked down at my printout and rattled off the addresses for Scali and Callahan. She again asked for our names.

'I'm Bill Buckner,' I said. 'And this is Mookie Wilson.'

She wrote down the names and walked back into the guard shack. Hawk didn't say a word but was smiling, which for Hawk was as good as slapping his knee.

A couple seconds later, the big metal gate swung open and I drove in as if our names had been Rockefeller. 'Always helps to tell the truth,' I said. 'We did come to see the properties.'

'Bill Buckner,' Hawk said. 'Ha.'

The developer of the Esperanza Marina did a lot to maximize the space of the lots. The Mediterranean Revival houses were jammed so close together you could pass a jar of peanut butter from window to window without ever stepping outside. The light stucco façades were topped with red barrel tile roofs. Some of the houses had names like Joe's Last Stand or The Carlisles' Reward.

'White people make me laugh,' Hawk said.

'Black people don't name their houses?'

148

'Shit,' Hawk said.

Scali's address was along Seagull Way, apparently the premier address of the development, as all the units faced the marina and onward to the Gulf. I pulled in front of a mailbox in the shape of a full-size dolphin. Hawk and I got out of the car and looked up to admire a three-story house.

'Look better when they put the windows in,' Hawk said.

The windows were covered in Visqueen that popped and bucked in the hard wind. When I walked up and peered inside, I saw that plywood still lined the floors and it didn't seem any of the fixtures had been installed. There was a pneumatic nail gun on the floor along with a level. The front door was locked, a realtor's key box on the handle.

'Maybe he ran out of money,' Hawk said.

'Or maybe he's in no rush.'

We walked a block over to the next address. The contractor had only recently poured the foundation of Callahan's place. The house had a realty sign staked out front. It was a different company from the one his wife and Scali's owned.

'What's it mean?'

'I'm not sure,' I said. 'I only thought they spent a lot of time down here.'

Between the two addresses, a long dock jutted out into the inlet lined with sailboats and Boston whalers, some larger live-aboard boats. A few of the big deep-sea fishing boats looked to be about fifty or sixty feet, made by Bertram and Hatteras, which was about the extent of my knowledge of boat makers. The engines on many were running, bubbling up seawater behind them. A guy who had skin the texture and color of shoe leather was filleting fish on a dock, ripping out the spine and guts to the sound of rock music blaring from the boat. He had the sleeves cut out of a T-shirt that read FLORA-BAMA and a long cigarette hanging from his lips.

'You wouldn't happen to know which boat belongs to Joe Scali?'

'Who?'

'Or a guy named Callahan?' I said. 'He's from Boston.'

He looked up from his work, hands bloody to the elbows, and pointed a couple times down the dock. He took a long drag from the cigarette and pulled it slow from his lips. 'That one of the judges?' he said, smoke escaping his mouth.

'It is,' I said. 'We're here to inspect his barnacles.'

'That seventy-seven-foot blue Hatteras down there,' he said. 'Biggest boat in the marina. Can't miss it.'

'Nice,' I said. I looked to Hawk.

Hawk whistled at the hulking shape of the ship. 'Pretty,' he said. 'Cost a few bucks?'

'A few bucks?' the leathery man said. 'How about a few million? I joke with them about it when they're down here. I don't think they've taken it out all year. The thing is brand-new. The captain is the luckiest guy I know. Doesn't have to do much but hose down the deck.'

'Callahan fly down a lot?'

'Every few weeks,' he said. 'Never see them here at the same time. What's the other one's name?'

'Scali.'

'He's kind of a weirdo,' he said.

'Yep, that's him.'

'Gives me the creeps,' he said. 'Those weird purple glasses he wears.' He flung some fish guts onto the deck and a couple seagulls fought over the mess. 'He's always yelling at folks who own the boats. Says they aren't following the rules. I don't think he knows one end of a boat from another. All he and his wife do is sleep aboard and get drunk.'

I thanked the man. The man put the cigarette, now smeared with fish blood, back to his mouth and resumed work.

Hawk and I stood at the bow of the judge's ship. The fighting chair reached up tall into the sky. Nautical flags flapped from stiff wires. The controls were covered in a tarp and, below deck, sealed with a padlock. I didn't need to get on board anyway.

Hawk crossed his massive arms across his chest. He shook his head and read the boat's name. *Reel Justice*,' he said. 'Boston, MA.'

'Poetic,' I said.

'You think that developer in Boston supplementing the judges' paychecks?'

'I do.'

'And that some way he's buddies with the DeMarcos?' he said.

'Yes, sir.'

'How many kids does Scali have to send to Fortune Island to buy a boat that big?'

'A few hundred.'

'So this is all about kids for cash.'

'Sure seems that way,' I said.

'I'd sure like to take those men fishing,' he said. 'Use their asses as bait.'

38

We returned to the Vinoy hotel and ate lunch poolside. I had on nothing but a pair of running shorts and my Sox cap. I rarely wore the Sox cap in Boston. Too much competition. But deep down in Florida, in enemy territory, it stood out like a beacon of hope. This time of year, the place was crawling with Yankees fans. I finished off the last quarter of a club sandwich and drank some Yuengling on tap.

'Man could get used to living down here,' Hawk said. A lot of glistening bodies sunbathed by the pool while he worked on a tall Bloody Mary, taking inventory.

'Maybe Scali and Callahan will take you yachting.'

'I dont think they want me in their club.'

'Bobby Talos has a boat in Boston,' I said. 'Keeps it at the Boston Harbor Hotel.'

'We can pay him a visit when we get back.'

'Not if his attorney has anything to do with it,' I said. 'Ziggy Swatek just left me a pretty nasty voicemail at my office. He threatened to sue for harassment.'

'We didn't threaten Talos,' Hawk said. 'Not yet.'

'He said I threatened Mr DeMarco and his business partners.'

'In other words, those crooks.'

'Well,' I said. 'Yeah.'

'This the attorney from Tampa?'

'Apparently he has offices in Boston, too.'

'What's his name again?'

'Ziggy,' I said. 'Swatek.'

'You're making that up.'

I shrugged and drank some more beer. A woman in a skimpy purple bathing suit and very large sunglasses shimmied by. It seemed as if Hawk had lost his train of thought.

I coughed. 'As I was saying.'

'*Hmm,*' Hawk said. 'I could get used to this.'

The pool was sprawling, with a man-made waterfall cascading and plenty of space for bodies to laze about on floats. Palm trees swayed. Cables on the marina boats clanked in the warm wind. The sky was big and blue, with fat white clouds only momentarily obscuring the sun. A waiter appeared. I asked for another beer.

'Maybe we should pay ol' Zig a visit,' he said.

'Confront him with what we know?'

'Why not?'

'He won't say anything about the DeMarcos.'

'Then again, he may not know we know about the judges taking payoffs from Talos.'

'Technically, we don't know. But I'd like to see his reaction.'

'Rattle that cage,' Hawk said.

I nodded. 'More than we have now.'

Hawk dove off into the pool. Several women watched him as he started to swim laps. His dark skin and muscular shoulders and arms made him seem as if he'd been born to the water. He did four laps across the pool before he was sidetracked by the woman in the purple bathing suit. She rested on a yellow float and turned sideways, keeping a tricky balance, as she moved to speak to Hawk.

Maybe I could bring Susan back here when things slowed down. We could thaw out for a while. Maybe catch a Rays game and the Dali

museum. Susan could shop. I could drink beer and eat blue crabs. It would be lovely.

About the time I finished my second beer, Hawk paddled up to the side of the pool. He rested his sizable arms on the lip of the pool.

'Making friends?' I said.

'And influencing the ladies.'

'I think her bathing suit was influencing you.'

'Both,' he said. 'She invited me to dinner.'

'Fast worker.'

Hawk grinned. I watched the pitch and fall of the sailboat masts in the harbor. The hotel stood pink and proud as it had back in Gatsby's day.

'Dont suppose we're down here to frolic in the water,' Hawk said.

'Even in the water, it's hard to imagine you frolic.'

'Where to?'

'Lets go see Zig,' I said. 'I don't know anyone else down here. I only know people in Miami.'

Hawk nodded.

'But it could be useful to check in with them,' I said. 'Perhaps they might offer an introduction.'

'Epstein?' Hawk said.

I nodded.

'Good to know some honest Feds,' Hawk said. He turned to look over his shoulder. The woman on the float raised a tropical drink in our direction.

'Meet you in the lobby in thirty minutes?' I said.

Hawk remained impassive behind his designer frames. 'Babe, that wouldn't do the lady justice.'

39

Ziggy Swatek's office was on the seventh floor of a building in Tampa that resembled a beer can.

'Everything looks like a beer can to you,' Hawk said.

'Maybe,' I said. 'But this building must have been designed on a very hot day.'

'*Hmm*,' Hawk said, standing with me on Ashley Street near the Hillsborough River. He looked upward, shielding his eyes and studying the tall, cylindrical shape. 'You just may be right, man.'

We rode up together on the elevator. My knee was giving me a little trouble, but I didn't acknowledge it. I start to complain about the knee, and soon Hawk and I would be trading cholesterol scores.

The Swatek Law Firm took up three office suites and had an interior that looked to have been designed by Marlin Perkins. Photographs of exotic animals lined the walls. The receptionist noted my staring and informed us Mr Swatek was a world traveler and an animal lover. Hawk leaned in and said, 'Reason he work with Jackie DeMarco.'

'Is Mr Swatek in?' I said.

'I'm sorry,' she said. 'He's not in the office. But his associate Sydney Bennett is in. Would you like to speak with her?'

'Terrific.'

'And your names, please?'

'Spenser and Hawk.'

'Mr Spenser and Mr Hawk,' she said, writing it down. 'And may I ask your first names?'

'That's all of it,' I said. 'Kind of like Madonna.'

'Or Prince,' Hawk said.

'Sorry,' I said. 'I was being racially insensitive.'

The woman studied us for a moment, not sure what to say, and picked up the phone. She let the party at the other end know a Mr Spenser and Mr Hawk were in the building. She put down the phone and gave an unsteady smile. Behind her was a picture of a cheetah chasing down a gazelle. Or maybe it was a small wildebeest. It was really hard to tell from the angle and all the blood. Another photo showed a herd of galloping giraffes. Hawk stood nearby, staring out the window at the river rolling by. A plaque on the wall noted that Swatek donated money to the Lowry Park Zoo.

After a minute or two, a young woman emerged from a hallway and walked out to the front desk. She was tall and moved with a lot of confidence, as if maybe she'd been an athlete in college. She had the build for it, maybe an inch shorter than me, with broad shoulders and muscular legs showing from a herringbone skirt. Her top was white silk and her shoes a modest black patent leather. She had bobbed brown hair and did not wear a lot of makeup. She offered her hand.

'You work fast, Mr Spenser,' she said. 'We only called you this morning.'

'Oh, well,' I said. 'We were in the neighborhood.'

She asked if we wanted water or coffee. I accepted a little coffee and she nodded to the secretary. Hawk didn't speak.

'This way,' she said. 'Please. We're looking forward to clearing up this matter.'

'We?' I said.

'Mr Swatek is just back to the office.'

'Ziggy,' Hawk said. 'Wow. Man sure moves quick.'

'Well, we weren't exactly expecting you,' Sydney said. 'I figured I'd be the one searching for you in Boston. I run the office there.'

'You don't say.'

'In Brookline,' she said. 'If we don't settle this matter today, I look forward to seeing you there. I fly back tomorrow.'

"When strangers do meet, they should ere long see one another again."

'Who said that?'

'Let's pretend it was Shakespeare and not Cary Grant.'

She didn't respond as we walked down a long hallway. The walls seemed to be made of tan suede. I looked back to Hawk and he ran his finger along the edge. He tilted his head and shrugged. She opened the door to a conference room and waved us in with an open hand.

At the head of an oval table sat an ugly man with a lot of white hair. He wore an ugly suit and had an ugly look on his face. If he'd been cast in ceramic, one might place him in a garden with a red hat to chase away evil spirits. His skin had an orange glow, contrasting weirdly with the cotton white of his hair. His sport coat was some hue of aqua over an open-collared white shirt. The shoes propped on the desk were pink suede.

'I'm guessing there was no court today,' I said.

'Who said that?'

'Your shoes,' I said. 'Your client would be guilty on many levels, Zig.'

He grinned. 'When I heard you were giving Mr DeMarco a headache, I had you checked out, Spenser.'

I looked to Hawk. Hawk nodded with appreciation.

'You've pissed a lot of people off,' he said. 'Your name is high on a lot of shit lists.'

'Shucks.'

'No, I mean it,' he said. 'You make trouble for people wherever you go. You have a history of stirring up things and pissin' in the punch bowl.'

'Man just can't help himself,' Hawk said.

'Who the hell are you?' Swatek said.

Hawk took off his shades and tucked them into his shirt pocket. He didn't change his expression. 'Better for you not to know.'

'Whatever,' Swatek said. 'Sit down. I got no problem with this. You want to come in and explain why you two come into Mr DeMarco's restaurant and start tearing up the place? Or do I need to call someone at Tampa police to come down and make an arrest?'

'Is there a third choice?' I said.

'I believe so,' Hawk said, smiling.

40

I sat down. Hawk sat down. The secretary brought in some coffee in a ceramic cup stamped with the firm's logo and set it in front of me. She turned and left as Sydney Bennett entered holding an identical mug of coffee and took a seat across from Swatek. Swatek removed his pink suede shoes from the desk and leaned back in his chair, waiting for us to explain his options. He didn't look very excited.

I sipped some coffee. Hawk pressed his hands together, both index fingers touching his chin. Hawk did most negotiation in silence.

After several moments of all of us staring at one another, Sydney tapped her pen on the legal paper and said, 'Two of Mr DeMarco's employees were badly injured by your actions. They required medical attention.'

I wanted to high-five Hawk. But I restrained myself.

'Call the police,' I said. 'And I'll call a friend at the *Globe*. I'm sure he'd be interested to know how the Mob is bankrolling a crooked developer and two crooked judges into selling kids to the prison system.'

'I got no idea what you're talking about,' Zwatek said. 'I represent Mr DeMarco. Are you saying he's in the Mob? You want me to file slander charges, too? Jesus.'

Hawk grinned. Sydney Bennett's face drained of color.

'Let's cut the crap, Zig,' I said. 'Jackie DeMarco has a hell of a rep. His dad had a record that would stretch from Boston to L.A. I don't really give a rat's ass whether he's selling his bootleg TVs from China or heroin from Mexico. I came across him because of a man named Bobby Talos, whom you also represent.'

Ziggy sat up straighter. He fingered his open collar and the little tuft of white hair sprouting from his shirt. He shrugged. 'I have lots of clients.'

'He's a sleazy millionaire developer who's figured out a scam with two greedy Blackburn judges, who also own a piece of DeMarco's bar in Ybor City,' I said. 'I want the judges. I don't care about DeMarco.'

'I don't know anything about Blackburn,' he said. 'All I know is you beat two men senseless yesterday at Mr DeMarco's bar.'

'You're wrong,' Hawk said.

Zig looked to Hawk.

'Man got to have sense before he can be robbed of it.'

'Funny,' Zig said. 'Hilarious. Sydney, get the police on the phone, tell them I have two men who tried to stick up a restaurant in Ybor City. We got your ass on tape.'

Sydney didn't move. She was biting her lower lip.

I pulled out my cell phone and twirled in on the conference call. 'You still taking the *Globe* on Sunday, Hawk?'

'Nah, man,' he said. 'I prefer *The Wall Street Journal*. Check up on my investments.'

'Go ahead,' Sydney said. 'I specialize in libel.'

Her words didn't have a lot of starch in them. Hawk cut his eyes toward me and then back at her and Zig.

'Tell DeMarco to stay out of this,' I said. 'This has to do with Bobby Talos and his prison out on Fortune Island. He's been greasing the palms of Joe Scali and Gavin Callahan so long they've gotten sloppy. They're going to bring all of this down, and Jackie is going to be following in the old man's footsteps making marinara and linguine at Walpole.'

'You're full of shit,' Swatek said.

'Man did go to law school,' Hawk said. 'Impressive vocabulary.'

'This thing is so incestuous it reads like a Greek play,' I said. 'How many other shell companies do they have besides the ones fronted by their wives?'

Swatek scratched his cheek. He looked to Sydney, who took a deep breath and turned away, and then back at us. He swallowed and said, 'This meeting is over.'

'Hold on,' Sydney said, raising a hand as Ziggy stood. 'What do you mean, "selling kids"?'

'Scali sentences kids in Blackburn for jaywalking,' I said. 'Or if they forget to wash their hands after using the bathroom. Each kid's incarceration is worth about eighty grand a year to the Bobby Talos Hilton.'

Sydney Bennett's jaw tightened. She pointed the end of a cheap pen my way. 'I think you're crazy.'

'Must be fun taking a ride on the *Reel Justice*,' Hawk said. 'Wind in your hair, champagne in hand.'

'We don't know anything about judges from Blackburn or Lawrence or Lowell,' Ziggy said. 'This meeting is fucking over.'

'What about the cops?' Hawk said.

'Oh, yeah,' I said. 'I wanted to be arrested again.'

Ziggy stood and marched to the door. He opened the conference room wide, back pressed to the wall as we exited. He did not look us in the face or speak as we passed. He straightened his aqua coat and looked away. Back in the conference room, Sydney Bennett had her head in her hands, brown hair dropping over her fingers and face. Her yellow legal pad sat empty in front of her.

Hawk had disappeared around the corner.

I turned back to Ziggy Swatek and said, 'Loved you in *Lord of the Rings.*'

'Get the fuck out of here,' he said.

I made the hand motion for him to call me and followed Hawk to the elevators.

41

I had not spoken to Epstein for some time, not since I'd found out something rotten about his predecessor in Boston last year. The predecessor was supposedly under investigation while Epstein remained in charge of the FBI's Miami office. I was shocked to learn he loved the Florida weather but hated the crime.

Hawk and I hadn't even left Tampa by the time he'd called back.

'Epstein?' Hawk said.

Hawk was driving the Expedition. I sat in the passenger seat as we cruised along Bayshore Boulevard, passing mansions, palm trees, and attractive people jogging along the waterfront. We kept the windows down.

'Yep,' I said. 'A guy named Jamal Whitehead is meeting us.'

'Jamal?' Hawk said. 'This the special brother in charge?'

'Could be a white guy named Jamal.'

'How many white guys you ever met named Jamal?'

'A lot of them on Cape Cod,' I said. 'Very preppy.'

'Haw.'

We killed the next three hours cruising around Tampa and the bayfront, ate Cuban sandwiches at a place called Brocato's, and Hawk bought a box of cigars at a place called King Corona. He was smoking a Partagas Black when Special Agent Jamal Whitehead walked out onto the open deck of Jackson's on Harbor Island. Hawk had also finished off a half bottle of Moët & Chandon Imperial while I had just started my second Yuengling.

We shook hands all around and introduced ourselves. Whitehead was a few years younger than us, a medium-sized guy with a strong handshake and a good smile. He wore a gray suit with blue ticking stripes, a light blue shirt, and a navy tie. As with most Feds, his lace-up dress shoes gleamed. When he sat down, Whitehead let out a lot of air, all but saying it had been a hell of a day.

'Epstein says if you two are here, I better watch my ass.'

'He's such a sweet guy,' I said.

Hawk blew out some smoke and reached over to pour some more champagne. 'Maybe we just on vacation.'

'Epstein says you two don't take vacations,' he said. 'He said something about you checking into the DeMarco family interests?'

I shrugged and offered my empty palms. Guilty as charged. I asked Whitehead if he'd like a drink, but he declined. He said he had to get home and let his dog out.

'What kind of dog?' I said.

'Would you believe a Yorkie?'

Hawk raised his eyebrows. I shook my head. 'Secret's safe with us.'

'I will take one of those sticks,' he said to Hawk. 'If you have another.'

Hawk produced another cigar from inside his coat pocket and handed it over to Whitehead. Whitehead stood for a moment, removed his suit coat, loosened his tie, and undid his top button. He had his own punch built into his lighter. Soon I felt like I was seated at the table of Cuban revolutionaries.

'So you know the DeMarcos?' I said.

'We're not on a first-name basis,' he said, cigar in his teeth. 'But I know them and they know me. 'Specially Jackie.'

'He's active down here?' I said.

Whitehead looked to Hawk and then to me. He gave a slow, delicate nod. From where we sat we had a nice view of the sunset where the river and channel met. A few boats puttered past the wide brick patio. The downtown reflected the sun's orange glow in mirrored glass.

'What got you into the DeMarcos?' he said.

There were other tables near us. But no one who looked connected with organized crime. Most looked like business professionals who'd walked over from the convention center. Some wore nametags.

'We ran into the DeMarcos,' I said. 'I was looking into a corrupt judge out of Blackburn, Mass. He sentenced the son of my client to nearly a year in juvie.'

'What'd the kid do?'

'Set up a Twitter account for his vice principal,' I said. 'Announced the guy had gotten his dick trapped in a VCR.'

Whitehead laughed loud. Hawk laughed, too, although he'd already heard the story.

'What's the judge's name?' Whitehead said.

'Joe Scali.'

Whitehead puffed on his cigar as he thought. I probably would have seemed more thoughtful with a smoke in my hand, too. Somehow a cold bottle of beer did not produce the same effect. He nodded a bit to himself. 'Epstein said I can trust you.'

'What about me?' Hawk said.

'Epstein wasn't so sure,' Whitehead said. 'Said it depends on the company you keep.'

Hawk sipped his champagne. 'Fair enough.'

'But since he's in such excellent company,' I said, 'perhaps you might lead us in the right direction.'

'I don't know Scali,' he said. 'But I do know of a judge from Massachusetts named Gavin Callahan.'

'Bingo,' I said.

Whitehead stared at me.

'Sorry. Sometimes I'm judicious about using the term.'

161

The federal man checked his watch and then looked back to us, enjoying the fine weather, the sunset, the smoke.

'Why Callahan?' I said.

'He and the DeMarcos are in cahoots,' Whitehead said. 'You must know that since you tossed a few of their people around in Ybor City.'

'You saw that?'

'Some of our people did.'

'You wouldn't have special agents in bikinis?' I said. 'Serving hot wings.'

Whitehead grinned and removed the cigar from his lips. He just smiled and shrugged a bit. A soft breeze passed over us. The sun was going fast; boaters were coming from the bay and back into the channel. 'Callahan and the DeMarcos are old family friends,' Whitehead said. 'Callahan was friendly with the old man, and apparently that extends to the new generation in Boston.'

'Classic,' Hawk said.

'Kind of missed those guys,' I said.

'Yeah, that guy Broz kind of shut down the old Mob,' he said. 'But the new ones, the younger ones, might even be worse. I used to work out of the New Orleans field office and got to know the old guard down there. This may not make a lot of sense, but some of them had a code about them. Does that make any sense?'

I nodded. Hawk didn't speak or make a gesture.

'These new guys,' Whitehead said. 'They have to be tougher and meaner, worse than the Asians or the Mexicans. You get soft with the Mexicans and you'll end up with your heart on a plate of enchiladas.'

'Ouch.'

Hawk finished off the champagne and plunged the empty bottle into an ice bucket. The sunset reflected off his sunglasses.

'Besides being in cahoots,' I said.

Whitehead shrugged. 'They operate some seemingly legitimate businesses together,' he said. 'If you believe it's ethical to have a judge into strip clubs and bars.'

'But of course.'

'We're pretty sure he's on the take,' Whitehead said. 'Besides the businesses we know about, Callahan receives huge payments for renting out his condo through a local attorney.'

'That wouldn't happen to be Ziggy Swatek, Esquire.'

Whitehead nodded, puffing on the cigar.

'Is this the condo that hasn't been built yet?' I said.

'Say,' Whitehead said, grinning. 'Not bad. Not bad at all.'

'What if I were to tell you that I don't think that money is coming from the DeMarcos but through one of Zig's other clients?' I said. 'You wouldn't happen to be interested in some major money laundering, racketeering, and bribes? All across several state lines.'

'That would definitely up the ante,' Whitehead said. 'Fill up more pages on the indictment.'

'We should probably keep in touch,' I said. 'I'm not sure how the DeMarcos fit into the scheme. But we're pretty sure about a guy named Talos sending kickbacks through Zig's office.'

Whitehead nodded, leaned forward, and ashed his cigar. In a low voice over the table, he said, 'I might know someone who can help us make that connection.'

I nodded.

'A contract killer who worked a bit with Jackie,' he said. 'He's sort of a nutjob trying to work out a plea deal. Not the kind of guy we want on the stand. But some of what he tells us deals with work he did in Boston. Interested?'

I looked to Hawk and nodded. 'All ears.'

'Okay,' Whitehead said. 'He's at Coleman. That's not far from Orlando. I can set you up for tomorrow.'

We all shook hands and he left just as the sun disappeared behind us. I ordered another beer to clear my mind. 'Champagne?'

'You buying?'

'Sure,' I said. 'Why not? Neither of us is getting paid.'

There wasn't much to Fortune Island. It wasn't that big, really only large enough to hold the three pod buildings, a cafeteria, and administrative offices. There was the West Shore with the beach, a couple acres of newly planted trees to the south, and a few mounds that the kids called the hills to the east. The hills had really just been trash mounds when the island was used as a landfill. Now it sprouted brown grass over the shit they shipped out of Boston. Someone had staked signs along the peaks saying it was now a natural habitat. Mainly the little mounds served as buffers from the wind. No one liked the wind out on the island.

The winter sun had set early. The boy sat with Dillon Yates on a bench watching a pickup game of basketball. They had already eaten dinner. This was supposed to be their rec period under the blaze of some hot lights set in the middle of the pods.

'Robocop make you swim today?' Dillon said.

The boy shook his head.

'I wondered where you were,' Dillon said. 'They cut you from our beach crew.'

'I got to unload shit from the boats,' he said. 'I did that all day.'

'He mess with you?'

The boy nodded. He didn't want to tell Dillon, or anyone else, about the things said and implied by Robocop. The man had some serious mental-health issues.

'Don't ever be alone with him,' Dillon said. 'I told you when you got here.'

'I didn't have a choice.'

'I think he messed with Tony Ponessa just like that,' Dillon said. 'When Tony first got here. Now he is, or was, his favorite son.'

'I don't speak to him.'

'Don't let him touch you.'

'It's not like that.'

The wind blew hard across the harbor and through the three block buildings and up and over the hills into the Atlantic. The boy pushed his hands deep into his pockets, feeling a little food he'd taken from the cafeteria. He wasn't supposed to take extra food, but he needed it. The fever had drained a lot of energy from him and made him weak.

'Everyone is talking about you,' Dillon said. 'They think you're the new Tony Ponessa.'

'What happened to the old Tony?'

'They got him cleaning shit off the south part of the shore,' Dillon said. 'Or that's what I heard anyway. People aren't afraid of him anymore. They know he's no longer top dog for Robocop.'

'What's wrong with that guy, anyway?'

Dillon turned to look at the boy. He shrugged. 'What's wrong with all these people?' he said. 'They all know it's wrong. They just want to punch the clock and leave this place. You see the look on their faces? All the guards and the people who serve that shitty food? They look like freakin' zombies. No one will look you in the eye. You notice that? They can't stand what they're doing.'

'I've gone long past caring.'

'You don't talk like that, 'Dillon said. 'You talk like that and they own you.'

'What do you know?'

'I know I'm getting out of here.'

'Same as you came?'

The wind came up hard again and Dillon pulled his jacket up higher onto his neck. He wore a knit winter hat that read **MCC.** Both boys had on a pair of cheap work boots made in China. Dillon spit on the ground. 'I'm freakin gone.'

'When?'

'Maybe tomorrow,' he said. 'I don't know. They pulled me aside today.'

'Why didn't you say so?'

'I don't know,' Dillon said. 'Not something you want to brag about.'

'Are you shitting me?' he said. 'I'd be jumping up and down if they said I could go. Shit, I'd swim across the freakin' bay to the aquarium and walk naked out onto Atlantic Avenue. Good for you.'

'My mom,' Dillon said. 'My mom did it.'

'Good for you,' the boy said. His voice sounded weak.

'I'll try and help.'

The boy watched the kids in heavy winter clothes playing a rough game. There were a lot of elbows and head butts before the ball would zing into the goal. The ball ricocheted off the back-board with a heavy, dull thud. The work boots on the concrete pounded loud and hard.

'Just don't come back,' the boy said. 'Promise me that. Don't ever come back.'

Dillon looked to the boy. He nodded.

'Maybe I can help.'

'Nah,' the boy said. 'I'll see it out.'

'My mom, she's smart,' Dillon said. 'If she can do it for me, she can do it for you.'

'All this is fucked up,' the boy said. 'I'll look you up when I get back.'

'I'll be gone.'

The boy smiled. Dillon offered an open hand and they shook as the guards called for final lineup before heading back to the pod.

42

Whitehead arranged for me to meet a convict by the name of Ray-Ray Barboza at nine the next morning. The Coleman state pen was about an hour and a half from St. Pete, and I left early, driving north on 1-75 with a cup of weak coffee and a cold bagel. Hawk was meeting the woman in the purple bathing suit for a leisurely brunch at the Vinoy. He mentioned omelets and fresh-squeezed juice.

I had the feeling, but no proof, they'd had dessert the night before.

The prison, like all maximum-security prisons, was a maze of many checkpoints. I checked in at the front gate, the front office, and through a few more posts before a guard ushered me to a meeting room. The room looked the same as they did in the movies, cinder-block walls, Plexiglas barriers, and an old-fashioned handset to communicate with the prisoner.

I left my gun locked in the rental. I came armed with only a smile and my winning personality.

I took a seat. In a couple minutes, a very unattractive middle-aged man sat across from me. He had longish, unruly black hair pulled into a ponytail, jug ears, and a busted nose. There was a big bruise on his forehead and scratches across his cheeks. Under his split lips, he kept the tiniest tuft of hair, which he stroked several times. When he looked directly at me, through the Plexi, I noticed he had both a brown eye and a black eye, giving him an almost canine appearance. I was relieved this wasn't my first experience with speed dating.

I picked up the phone.

He did the same.

I told him Jamal Whitehead had sent me to him.

He shrugged and picked his nose. We were off to a famous start.

'I understand you used to work with Jackie DeMarco?' He met my eyes again. The two colors gave me a slight case of the creeps. He nodded. I continued. 'And I heard you're from Boston?'

'Revere,' he said. 'I grew up in Revere.'

If he hadn't said it, I might have guessed it by the accent. 'You miss Kelly's?'

He smiled, the effort of the broken lips seeming to hurt a little. 'I'd freakin' kill for one of those sandwiches about now,' Ray-Ray said.

I smiled back at the assassin. I couldn't help myself.

'Maybe that's a bad choice of words,' he said. Ray-Ray was no longer smiling, and sat stoop-shouldered and watching me from under a pair of bushy eyebrows.

I shrugged. 'But you were down here doing some work for up there?'

He shrugged. Maybe we didn't need the phone. Maybe we could communicate in a series of shrugs and nods, maybe a shake of the head. I could even tap out the Morse code I'd learned in the Army on the glass.

'Jackie set you up?' I said, already knowing the answer.

He nodded. 'Flushed me down the freakin' toilet.'

'Ever hear of him working with a guy named Gavin Callahan?' I said.

He shook his head.

'Joe Scali?' I said into the mouthpiece.

He again shook his head. I nodded. 'How about a rich guy named Bobby Talos?' I said. 'He's a developer back home.'

I thought the *back home* was a particularly good touch to build a rapport. After Kelly's, I planned to talk to him about how much the Sox were going to suck this year. Maybe tell him about the new indigo line on the T.A. ; hundred years from now, it should be running smooth and on time. Someone could push his wheelchair up onto the platform.

'I don't know those guys,' he said. 'Sorry. What's this about anyway?'

'Your old pal Jackie,' I said. 'And two corrupt judges.'

He nodded. 'Is there any other kind?'

'I thought you pled out,' I said. 'To get out of... you know.'

'The death penalty?'

'Yeah,' I said. 'That.'

Ray-Ray nodded in agreement. 'I only did those two of the four they say,' he said. 'But I was just the instrument, man. I wasn't calling the shots.'

'And DeMarco is walking free.'

'Never so much as a Christmas card or a "Hey, how you doing?" You know? He washed me off like I was shit on his Guccis.'

'Self-preservation,' I said.

'That's why I agreed to help the Feds,' he said. 'They don't think I'll be good on the stand because of things I done. And some lies I may have told. But they can make my life easier inside. If it puts the screws to Jackie down here? That works.'

I nodded. 'What kind of stuff are they into down here?' I said.

'Making money,' he said. 'Jackie owns six strip clubs, a few restaurants, and a bunch a boats. He takes people out on dolphin cruises and shit. Does some deep-sea fishing. He gets pills brought in off the twelve-mile limit. I don't know why, but it's easier to slip through down here. Like I said, if it's about money, he's interested. I seen him one time buy a cargo hold of bootleg Barbie dolls from China.'

'A true entrepreneur,' I said.

'Yep,' he said. 'And a real asshole.'

'Do you know if he had much interest in Blackburn?'

'Blackburn, Mass.?'

No, Blackburn, Oklahoma. 'Yeah, back in Mass.'

'Not much,' he said. 'Like I said, he's into money, and there ain't a lot of money in Blackburn. Probably some drugs. But I really don't know. I can't remember.'

I nodded.

'There was this one thing in Blackburn,' he said. 'One time. But I didn't kill him. Okay? I saw it and this is the way it happened. But no, I didn't kill the old guy. I was just supposed to scare him and this freakin' guy just keeled over after I popped him a few times. I thought he was crapping his pants or something, but he grabbed his arm and said he was having a heart attack. I didn't know what to do. So I got the hell out of there. I read the guy had really died.'

'Jim Price,' I said. 'He was a judge.'

'Yeah,' he said. 'Yeah. How the hell did you know about that? I hadn't told no one about that. They'd try and pin that on me, too.'

'I used to rent an office of a clairvoyant,' I said. 'Must be osmosis.'

'What's that?'

'It means I picked up her talent.' Ray-Ray Barboza stared at me with amazement and awe. I think he believed I might just pull a Playboy Bunny from my Red Sox cap. 'How many did you kill for DeMarco?'

He shook his head. 'Whitehead knows,' he said. 'But that's between me and him. I was told to help you. Not tell my life story.'

'Fair enough,' I said. 'Ever hear anything about DeMarco making money by building prisons?'

'That's a laugh,' he said. 'Why would Jackie build a prison?'

'For kids.'

He shook his head. 'Nah,' he said. 'I don't believe that.'

'Did Jackie say why he wanted to scare Judge Price?'

'I figured it was a favor to someone,' Ray-Ray said. 'He didn't seem to know a lot about the guy. He just told me to screw with him a little. Gave me an address and said go slap him around until he shut his mouth.'

'And it worked,' I said.

'Yeah,' he said. 'Sometimes you get lucky.'

I folded my arms across my chest. Ray-Ray turned his head behind him to check the time. He shuffled a little in his chair. I wondered what kind of omelet Hawk had at brunch. I wondered if it was poolside or bedside. I checked my watch and nodded to Ray-Ray.

'And you worked with Ziggy?'

'The freakin' Jew lawyer?' Ray-Ray said. 'That piece of shit. He'd sell out his own mother for Jackie. But Jackie never trusted him.'

I shifted in my seat, crossed my left foot over my right knee. I wiggled my foot a little and waited. 'How do you know?'

' 'Cause he talked to me about it,' Ray-Ray said. 'He had a plan in place for Ziggy before I got popped.'

I leaned toward the glass. I smiled. 'I have time, Ray-Ray. How about you?'

43

'Did you get what you need?' Hawk said.

'Did you?'

'And then some, babe,' Hawk said. 'And then some.'

'Oh, hell,' I said. 'I'm more interested in your breakfast. But you missed a real class character today. He had two different-color eyes.'

'A damn shame.'

'And a mullet,' I said. 'Of course, I think it was a mullet. He had it pulled into a ponytail.'

'Classy.'

We were at the poolside bar at the Vinoy, enjoying some poolside beverages. I broke the beer streak for a margarita in honor of Susan. Hawk drank ice water with lemon. A nice breeze lifted off the water, shaking the leaves of the palms and sprawling banyan trees. Many sailboats had left their moorings for some sport out in the bay. A lot of dazzling colors and activity out in the big empty sea.

'What'd that convict say?'

'He told me he'd kill for a roast beef sandwich from Kelly's in Revere.'

'Man works for cheap,' Hawk said.

'Indeed,' I said. 'He also told me he'd put the screws to a judge named Jim Price before being thrown in the clink. Jackie DeMarco had sent this guy to Blackburn to scare him to death. And the good judge ended up having a heart attack.'

'Your judge?'

'My dead judge,' I said. 'The one wishing reform for the kids.'

'You really believe he died of fright?'

'I dont know,' I said. 'I'm surprised you hadn't heard of him. Ray-Ray Barboza.'

171

'Ain't no union for what we do, man.'

I nodded. I left it at that. I never liked to know more about Hawk's work than necessary.

'Ray-Ray told me that he'd taken the fall for a couple jobs DeMarco pulled himself,' I said. 'And two that DeMarco ordered.'

Hawk nodded. In the center of the pool, the woman he'd met yesterday lay chest-down on a float. Her bikini top had been untied, but I noted she now wore red bottoms. Her back was very tan and she had one long arm trailing along in the water. She wore enormous sunglasses and I couldn't tell if she was awake. Suddenly a hand shot up and she waved to Hawk.

Hawk waved back. In truth it was more of a salute.

'Before I left Coleman, Ray-Ray confided his last job concerned our pal Ziggy Swatek.'

'On,' Hawk said. 'Or for?'

'DeMarco thought Ziggy's associate, Sydney, might have turned. Apparently Sydney had raised an army of red flags about what they were doing for the DeMarcos. Zig told her to take a walk. But she stayed. DeMarco thought she might have been working for the Feds.'

'Is she?'

'Maybe,' I said. 'Might be worth mentioning to Agent Whitehead.'

'C'mon, man,' Hawk said. 'You can call him Jamal. It's cool.'

'I'd like to run it past Jamal and I'd like to run it past Sydney.'

Hawk took a sip of his ice water. The ice rattled just a bit in his glass. The woman in the red bikini, that being her new name, twirled and floated out in the big pool. Another breeze washed over us and shook more palm fronds.

'Back to Tampa?' he said.

'I'd rather catch her in Boston.'

'So our work here is done?' Hawk said.

'You tell me,' I said. 'We could catch the three-thirty nonstop to Logan.'

Through his dark sunglasses, Hawk's gaze seemed to be at the pool and the woman. 'How long would that give me?'

'Couple hours,' I said. 'I was going to work out, call Susan, and then pack.'

'It'll be close,' Hawk said. 'But okay. I'll make it work.'

'You're a real pro, Hawk,' I said.

'Ain't it the truth?'

44

Hawk and I parted at Logan. I drove back to Marlborough Street to drop my bag and change into a less wrinkled shirt and a blazer. An hour later, I strolled into Rialto and found Susan at the bar talking to Jody Adams. Jody was owner and head chef. I hugged Jody first and then Susan. My hug with Susan lingered a little longer, perhaps bordering on a public display of affection.

Before my backside even kissed the bar stool, a cold draft was set before me. I winked at Jody, and she disappeared into the kitchen. I put a hand on Susan's knee. I used the other to lift the beer.

'Are you meeting someone?' I said.

'Perhaps.'

'Is he tall, dark, and handsome?'

'He wasn't so dark before,' she said. 'But I see that's changed.'

'Should've used more sunscreen.'

'Lucky you.'

I drank some of the beer. Susan had a vodka gimlet.

'If I'd sent you a postcard,' I said, 'it would have read: "Having a great time. Huckster lawyers, hoods from back home, and a very talkative hit man. Wish you were here".'

'Sometimes I wish I didn't know these things.'

'The hit man was toothless,' I said. 'An inch of Plexiglas separated us.'

She nodded. She put her hand over my hand and squeezed my fingers.

'Not the same?' I said.

'I've eaten here twice.'

'Without me?'

'If it weren't for the hot sex,' Susan said, 'this place has a slight edge on your kitchen.'

We mooned over each other for a bit. I finished the beer in less than two minutes. Susan might have had an eyedropper full of the gimlet. The hostess led us back to the booth, or, more appropriately, Susan's booth, among the billowing curtains and soft music. 'So let me guess,' Susan said. 'The case is solved, bad guys thwarted, and all is right in the world.'

'They gave up,' I said. 'They found out Spenser and Hawk were in the Sunshine State and the bad guys tossed their guns into the Gulf.'

'Are we clear on who are the bad guys?'

'In living Technicolor.'

'Can you now hand it over to the police?'

'It would be federal,' I said. 'Since it involves the DA in Blackburn and money moving across two states.'

'Then the Feds?'

'Boston's special agent in charge and I have a strained relationship.'

'Not to mention he's a shit heel and you can't trust him.'

'True,' I said. 'But if I push a few things a bit, I may make it work through the Feds down there.'

'Your powers never cease to amaze,' she said. 'But how exactly would that work?'

'You remember Epstein?'

'Yes,' she said. 'You liked him.'

'Epstein introduced me to a guy in Tampa,' I said. 'He's already onto one of these judges and a good local boy from Revere.'

'Great.'

'But its not enough yet,' I said. 'He needs more before they'd even think about arresting this guy Callahan or my dear and personal friend Joe Scali.'

'But you have an idea?'

'Don't I always?'

'Do you wish to share it?'

I thought about it. I shook my head. 'I've been on an airplane for more than four hours,' I said. 'I feel like I've been in the clothes dryer on low tumble. I'd rather eat, drink another beer, and then pick up a wild and uninhibited woman and take her home with me.'

'My place is much closer.'

'Or let her take me home with her.'

She picked up her gimlet and took a long sip. Her dark eyes were very big and very adventurous over the rim of the glass. My swig on the pint was considerably less sexy.

I ordered the smoked chicken grilled under a brick with ginger, beets, cracked wheat, mushrooms, and goat cheese. Susan had the lobster bucatini with red and green tomatoes, chilis, and saffron. When the waiter left, I leaned over and asked when Jody would ever put a bologna sandwich on the menu.

Susan said, 'I'm sure she'd be glad to substitute the bologna for chicken.'

'Not just any chicken,' I said. 'But a chicken that's been humiliated. Under a brick.'

'Do you and Hawk talk like this?'

'Hawk doesn't talk much,' I said. 'But he did meet a friend in Tampa.'

'Hawk does make friends easily.'

'He would agree.'

I recognized the song overhead as Satchmo singing with the Duke. 'Do Nothin' Till You Hear from Me.' A personal favorite. Satchmo, Susan, and suds. A regular trifecta.

'So,' Susan said. 'Can you and Hawk get these people?'

I nodded.

'Good,' she said. 'Because in your absence, I've made some calls and checked in with some old friends.'

'Anything I can use?'

'Just that this place in the harbor shouldn't be licensed,' she said. 'That place does so much business, there's a waiting list.'

175

'Not surprising.'

'I also checked out Massachusetts Child Care,' she said. 'I learned a lot about their corporate philosophy.'

'And?'

'It's all bullshit,' Susan said. 'Taking children from their parents and their schools should be the very last step. Not the first. It interrupts their education, exposes them to all kinds of trauma, gets them mixed up with delinquent peers, and mainly stigmatizes them. The whole philosophy of scared straight doesn't work. Studies have proven it. It's a lie that keeps places like this filled.'

I nodded. I kept my mouth shut. I had a better chance of stopping a locomotive with my teeth than backing Susan off a tirade.

'Did you know juvenile crime is at an all-time low, but the incarceration rate for kids has stayed the same?' she said. 'Who wants to explain those numbers?'

'This problem may be bigger than Blackburn,' I said. 'But this is where you start,' she said. 'Expose this and maybe the light shines through?'

'One would hope.'

'Lousy bastards,' Susan said, before taking a dainty sip.

'You said it.'

45

Sometime while Hawk and I had been crossing the bluish-green waters of Tampa Bay, Dillon Yates had been released from the MCC facility on Fortune Island.

I'd invited Iris Milford to meet me at the Yates' apartment, a two-bedroom unit in a development just out of downtown called Old English Village. Not much had changed since my last visit to Blackburn. The Merrimack was still frozen and winter seemed like it might last another hundred years.

Sheila Yates met me at the door. I introduced Iris, and Sheila was a little less than enthused. 'A reporter?' she said. 'I don't know. Dillon's just home and there were conditions of his release and promises made. I don't think this is a good idea.'

'Miss Yates,' Iris said. 'Your son is one of the lucky ones. People keeping to themselves is how this whole mess started. You can keep quiet. That's up to you. But knowing what goes on in that place is going to help out those other families. Or y'all want to keep this a private matter?'

Iris Milford had a very direct, authoritative way of speaking. Sheila swallowed, looked to me, and then nodded back at Iris. 'Okay,' she said. 'Come in.'

We walked back to a small kitchen table with a fine view of the parking lot and other similar apartment units. They were all new-ish brick, two stories tall, with white vinyl dormers. The chosen landscaping was of the type to survive a nuclear winter. Arthur Treacher's Fish & Chips had more British charm than Ye Old English Village. I turned away from the window as Sheila disappeared into a back room. Iris set out a digital recorder and her notepad. I touched my temple with an index finger and said, 'Steel trap.'

'You really remember everything?'

'Everything.'

'What was I wearing when we first met?'

'A dashiki,' I said.

'Hmm,' she said. 'Could be. I can't remember myself. But that sounds like something I would've worn back then.'

'I once wore a leisure suit.'

'Burn the pictures?'

'You bet,' I said.

Iris smiled as a back bedroom door opened and out walked a big sleepy kid wearing gray sweatpants and an oversized white tee that fell to his knees. He didn't wear shoes, and his feet were bigger than mine. He looked thinner than he had in the photographs I'd seen, different somehow, or maybe it was just the hair. His thick, curly hair from the pictures had been cut shorter than Daddy Warbucks's.

He took a seat at the head of the table and widened his tired eyes at us. I waved. Sheila put a hand on his shoulder and introduced us. Dillon blinked a few times and sat up a little straighter. He wiped his eyes a bit and nodded, staring right at me. 'You were the one who got me out?'

I shrugged. 'Mostly it was a tough attorney named Megan Mullen,' I said. 'You'd like her. She's about your age.'

'What?'

'He's kidding,' Sheila said. 'Spenser helped her with some information. You and a lot of other kids were being sent away without an attorney. You can't do that. You can't do that to anyone.'

Dillon's face hardened. He nodded along with his mom, his eyes flicking back and forth between me and Iris.

'What's it like?' Iris said. 'Out there on that island?'

'It sucks.'

'Can you tell me in more detail?'

'It sucks hard,' he said. 'It's colder than shit.'

I looked at Iris. 'You writing all this down?'

Iris nodded, took a long breath, and pushed the digital recorder closer to Dillon. 'Were you abused?'

'Me?' he said. 'No.'

'Did it straighten you out?'

'For setting up a Twitter page?' Dillon said. 'It may have been stupid. But no one should get treated like I was.'

'How were you treated?'

'Like a freakin' prisoner,' Dillon said. 'What do you think? They made me take a chemical shower and then shaved my head. I was stuck in this room with a bunch of kids who were in for real crimes, real violent crimes. One of the kids had nearly killed his old man with a ballpoint pen. A few others actually killed someone. We were told to shut up, don't do anything, stick around and watch a crappy TV until they turned the lights off.'

'What about school?'

Dillon snorted out his nose. 'That's a joke.'

178

His mother had not moved, standing with a hand still on his shoulder. Sheila again wore her signature perfume and a lot of it.

'Dillon said he was sent to a room for thirty minutes a day for study period. Study period was pretty much keeping quiet and doodling in old workbooks. Almost all the books had been filled in, front to back.'

'How about counseling?' I said. 'Did you meet with anyone?'

'There was this weird guy I saw a couple times,' Dillon said. 'We called him Dr Feelgood. He was an absolute idiot. I'm pretty sure he was on drugs. He was zoned out. You know? I think he was taking the drugs meant for the kids who needed them. If you got to be a problem, he'd give you some kind of pills. Some of the kids would act wild and give guards trouble just to get the scrip.'

'So no school, no real psychiatric care,' I said. 'They must have some terrific cultural activities.'

'Oh, yeah,' Dillon said, grinning. 'We got to hum a little while we picked up shit on the beach.'

'Dillon,' Sheila said.

'What else can I call it?' he said. 'We were on garbage detail. We cleaned up the beach every day until we had two sacks full of the stuff. Sometimes we'd add in seaweed and crap to make it all go faster. They didn't really care about the cleanup. It was just busy work. Everything we did was about checking the box. School, the doc, recreation time. Even the food. I wasn't exactly expecting great stuff, but I wouldn't feed a dog the kind of stuff they dished out.'

'My dog has gourmet tastes.'

'Well, your dog wouldn't last on Fortune Island,' he said. 'It's not a place to live. You just sort of exist. It makes you feel like you've been put on hold, and nobody gives a shit anymore. I know that's not true. I know everything my mom was doing. But they want you to believe that you're nothing and no more important than the crap that washes up on the beach.'

I nodded. Iris kept writing down notes. Sheila started to cry a little. She told us she'd already found a new place for them to live. They'd never come back to Blackburn. Ever.

'Did you meet other kids like you?' I said. 'Given a sentence for a minor offense.'

'How long you got?' Dillon said.

'Long as you want to talk,' Iris said. She had on severe black-framed glasses that gave her a serious and focused look. Not that Iris Milford had ever been a wallflower.

'Listen,' Dillon said. 'I'll tell you whatever you want to know. I'll tell you everything that happened to me. My mom and I already talked about it. If I shut up, then people like Judge Scali have won. I'm not ever going back to that school and we're moving out of this town. But I have a favor to ask, Mr Spenser.'

I nodded.

'I met a friend out on the island who had it a lot worse than me,' Dillon said. 'He's from Blackburn, too, but a senior. He was a wrestler and a real good guy. I knew who he was before the island but we really didn't know each other. He did something real stupid but not violent. He got sent to the island and when he was there he wouldn't get with the program. I respected him for not letting the guards beat him down.'

'What's his name?'

Dillon told us.

'How can we help?'

'If you don't get him off that island they are going to freakin' kill him,' Dillon said. 'These guys, the guards, they don't give a shit. Sorry, Mom. But they don't. They'll shoot him and throw him into the harbor and no one will ever find him. I'm worried they may have already done it.'

'Why him?'

'Because the kid won't quit,' Dillon said. 'They can't break him. And the guards don't know how to handle it.'

I lifted my eyes at Iris. She was taking notes. She met my eyes and just shook her head.

'Okay,' I said. 'Tell us all you know.'

Sometime in the morning, before the other kids were up, Robocop kicked the boy awake. He told him to get dressed and follow him to the security check. This time Robocop didn't watch him dress. The boy did as he was told and soon he was following the man down a rutted path to the docks. There were two small boats teetering in the lights where two guards unloaded boxes and set them into the back of a small pickup truck.

'What?' Robocop said. 'You need a fucking invitation?'

The boy walked to the boat, where a fat man in an MCC uniform handed him a heavy box. He loaded it onto the truck and kept on with the boxes until they were gone. The truck drove off. The boy was sweating under his clothes. He stood alone with Robocop on the long, weather-beaten dock. They could see the outline of Boston's lights clear from where they stood. He thought about what he'd told Dillon Yates, and for a half a second he thought about jumping and trying to swim. But then he saw the jagged pieces of ice and the high breaking waves on the beach.

'Okay,' the boy said. 'What now?'

'Follow me.'

Never be alone with the guard.

'I don't like being out here.'

'I don't give a shit.'

'You have to have other guards around,' the boy said. 'That's the rule.'

'Someone will come back.'

'I want someone now.'

The man wore an old Army jacket and a black ball cap. He hadn't shaved and the whiskers on his chin looked dirty. From across the boat, he could smell the alcohol on the man's breath.

'Sit down.'

'I'm fine.'

'I said sit down,' Robocop said. 'Or do you want to go swimming again?'

The boy sat. The boat rocked up and down, unstable on the two lines tethering it to the dock. He caught his breath, feeling the sweat under his clothes and the tight frozen feeling on his face. He wiped his nose. He looked far across the harbor of Boston.

Robocop lit a cigarette. A deep purple light shone from over the old trash mounds beyond the pods. The guard blew some smoke into the wind. He scratched the back of his neck. The cold silence, the rocking of the boat, made the boy feel uneasy. He wanted to get back to the pod and join the others. Dillon was gone.

He heard a new boy was coming in today.

'There's no reason we can't be friends,' the man said. He spoke the boy's name. 'Wouldn't you like that?'

The boy shrugged. The man smiled and turned his head over the edge of the boat and spit. The boat rocked some more. The man rested his arm on his thigh, tight and immovable in the silence around them.

He smoked down the cigarette, tossed it into the harbor, and walked over to the boy.

The boy stiffened. The man, bony and now reeking of booze, sat down next to him. There was no space between them. The boy moved over. The man laughed. He offered the boy a cigarette. And the boy shook his head.

'No reason not to be friends.'

'What do you want?'

'Good to have a boy in charge,' he said. 'You know. Like Tony.'

'Then keep Tony in charge.'

'Can't have that.'

'Why?'

' 'Cause he's weak,' the guard said. 'He's not like you. You showed him up.'

The boy swallowed. His hot breath turned to smoke in the cold harbor air. The guard smoked some more and then reached into the pocket of his dirty coat. He pulled out a pint of whiskey and put it into the boy's hands. 'This makes things easier.'

'I don't want things to be easier.'

'Yeah,' the man said. 'You do.'

He didn't wait a beat before grabbing the boy by the scruff of the neck and sticking the neck of the bottle into the boy's mouth. He felt the hot burn of the booze in his throat as he tried to knock it away. The man suddenly thought he'd had enough and yanked the bottle back. He laughed some and took a swig. The boy wiped his chin.

The boat kept on rocking. Somewhere on the other side of the harbor, people were going about things in Boston. Having normal lives. Doing normal things.

'It makes it easier,' the guard said. 'The thing about you? I see you're a lot like me.' Robocop swallowed a bit more and tucked the whiskey bottle into his oversized Army coat. The boy looked to the boat steps, the hard line of the ropes trying to keep everything close to the dock. The rope squeaked and ached with the pressure.

'Come on,' Robocop said. 'I ain't so bad.'

The older man reached out and touched the boy's knee. He then gripped the back of his neck, squeezing hard with his big fat hand. The boy recoiled, jumped up, and jackrabbited off the boat. He leaped over the steps and onto the beaten dock. He tripped and fell, caught on a loose nail. But he was up again. You never stayed down.

Robocop yelled obscenities at him. He ran after him, off the dock, and onto the shore. The older man threw the bottle at him and it shattered in a million pieces. The boy was on the path toward the pods and then decided to break away and run toward the South Shore and into the grouping of trees weirdly rooted in the old landfill.

He ran fast, tried to keep his breathing under control. You kept moving. You didn't stay down. You kept moving.

He couldn't hear the yelling anymore.

There was only the wind breaking and fluttering the bare limbs of the trees and the crashing of the harbor surf. Jesus Christ. He was dead. The guy would kill him.

46

After Iris and I compared notes, I drove back to Boston. Iris was working on a story about conditions on Fortune Island while I followed the money trail from Bobby Talos Jr. to the pockets of Judge Joe Scali. Since I'd left Tampa, I had tried to get in touch with Sydney Bennett outside Ziggy Swatek's office. I had left three messages at her Boston office and two at her home number. I said I had something important to tell her, knowing being told you were on a hit man's punch list was something best done in person. I was pretty sure Hallmark didn't make a greeting card for that purpose.

I tried again. The call went right to voicemail. Being a persistent investigator, I drove to her office in Brookline. Ziggy Swatek kept his Boston office in the heart of Brookline Village. The building was decidedly less grandiose than the beer-can building and was located on the second floor of a short brick building on Harvard Street.

I bought a corned-beef on rye at Michael's and ate while I watched. I knew her car tag and her car, parked five spaces away. I didn't really get bored until three hours later. The sandwich was gone, as were the chips and a pickle. I used my branch office, the closest Dunkin', for the facilities and bought a coffee.

I listened to 'Here and Now' with Robin Young. I watched the world stroll by in their heavy coats and ski hats. A woman in a white puffy coat and blue jeans walked a high-strung black Lab on a red leash. The woman had on aviator sunglasses and had a blond ponytail that fell the length of her back. The Lab bounded and jumped, grabbing the leash with its mouth, wanting to take the lead.

After nearly four hours, Sydney Bennett emerged from the office building, waited for traffic to pass, and then crossed Harvard Street to her car.

I waited until she'd backed out and then started mine. I followed her west on Route 9 for fifteen to twenty minutes. I kept a decent distance away from her Lexus, although she had no reason to know my vehicle. I kept out of sight more as a professional courtesy than anything.

I still had some cold coffee and drank it. I turned off the radio and turned on the windshield wipers, as it had started to rain. The rain was cold, the day was gray and miserable, and soon the roads would turn to ice. But I felt comfortable back in my native habitat.

Traffic was slow and sluggish as we passed the Brookline Reservoir. I knew she wasn't headed home. I had her address in an apartment in the South End. I had resigned myself to the fact that I might be spending the day in Framingham or Worcester when she pulled into the Chestnut Hill Mall. Again, familiar turf. Susan had propped up the gross national product of Guatemala in those hallowed halls while I'd drunk beer at Charley's.

Sadly, Charley's was no more. And lately Susan had preferred dragging me around Copley Place.

Sydney parked near one of the Bloomingdale's that bookended the mall. Since I was well versed on the turf, I knew this was the one that sold women's clothes. I was good, but blending into the intimates collection might prove difficult.

I waited until she disappeared inside and then followed. I was dressed differently than I was when we met in Tampa. I wore a leather jacket and a ball cap. I wore the ball cap down low to obscure my face. I tucked my hands in the pocket of the jacket and walked with my head down. I strolled inside and spotted her right off in the ladies shoes department.

I hung back with Ralph Lauren. I pretended to shop as if I were shopping for Susan. I would never shop for Susan. She once told me my taste seemed more fitting for Gypsy Rose Lee. I thumbed through a rack of herringbone jackets. I became immersed in a stack of navy silk blouses. I was about to move on when a perky sales clerk wandered up to me and asked if I'd found anything.

'Do these come in a double XL?'

'Men's section is at the other end of the mall, sir.'

'Darn,' I said. 'And I was starting to feel so pretty.'

When I looked up, Sydney Bennett was gone. I made my way through the shoes and into cosmetics and spotted her just as she stepped out of the store into the rest of the mall. It was a weekday and the mall crowd was thin. Even with Susan, my patience with shopping lasted only a good twenty minutes.

Not far from the Bloomingdale's entrance, Sydney had stopped to check messages on her phone. There was a grouping of leather furniture nearby, close and comfy to keep you prisoner in the mall with the offer of Wi-Fi. As she tucked the phone into her purse, I stepped up next to her.

'Hello,' I said. 'Again.'

She did not look in the least bit surprised. I think I'd have been more pleased if I'd actually startled her. She might have been easier to work with if she wasn't sure what to say or do. But there was a reason she was second in command to a huckster like Ziggy Swatek.

'I have nothing to say.'

'"Then follow me and give me audience".'

'Is that a quote?'

'Yes.'

'By whom?'

'You'd rather not know,' I said. 'It might lead to suspicion.'

'I am already more than suspicious, Mr Spenser,' she said. 'You followed me here.'

'Yes.'

'Because you believe I will tell you something about my client?'

'No.'

'Then why else?'

Two old women in small pink ball caps wandered by, hoisting packages in old frail fists. They sat down at the little grouping of leather seating, ruining our private place to talk, and complained about their poor, aching feet.

'Perhaps we can go elsewhere,' I said.

'I have nothing to say,' she said. 'And frankly, I am—'

'Do you know the name Ray-Ray Barboza?'

'No,' she said. 'Why should I?'

'Or perhaps Raymond Barboza,' I said. 'I believe Ray-Ray to be his professional name.'

'What kind of professional?'

She looked annoyed and impatient, and reached into her purse for her phone. She looked at its screen and then back at me. She typed out something and then replaced the phone. She looked even more lawyerly today, wearing a fitted navy pin-striped suit with a pearl-colored silk top under a heavy blue wool coat. Her leather boots were tall and seemed like they may have been designed by the Luftwaffe.

'If you click your heels together, I bet those things make a hell of a racket.'

She turned to leave. I touched, not grabbed, her arm.

'Jackie DeMarco isn't a nice man.'

'Is that what you came to tell me?'

'He feels you may be working with the Feds.'

'Yeah, right.'

'And he hired Mr Barboza to make sure you would stay quiet.'

'That's a lie.'

She turned up her small chin to look at me. She might've been pretty in another place and under another circumstance. It's hard to find beauty when someone looks like they just might clock you with their purse.

'I don't know if you're working with the Feds,' I said. 'But you know what Talos and the judges are doing with those kids is wrong. You didn't sign on to work with a creep like Judge Scali.'

'You draw a lot of imaginary lines, Mr Spenser.'

Her mouth twitched a bit, and as in the Tampa office, her words had little starch. She just upturned that little chin and shook a little. I placed a hand on her shoulder. 'Let's go somewhere,' I said. 'I'll tell you all I know, and then you can make up your own mind.'

I waited for the purse to clock me with all the ferocity of Ruth Buzzi. Instead, she simply nodded.

47

I told Sydney Bennett all I knew at the Café Vanille inside the mall.

She drank coffee and listened. Although the dark chocolate croissant looked terrific, I knew it was just a fancy donut. I had coffee, too. I was within a few pounds of my target two hundred and ten.

'I'm supposed to believe the word of a convicted killer.'

'No,' I said. 'Only believe me. I think you got a queasy feeling about this whole business long before we met.'

She was silent. She stirred her coffee for the umpteenth time.

'Even if I had concerns about a client, I would be disbarred for speaking with you.'

'Perhaps.'

'Not perhaps,' she said. 'Absolutely.'

'What if you only told me about the judges?' I said. 'You said they aren't your clients. I have a pretty good idea on what the DeMarcos are all about.'

'Oh,' she said. 'Do you?'

She said it condescendingly, with a sharp edge. I shrugged and let the words hang there for a moment. I took a sip of coffee to keep my mind working to decide on what my mouth should do next. I nodded. 'I knew Jackie DeMarco's old man,' I said. 'I knew the guy who sold him out and sent him to prison, too. Over my many years in this business, I've had the dishonor of meeting a thousand guys like Jackie. Jackie does for Jackie. I doubt he's even conflicted about it.'

'You don't even know my client.'

'Jackie will steal, rob, and cheat until he creates his own noose. I'm more concerned about two men who swore an oath to uphold the law. You lead me in the right direction and I walk away.'

'And why on earth would I do that?'

'Because you don't like this any more than I do,' I said. 'You don't mind playing the game for the DeMarcos, but you want out of this.'

She looked at me, mouth open, as if about to speak. She then shut her mouth and just stared. 'You got me,' she said. 'Where do I sign up to unburden myself?'

'You are a tough nut,' I said.

'I have a job to do, as do you,' she said. 'You keep following me, and I'll file a restraining order.'

'Then why did you sit down with me?'

'Why else?' Sydney said. 'To find out what you know. To learn what kind of an agenda you have toward my client.'

'The judges,' I said. 'Sydney, I just want the judges. You can help.'

'Goodbye,' she said. 'Thanks for the coffee.'

'May I offer you a maple scone?'

She stood, snatched her big bag, and turned back toward Bloomingdale's. I paid and followed her out. Outside, the rain had indeed turned to sleet, and the wet asphalt turned slick. The sleet pinged off my hat and jacket as I walked to my car, spotting Sydney Bennett getting into her Lexus, lights blazing on, and then sitting there watching me. For a moment, I thought she might have a change of heart. But soon she drove off and I was left standing there.

I got back into my Explorer.

It was late. I could head back to my apartment and finally unpack. I could return to my office and shuffle through unpaid bills. Or I could go to the Harbor Health Club and see how much damage had been done to my knee.

When I started the engine, I felt a firm forearm wrap around my throat and the familiar click of a revolver in my ear.

'You boys take mall security seriously.'

'Drive, fucknuts,' said a familiar voice.

'Hello, Arty.'

'You say another word and I'll ruin the leather interior.'

'Yikes.'

'Say it again.'

'You want to remove your arm or are you looking to go steady?'

'I said drive,' he said, removing the arm and reaching down on my hip for the .38. He removed my gun but kept his gun screwed behind my ear.

I drove. I nosed the car back out to Route 9.1, idled at the stoplight, unsure of which way to turn. 'Back to the city,' Arty said. 'Back to the city.'

'This time of day it'd be much faster to hop on the expressway.'

'I'll tell you where to go,' he said, settling in behind me. We drove around for a long time in complete silence. I wanted to turn on the radio but feared we would have a disagreement on the music. Arty LeBlanc struck me as an easy-listening kind of guy. Or maybe smooth jazz.

'You like smooth jazz, Arty?'

'What part of "shut the fuck up" don't you understand?'

'You still sore about Tampa?'

'Goddamn right I'm sore,' he said, just as we passed Pru Center. 'That nigger sucker-punched me.'

'I'll pass along your complaint to Hawk.'

'I'll deal with him soon enough.'

'I thought you'd been around, Arty.'

'I been around,' he said. 'So what?'

'You sure don't know much about Hawk.'

Arty Leblanc stayed silent until we passed through Back Bay and drove along the Common. He told me to turn on Tremont and head into the South End, where we crossed the channel into Southie. We drove along Dot Ave and deeper into the old neighborhoods, cutting along the destruction site of the Old Colony Housing Projects, where some good people I'd known had grown up. And several crooks, including Joe Broz.

'Turn here,' he said.

I turned.

'Turn there.'

I turned there.

We rode the long length of a chain-link fence with a lot of NO TRESPASSING and PRIVATE PROPERTY signs. He told me to drive to the gate and wait. Soon the chain-link gate slid open and I drove past a big sign reading DEMARCO TOWING.

'I get to finally meet Jackie,' I said. 'Hot damn.'

48

Two junkyard dogs pulled at anchor chains set near two old construction trailers. They yelped and barked, claws scratching into the broken asphalt as sleet pinged off the ground. The door of one trailer opened and a thick-bodied guy with a lot of black hair and a hook nose descended a short flight of handmade steps. He wore a slick Pats jacket and an orange watch cap and stopped halfway between us and the trailer to light up a smoke. He had thick legs and a big gut. He was built like a Bulgarian power lifter gone to seed. 'This him?' he said, clicking a Zippo closed.

'Yeah,' Arty said.

'Don't look like much,' he said.

'C'mon, Jackie,' I said. 'Don't hate me because I'm beautiful.'

Arty shrugged and walked over to one of the two dogs and rubbed the pit bull's nub ears. On one knee, he spoke to the dog like the animal was a child. The pit bull flopped over on its back for a belly rub.

'You Spenser?' Jackie said.

'Jesus Christ,' I said. 'Arty just told you I was and then you said, "He don't look like much." And then I said, "Don't hate me because I'm beautiful".'

I was ready for it, but the punch in my gut still took a little air from me. I returned with a rabbit punch to Jackie DeMarco's kidney and then another into his bloated gut. It felt like I was punching into a lumpy mattress. By that time, both doors to both trailers had opened and both Howdy Doody and Baldy ran from the steps and pointed guns at me. They were joined by a skinny guy in an open parka, jeans, and no shoes holding a shotgun.

'The gang's all here,' I said. I rubbed my stomach. Jackie DeMarco gave a good punch. I nodded my respect toward Jackie. The dogs were barking again and digging at the asphalt, trying to break their chains to get to me.

'At your office,' Arty said, 'didn't we tell you to get lost?'

'You did.'

'And in Tampa?' he said. 'We let you go with a warning.'

'I don't recall you saying much, Arty,' I said. 'After Hawk knocked you out.'

'Shut up,' Arty said.

Jackie DeMarco lit another cigarette, clicked the lighter closed, and then eyed me with a little humor. Baldy had slipped the auto back into his belt. Howdy Doody had dropped his pistol, too. Only the new guy, Shoeless Joe, kept his gun aimed at me. He walked around in a wide circle while I talked with Jackie and Arty Leblanc. He had the jittery look of a meth head with an itchy trigger finger. I kept in close to Jackie and Arty. If he were to spray buckshot, it would be nice if we all got it. The pinging sleet gave the air an electric feel in the graying day.

There must have been more than a hundred impounded cars parked out into the spaces behind the trailers and a fleet of a couple dozen tow trucks, DEMARCO's proudly displayed on the doors.

'I guess we're at an impasse,' I said.

'What?' DeMarco said.

'An impasse,' I said. 'You want me to quit with those two judges. And I won't.'

'Maybe so,' DeMarco said. 'But nobody is really going to care when you disappear, Spenser. You know how many guys I know who will throw a freakin' party when you're gone?'

'How many?' I said.

'Lots.'

'But we'll need a head count,' I said. 'Appetizers. Cocktails.'

'Arty?' DeMarco said.

Arty looked up. Howdy Doody and Baldy had joined him to stare at me as Jackie DeMarco shamed me so thoroughly. My face felt stiff

192

and waxen in the cold. The sleet fell harder. The dogs pulled at the chains, reaching their limit, but still clawing, yelping. DeMarco took one last puff on the cigarette and tossed it to the ground. 'Kill this son of a bitch,' he said, tossing Arty some keys. 'Take that old Buick somewhere and burn 'em both up.'

Arty pocketed the keys and reached into his black leather coat for his gun.

I heard the boom of the rifle a millisecond after Arty's head exploded. The three flunkies pulled their guns and started firing out into the wide-open space of the impound lot. I'd dropped to the ground and snatched back my gun and Arty's stainless-steel Taurus. He'd fallen ugly and dead onto his back, his fingers just in reach of one of the dogs. The dog was in a yelping frenzy, biting and pulling Arty by the digits closer toward him. Blood spilled across the ground. Jackie DeMarco had come out of the trailer holding a shotgun. Two more blasts of the .44, one ripping into the skin of the trailer, and DeMarco was back inside.

I ran for cover behind a tow truck, one of those big ones that can slide a Patton tank up onto the flatbed. I exchanged a few shots with Baldy. He was behind the hood of a black Jeep Wrangler, popping up every few seconds like a game of Whack-A-Mole. Jackie DeMarco had a window opened in the construction trailer and was firing out into the lot. Another rifle blast from the lot silenced him for a bit. For a good twenty seconds, gunfire ringing in my ears, all I could hear were the pin sounds of ice needles hitting the ground.

Baldy fired at me again and then ran for a long line of impounded cars. I could hear the thud of his boots and his heavy breathing as another rifle shot sounded and he was cut down at the legs. He screamed and yelled obscenities and rolled around on the ground. I looked up over the edge of the flatbed and saw and heard nothing else but the guy's pain. The automatic spent, I laid it on the ground and held my .38. I moved toward the cab of the tow truck, trying to keep quiet, trying to listen. In the big oversized sideview mirror, I saw the flash of red hair and turned to see Howdy Doody pointing his shotgun at me.

I shot him three times. His body jerked and spasmed like he was being jolted by an electric wire.

The ringing silence broke with the sound of a big engine starting and the squealing of tires. A big black Ford F-250 raced by the tow truck, slamming on brakes before it came to the closed gates, the gates slowly clanging open. One of the doors opened and the skinny guy with no shoes jumped in the passenger side as the truck raced off into Southie.

I stepped over Howdy Doody's body, which now looked like a broken marionette. I felt an acid rising up in the back of my throat. I spit into the lot and kept walking forward, trying not to look over at the two dogs fighting over different pieces of Arty Leblanc. Baldy was screaming in pain. Everything was dirty and messy, but I preferred this to being burned up in the back of a Buick as Jackie DeMarco had instructed.

Hawk wandered out of the maze of impounded cars, propping a .380 hunting rifle over his shoulders like old stills I'd seen of Woody Strode.

'You want to call Quirk?' he said. 'Or split.'

'Call Quirk.'

'Then I split.'

I nodded at Hawk. He nodded slightly to me and disappeared out the gate and into Southie. It was another ten minutes before I heard the police sirens.

49

'You know, I saw this movie once,' Frank Belson said. 'The private eye kills a bunch of hoodlums before the police show up. And you know what the detective does?'

'What's that, Frank?'

'The guy gives the shamus his weapon back,' he said. 'No questions asked. He tells the boys on patrol, "He's okay, guys. No problem." Our hero rides off into the sunset or drives his fucking sportscar, or whatever.'

'And that's what you're going to do for me, Frank?' I said.

'Ha,' Belson said, plugging an old cigar into his mouth. 'Ha, ha.'

There were a lot of BPD cars and a lot of cops scouring the impound lot. I spotted an ambulance, two hearses, and a lot of unmarked units parked inside or near the chain-link fence. It was night now and the sleet had stopped. I wanted to go home very badly. Belson kept laughing.

'Something funny?'

'I don't give a crap if this is Jackie DeMarco's impound lot or Lucky Luciano's,' he said. 'You got a lot of explaining to do, hotshot.'

'I had just run in to get some takeout,' I said. 'I didn't even see the meter.'

'And so you got pissed about them towing your ride and killed two guys and sent another guy to the hospital?'

'How's he doing anyway?' I said.

'Do you care?' Belson said.

'Nope,' I said. 'Not really. They had just offered to snuff out my candle and burn me up in the trunk of an old Buick.'

'The indignity,' Belson said. 'I would've figured you for a Cadillac.' He looked over my shoulder to a couple uniformed cops walking the impound lot. One of them held up a thumb, finding the place where DeMarco's crew had returned shots with Hawk. They set little tags on the hood and windshield for the bullet holes.

'Who was with you?' Belson said. 'Hawk, Vinnie Morris? Or was it that Indian kid you're training these days?'

'I ride alone.'

'Bullshit,' Belson said. 'I don't need some tech people to tell me they're pulling rifle slugs out of that one on the ground. The other one, Jesus Christ. I saw he'd been shot, but son of a bitch. What that dog did to him. They had to tranq the fucking dogs and send 'em to the pound.'

'His name is Arty Leblanc,' I said. 'He used to work with Broz. Back in the day.'

'Not many of you guys left,' he said. 'Maybe I should salute or something.'

I shrugged. Despite my history with Frank Belson and the guys in homicide, they took my .38 and the Taurus I'd pulled from Arty Leblanc. They would test the weapons, conduct autopsies, draw maps and diagrams, and ultimately pull me into an inquest. The inquests were seldom interesting or helpful to me. I'd sat through many before. I'd be cleared but not without a lot of questions from the Suffolk County DA.

In the darkness, the impound lot and the triple-deckers and remnants of Old Colony that surrounded it seemed as welcoming and homey as a foreign planet. Despite my protests, Belson fired up his old cigar. The smoke looked and smelled like a piece of old rope. He made an effort to exhale in my direction. The lights over the lot shone down on the iced hoods and windshields in colorful bright patterns.

'Where's Quirk?'

'He's coming.'

'Goody.'

'He was off this week,' he said. 'Spending time with grandkids.'

'It's been a while,' I said.

'Not long enough.'

'And you think he'll be upset?'

'He'll be more than upset,' Belson said. 'He'll be fucking pissed.'

'Terrific.'

'Who was the other shooter, Spenser?'

'Beats me,' I said. 'Rough neighborhood.'

'Do you know how much you make my ass hurt?'

I walked over to the steps to the trailer and sat down. They'd been made inexpertly with some two-by-fours and penny nails. Belson pulled out a notebook and asked me to go back to the beginning. 'At the mall,' he said. 'When exactly did this guy Leblanc pull his weapon?'

50

I was lucky to get to Susan's a little after ten that night. I had called and she was waiting up. Pearl was very happy to see me, her nubbed tail moving as fast as hummingbird wings. Susan set out a bottle of Eagle Rare bourbon on the kitchen counter. I added some ice to a glass and poured out three fingers of whiskey.

'Bad?'

'Worse,' I said.

'How many?'

'Three dead,' I said. 'Two got away.'

'Same men from Florida?'

'Same men.'

'And now?' Susan said.

I removed my jacket and my ball cap. I wandered over to her leather couch and set down my drink. Pearl hopped up beside me and nuzzled her head into my lap. Dogs had a sixth sense for knowing when their pals were down. I rubbed her head and patted her lean, muscular flank. She sniffed at my shirt and my hands. I wondered how much the smell had told her.

'You don't want to talk about it,' she said.

'I've been talking about it for the last four hours with Frank Belson and Quirk,' I said. 'Quirk was about as mad as I've ever seen him. He said I put him in an irregular position with the commissioner.'

'Irregular?'

'Yep,' I said. 'Well, actually he said "fucking irregular" because that's the way Quirk talks.'

I leaned forward, Pearl still huddled close to me, and picked up the glass. I drained a lot of the whiskey. I could feel the alcohol hitting the bloodstream and dilating the capillaries. The tension in my trapezius muscles started to unclench. Susan sat on the other end of the couch and watched me as I stared and drank. She had on silk pajama bottoms and one of my old BU T-shirts.

The television was on, but she'd turned down the sound. She'd been watching some kind of cable drama show where people were throwing things and crying. A vintage movie poster for *The Gay Caballero* hung close by. Lee Farrell had given it to Susan as an inside joke. Cesar Romero as the Cisco Kid. I wondered if the Cisco Kid or Gordito ever had problems with shooting outlaws. Or was it his sidekick Pancho? I couldn't recall. I mainly remembered Gilbert Roland as The Kid. He had a hell of a fancy suit.

'Are you hungry?'

'Nope.'

'Have you eaten?'

'I almost had a chocolate croissant at the Chestnut Hill Mall.'

'And before that?'

'A nice corned-beef sandwich from Michael's.'

'You know you don't have to eat kosher just for me.'

'I do it for the pickles,' I said. 'Jews make wonderful pickles.'

Susan stood up and gently pushed Pearl aside. She sat in my lap and wrapped her long legs around my torso. 'Can I do anything to make you feel better?'

'This may be the first time I've said this,' I said. 'But I want to take a shower and go to sleep. I feel lousy as hell.'

She bit her lower lip and nodded. I wrapped my arms around her and rested my head on her shoulder. 'What about the woman?' she said. 'The lawyer? Will she help?'

'I'm pretty sure she's the one who tipped the men off to snatch me.'

'But you already knew that,' she said. 'Why you had Hawk following you.'

'I had doubts about her integrity.'

'What about now?' Susan said.

'What do you mean?'

'She's in a different situation,' she said. 'If she had any doubts about covering for the judges, perhaps this may have put her over the edge.'

198

'I doubt it.'

'The shootings made the news,' Susan said. 'If she isn't a complete sociopath, this will rattle her a great deal and could make her more likely to discuss private matters with you.'

'She knew she was setting me up.'

'How do you know?'

I didn't say anything for a moment. Channel 7 news teased SHOOTING IN SOUTHIE. Three dead. Local reporter Hank Phillippi Ryan was at the scene.

'I could ask her,' I said. 'I know where she lives.'

'I could go with you,' Susan said.

'Moral support?'

'Push her some,' she said. 'I could perhaps persuade her in a way you couldn't.'

I nodded. 'Therapeutic talk?'

Susan shook her head. 'She needs to be slapped around,' she said. 'She almost got you killed. You can't physically threaten her. But I can.'

'Maybe I should go alone.'

Susan looked thoughtful for a moment. 'Perhaps that would be best.'

'Can't have shrinks slapping around vulnerable people.'

Susan took me by my chin and kissed me full on the mouth. 'You look kind of vulnerable right now,' she said. 'I kind of like it.'

Susan wandered back to the bedroom. She left the door wide open.

I took a long sip of the bourbon.

And followed.

He slept outside all night. No one came looking for him. The guards must've thought he had nowhere to go and would eventually turn himself in. But he didn't. He kept moving, finally settling into a small island of trees on the south side of the island at the bottom of the big hill facing the ocean. He found part of a blue tarp to use as a blanket and some pieces of cardboard to make a little shelter against a young tree. The sound of the ocean was strong, and at night, when the lights went off on the island, Boston looked like a bright jewel. He had nothing to eat. The fever and the shakes were coming on again.

But he couldn't be sure if he shook from the sickness or the cold. He crawled out of the shelter sometime in the early morning where the hills had eroded into the beach. He searched through the pieces of trash that had spilled from the old landfill. Looking for anything to keep him warm. He found some ragged but dry pieces of cloth, maybe part of old pants and a shirt, and used them to make a nest to sleep.

He couldn't sleep. The wind blew stronger. And at one point, a hard gust toppled his whole shelter. It took an hour in the full dark to rebuild and settle back into the nest. Everything smelled of garbage and rot. He didn't care. He buried his head deeper in the mess. He tried to sleep. He had a fever but couldn't sweat in the cold. He wanted to throw up. But his stomach was empty.

The cold was too much to take. If he could have moved, he would have walked back. He would have quit. But he was weak and the cold was so deep and paralyzing that he was pretty sure he'd die out here. He knew they'd kick him into the sea or bury him deep with all of the city's garbage from years ago. They wouldn't find him. He'd be nothing.

The sun is what kept him going. He lay facing the hills when the black became a bright, electric blue. He staggered to his feet and dragged the ripped blue tarp on top of the hill. He wrapped the tarp around him, still sick and breathing hard. He tried his best to will the sun to come on faster to warm things up even just a little, hard waves beating against the thin cut of beach. A hollowness turned in his stomach. There was a prick of light coming on. The blue light shading into orange. Just a wisp of clouds over the ocean, a light roll of the waves. The little light became a small ball shooting out spectrums of light, turning the entire horizon orange. The boy made it to his feet. He wore the tarp over his shaved head, wind rattling around him.

'Isn't that pretty?' a voice said behind him.

It was Robocop.

The boy turned. He wavered on his feet, not from being afraid but from the hunger and the sickness.

'I thought you'd be dead by now.'

The boy didn't say anything. Only the wind off the Atlantic answered.

'I hoped you were dead,' he said. 'Come on.'

The boy didn't move. Couldn't move.

'I said come on.'

The boy shook his head. The light bled up over the beach and onto the hills, crossing the shadows of his feet and the space that separated them.

'You'll take what's coming to you.'

The boy shook his head.

The guard pulled out a police baton and walked fast, trampling the sun in the dead grass. 'Come on, you little fucker.' He raised the baton, and as he wavered over the boy's head, the boy snatched it from him and thwacked the man on the side of the head.

The man yelped in pain. The boy did not stop. He hit the man again and again until he saw the blood. The man was on his knees when he heard the yelling. A fat woman in uniform and an old guy holding a gun ran up onto the hill. The old woman was out of shape and breathing hard when she told him to drop the weapon. The boy waited a beat and then tossed the baton off the hill and down to the narrow beach. He felt empty, spent, almost hollow with lack of sleep and food.

Robocop got to his feet and wiped blood off his mouth. He snatched a Taser from the fat woman's hand, and before he had time to react, shoved it up under the boy's arm. The pain of it nearly lifted him off his feet. He clenched his teeth, not wanting to show the pain, as the man zapped him again.

He fell with a thud. Robocop looked down at the boy. He spit in his face.

'Get this piece of shit back to the compound,' he said. 'He tried to fucking kill me. That's attempted murder.'

The boy fell to his back, trying to catch his breath. He looked up at the bright sky. The fat woman, the old guy, and Robocop grouped in a sloppy circle. The kid just tried to breathe.

'He's screwed,' the fat woman said, her voice gaspy and excited. 'That's attempted murder. He ain't never getting home.'

51

Sydney Bennett lived in the South End on the second floor of an old redbrick row house. Hawk and I drove past the address the next morning. Hawk sat in the passenger seat and stared right ahead, and we drove along Appleton at a slow, yet confident, pace. A lot of cars had been covered in the sleet and snow overnight but the streets had been scraped clean as a fat man's dinner plate. 'Someone's minding the woman,' Hawk said.

'Looks like it.'

'Guess you figured that,' Hawk said. 'Since she didn't show for work.'

'White BMW,' I said. 'Two guys up front.'

'That's them.'

'You think you could redirect their attention while I attempt to talk to Miss Bennett?'

'Be my pleasure, bawse.'

'You do a good job,' I said, 'and I'll let you wax the car later.'

'Lawdy,' Hawk said. 'You just too good to me, Mista Spensah.'

'Is that really necessary?'

'Sometimes it's important to underscore the racial dynamic to our relationship.'

'Well, in that case ...'

I found a parking space two blocks away and settled in while Hawk got out and disappeared around the corner, doubling back on Lawrence. I waited ten minutes, got out into the cold, and then strolled back toward Sydney Bennett's town house. Steam rose out of sewer grates. A few cars zipped along the street. The white BMW had disappeared. I walked up to the front door and mashed a few buzzers. Someone let me in and I made my way into a warm marble entrance and up a flight of stairs.

I knocked on Sydney's door, took off my hat, and turned to look in the opposite direction so as not to be seen in the peephole. Thirty seconds later, she opened up. She was wearing a blue terrycloth robe with a white towel wrapping her head.

She took one look at me and then started to close the door. I stuck the steel tip of my Red Wing into the door frame and held firm.

'Goddamn you,' she said.

'Lovely morning,' I said. 'Did you sleep well?'

'Get your foot out of this door or I'll call the police.'

'Be my guest.'

'Seriously,' she said. 'You better get out of here. If you don't want to get hurt.'

'You mean Mr DeMarco's friends in the Beamer?'

She stared at me and didn't say a word. I slipped my ball cap back on. 'They've gone out for a ride with a pal of mine,' I said. 'I don't know when—or if—they will return.'

'You son of a bitch.'

I shrugged. 'I smell fresh coffee.'

Sydney Bennett made a grunt and turned from the door. I pushed the door open, walked inside, and shut it behind me. The apartment had probably been a crack den twenty years ago. Now it was high-end. Refinished hardwood floors, stainless-steel appliances, and a commercial stove larger than my kitchen. She had a nice mix of new leather furniture and antiques. She'd hung a lot of old family photos, some sepia-toned, on a gallery wall between two large windows. A lot of stern old white men with impressive mustaches.

Sydney walked back to the kitchen. She'd taken the towel off her head and was pouring coffee.

Unless she planned to throw scalding coffee in my lap, I took this to be a good sign. I had a seat and waited. At the end of a long hall, the door was open and I spotted an unmade bed. I listened for sounds of anyone else in the apartment but heard nothing. I had brought a new gun with me just in case. Not that I had any reason not to trust Sydney.

She thunked down a mug of coffee so hard some of it sloshed onto her coffee table.

'What do you want?' she said.

'You set me up.'

She sat down in an oversized leather chair close by. She held the front of her robe shut with one hand, her thick, naked calves poking out below. She had calf muscles like an athlete, wide shoulders, and large hands for a woman.

I sipped some coffee.

She tucked her large feet up under her. She waited.

I didn't say anything.

'I didn't have a choice,' she said. 'I think you know that.'

I nodded. I was the master of stringing out the silence. And I think the disappearance of DeMarco's men had left her a little off guard.

'Why didn't you tell the police about me?' she said.

'How do you know I didn't?'

'Because I haven't seen any police,' she said. 'No one has come to talk to me.'

'Besides Jackie.'

'Yeah,' she said. 'Besides him.'

'So how exactly does it work?' I said. 'Who's on first?'

'What?'

'Where does the money start and where does it flow?'

'I would have thought you'd had that all figured out by now.'

'I think the judges get a piece of whatever plans DeMarco and Talos have cooked up.'

She shook her head with great disappointment. I'd had that reaction from only a few women. It felt strange. I crossed my legs, ankle across my good knee. I sat up straight and drank a little more coffee. 'I can always tell the police about your involvement in the shooting yesterday.'

'That you were stalking me at the mall? Go ahead. That's all I know.'

'You texted DeMarco and he sent Arty Leblanc and his crew.'

'So you say.'

'It doesn't bother you that Jackie DeMarco wanted to have you killed?' I said. 'That Callahan and Scali were scared shitless you'd turned on them?'

She didn't say a word. She rubbed the back of her neck and leaned back farther in the seat. She took a long, good breath and settled in.

'Are you working with the Feds?'

'No,' she said. 'Of course not.'

'Would you?'

She looked as if I'd poured ice water onto her head. 'Excuse me?'

'Would you work with the Feds if you knew you could escape being roped into this mess?' I said. 'At best, you'll be disbarred. At worst, they'll kill you.'

She leveled her large brown eyes at me and ducked her chin. But she offered no response. I took her moment of thought to warm my hands on the mug. The coffee was terrible. It tasted like the kind of coffee you get free with an oil change.

'Did they say you were being protected?' I said. 'Or watched?'

She cleared her throat and shook her head. 'Nobody told me anything,' she said. 'I saw the men outside and I was afraid to leave.'

I nodded.

'I saw the news last night,' she said. 'I saw all those men had been shot. I didn't know they were trying to kill you. I wasn't told anything other than to let Arty know if I was being harassed.'

'Any of DeMarco's people threaten you?'

She shrugged.

'How does Talos figure into all this?' I said.

She swallowed. Her hair had started to dry and curl, shining after a good wash. She wiped her eyes and nodded. 'You're going to get me killed.'

'Or save your life.'

'How'd you know they'd threatened me?'

'I spoke with a former employee of the family, remember?'

'And he told you about the judges getting greedy?'

I leaned forward, picked up the coffee mug, and took a sip. As natural as can be. I nodded with a lot of confidence that this had been my plan all along.

'They weren't happy with the initial deal with Talos,' she said. 'Callahan wanted a lot more and Scali sided with him. They couldn't get enough money after the island facility was built. They threatened to send kids somewhere else and leave Talos with a big white elephant.'

'You can't have that.'

'No,' she said. 'And so a new deal was made. Talos first balked, but then. Well, you can imagine what happened.'

'Jackie DeMarco.'

'Ziggy didn't want to be involved in this,' she said. 'He had no interest in anything but setting up some shell companies for the judges. He's not a bad guy. Really.'

'Forgive me if I'm skeptical.'

She nodded. She dropped her head into her hand and started to cry a little. I stood up and walked to the kitchen. I pitched the rest of my coffee into the sink. I walked to the big window and looked down on the street. I saw Hawk standing in a fur coat outside the BMW. The BMW looked empty. Hawk was smiling.

'I know someone in Tampa,' I said. 'He's a good man and can help you out of this.'

'Ziggy,' she said. 'That dumb bastard. I busted my ass in college and law school, all to end up stuffing FedEx boxes full of cash in the back room of his practice. When I told him I wanted to quit, that's when they started to follow me. No one made threats.'

'They didn't have to,' I said. 'They were implied.'

'I want out of this.'

'I know you do.'

'I feel like I'm a prisoner,' she said. 'I can't go anywhere without being watched. People following me around. I don't even have a life anymore.'

I nodded. She wiped her eyes and looked at me.

'Just imagine how the kids feel,' I said.

52

Two nights later, I was back in Florida watching two Feds test a wire on Ziggy Swatek. It wasn't pretty. Ziggy had taken off his shirt, showing off a pudgy pale body and thick black hair on his chest, back, and weirdly long arms. If he were running through the woods, hunters might have mistaken him for a small bear or a large ape.

'Do we have to use the freakin' tape?' he said.

A female agent in a blue suit nodded. She tore off more tape and patted a microphone to his chest. She was short and stocky, with cropped, frosted hair and little makeup. As she worked, I noted the impressive government-issue auto she wore on her hip. The other agent was tall and gawky, fidgety, as he tested a signal on a laptop. When finished, he gave the woman a thumbs-up.

'What if they make me take off my shirt?' Ziggy said.

'They'd be sorry,' I said. 'Ever hear of manscaping, Zig?'

'Man-what?'

'You might want to invest in a Weedwacker.'

'Screw you, Spenser,' he said. 'Who the hell invited you?'

I nodded to Special Agent Jamal Whitehead, who stood near two French doors facing the Gulf. He was talking on a cell phone. Outside, it was raining, and a little thunder growled overhead. The newly planted palms at the judges' planned community whipped around in the tiny squall, rain tapping at the glass. But the weather was tropical and pleasant, and the warm air had felt good as soon as I'd landed that morning. Whitehead had picked me up at Tampa International.

We had gone to see Zig. At first, Zig had threatened. And then Agent Whitehead had run down his short list of options. Zig finally agreed to give up the judges. He wouldn't even mention Jackie DeMarco's name.

'What if they try and throw me overboard?' Ziggy said. 'I can't swim.'

'We're on a boat two slips down,' the female agent said.

'And we have a net,' Whitehead said, pocketing his cell phone in his gray pants. He had on a tailored white shirt with his initials on his pocket and a black knit tie. 'We'll pull you in with the rest of the sea creatures.'

'If you want to be an asshole about this,' Ziggy said, 'I can walk away right now.'

'What time does Jackie DeMarco's plane land?' Whitehead said.

'Ten in the morning,' the female agent said. 'Should we meet him at the gate?'

'What do you think, Zig?' I said. 'Fair offer.'

'Jesus,' he said. 'Okay. Okay. What do you want me to say?'

'You said Callahan and Scali wanted to meet,' I said, looking to Whitehead as I spoke. 'And you persuaded them Boston was too hot. So here we are. And here they are. All you got to do is facilitate some fascinating conversation.'

'On the fucking boat?'

'*Reel Justice*' Whitehead said. 'It's gonna look great in print.'

'Not my name,' he said.

'Not now,' Whitehead said. 'Not until the trial.'

'My career is over,' Ziggy said. 'Hope you're all happy about that.'

Whitehead smiled and nodded. I nodded, too. I was very happy how it all worked out.

'How'd you know about me being shaken down?' Ziggy said. 'Sydney tell you?'

The rain hit the glass a little harder now. The palm fronds shook and the boats rocked out in the marina. A man and a woman darted off the long pier and ran to the parking lot. I saw the taillights click on as they U-turned out of the lot and drove away.

'I don't believe Scali and Callahan would've had it any other way,' I said. 'A big boat like that takes a lot of gas. They'd need gas money.'

'Someone on the inside tipped you,' he said. 'Who the hell was it?'

Whitehead held up his hand in a polite gesture to tell Ziggy to shut his mouth. He leaned over the young agent who was working on the laptop and looked up to the female agent finishing with the tape. Ziggy stood there, pale and hairy, a pink silk shirt hanging across a rattan chair. I almost felt sorry for him. Almost.

'Get them talking straight and exact,' Whitehead said. 'They start talking in vague terms, or in code, we won't make a move. Don't have them hemming and hawing around the point. You understand?'

'What do you mean?' Ziggy said.

'I once worked a case with some guys who called money fish,' Whitehead said. 'They'd make plans for a deal and talk about all the fish they'd need. I don't want the judges talking how much flounder they plan on netting. You got it?'

Ziggy nodded.

'Ask them straight out about this new deal they want with Bobby Talos.'

'Bobby is a good guy,' Ziggy said. 'A class act. He don't deserve this.'

'Zig, you are the true Good Housekeeping Seal,' I said. 'If only Bobby Junior could be with us today. I'd love to finally meet him up close and personal.'

'Mr Swatek here comes through and we'll get all we need to indict Mr Talos,' Whitehead said. 'Only thing that's not clear is who came up with the whole plan? Did Talos go to the judges or did the judges go to Talos?'

'Joe Scali reached out,' Ziggy said, reaching for his pink shirt and thankfully covering up his less-than-impressive physique. 'He came to Bobby. He said he and Callahan could close down that shithole in Blackburn and they could steer business his way. It was all supposed to be a straight deal until they came back for more. And then more again.'

'And the DeMarcos?' I said.

'The who?' Ziggy said, smiling and buttoning up.

'One step at a time,' Jamal Whitehead said. 'One step at a time.'

'Jackie was going to have Sydney killed,' I said. 'Doesn't that mean anything?'

'Yeah,' Ziggy said. 'It means I'd have to look for a new partner who wouldn't put my dork in the broiler.'

I shook my head. Ziggy tucked his pink shirt into his black pants. His face was red and sweaty. I handed the strange little man a hand towel. He just looked down at it like he didn't know how to use it.

'Always a lovely sight to see a man saving his own ass,' Whitehead said, checking his watch.

I just watched Ziggy the way you might examine an animal at a zoo. Endlessly fascinating.

A folding table had been set up in the middle of the condo. On the table, six laptop screens showed various locations around the boat, cameras mounted on neighboring slips. Whitehead leaned in and studied the screens, the other Feds making the final prep for the meeting. In panoramic clarity, I watched Joe Scali board the fishing boat and run into the wheelhouse. He had on a polo shirt and shorts showing off his short, skinny legs. He was alone, closing an umbrella and surveying the gulf with a big smile, before opening up a cooler and pulling out a cold beer. Miller Time. He drained half the bottle while sitting up high in the captain's chair.

'You gonna stick around?' Whitehead said. 'Gonna be a hell of a show.'

I shook my head. 'I better get back to Boston.'

'More with the DeMarcos?'

'Nope,' I said. 'Just a promise to keep.'

53

I didn't sleep, making two phone calls and changing clothes before driving down to the Seaport to meet Sergeant Danny Long, harbormaster for the Boston Police. One day you're staring out into the deep green of the Gulf of Mexico and the next at the choppy gray waves of the Boston Inner Channel. Long waved me aboard and shook my hand as I set foot on deck. He was built like a heavyweight from another century, with a big Irish head, smiling green eyes, and a lot of thick black hair. He had on a heavy coat, as Long mentioned today was cold as a bastard. A blue ball cap noted he was indeed harbormaster.

'Commander Quirk says you got a wellness check?'

'Sure.'

'And you don't want to call ahead to the facility?'

'I believe phone lines are down.'

'Oh, yeah,' Long said, chewing gum, smiling. 'I heard that, too.'

'You know the island?'

'Of course,' he said. 'It's part of our patrol. A little past Thompson Island. Not much to it. Used to be a trash dump before the city leased it to the jail.'

'You know anything about it?'

'I've seen some kids picking up garbage on the beach,' Long said. 'We had a kid last year went missing. They said he was trying to escape. You know, like it was fucking Alcatraz.'

'Alcatraz may have been more fun.'

'No shit?' Long said.

'None at all.'

'Most of the kids aren't even from Boston,' he said. 'It's part of some program to extract them from problem areas and get them back to fucking nature.'

'That's what they say.'

'What's the boy's name?'

I told him. He nodded, chewing his gum, and asked if I'd untie the two lines attached to the dock. I saluted him and untied the boat, coiling the ropes as I'd learned from my uncle Patrick, who'd settled in Mattapoisett to build boats. He revved the engine in reverse, chugging slow out into the channel, and then once we were all clear, throttled us forward and out into the harbor.

Sergeant Long had lied. It was colder than a bastard. I had on a pair of thermal underwear, jeans, a flannel shirt, and a peacoat with a watch cap. But I still kept in the wheelhouse, turning back to see Boston fading from view. The pilot boat skipped over the small waves and over hard chunks of ice. As he kicked the engine into high gear, hitting about thirty knots, he'd turn to stare at me when I wasn't watching.

'You're the guy.'

'What guy?'

'When Quirk said your name, it didn't click,' he said. 'But now. You're the guy from the papers.'

'Boston's Most Handsome Professional?'

'No,' he said, kind of yelling over the whine of the motors. 'The guy in the shootout with those shitbags who worked for Jackie DeMarco.'

'Just a simple misunderstanding.'

'Misunderstanding, my ass,' Sergeant Long said, destroying his chewing gum. 'What? Were they trying to whack you?'

'They got a little agitated.'

Long nodded. He steered with one hand. He had his ball cap down in his eyes so the wind didn't kick it up and out to sea. 'DeMarco mixed up in this kids' prison?'

I nodded.

He stared straight ahead, the shapes of a couple harbor islands coming into view, shrouded by a thick fog. 'When I was a kid, I used to see his old man hand out candy in the North End,' he said. 'He had a big coin laundry there.'

'Lovely man.'

'Yeah,' Sergeant Long said. 'Lovely if you're his pal. If you're not, you're toast.'

'And the kid?'

'Ha,' he said. 'What do you think?'

'He's a real charmer,' I said. 'He'll go far in this town.'

'Jesus Christ.'

It didn't take long to pass the other Harbor Islands: Thompson, Spectacle, Long, Gallops, and Lovells. I didn't know each one; Sergeant Long pointed them out along the way. I'd spent some time out this way fishing with Henry Cimoli after he moved to Revere and bought a boat. But we'd fished more for beers than we had actually

213

searched for haddock. Fortune was situated a little outside Green Island and Outer Brewster. By the time we got there, I felt a little like Jim Hawkins.

Long slowed the boat when we spotted the docks. There was a narrow slice of a rocky beach and an industrial-looking building situated up a little hill. He pointed it out as we slid into the dock. The wind would've taken less hardy men out to sea. But even without breakfast, I stood firmly rooted on deck and hopped out onto the dock. I tied the lines. The motor settled into a putter, the exhaust chugging into the cold air.

Once the boat was tied up, we walked together up a narrow pebble path to signs pointing out the direction to the MCC office. Since the building took up a third of the island, the signs were a bit superfluous.

'Downed phone lines?' Long said.

'Yep.'

'You know, cell phones work out here,' he said, checking his phone. Grinning.

'You don't say.'

Long shrugged in a noncommittal cop way and followed the path around the large building surrounded by chain link topped with razor wire. I couldn't imagine a homier environment for troubled teens except for maybe a classic British workhouse. There were three large brick buildings and a smaller one serving as the entrance. A sign read OFFICIAL MCC PERSONNEL ONLY. NO VISITORS.

Sergeant Long opened the front door wide and held it for me. Three men and a fat lady were lounging in office chairs and watching the morning news. There was an empty box of donuts on a table. They all wore blue uniforms with patches on their shoulders. No one stood up or said anything. They all just kind of looked at one another. A wiry guy with a thin face and a purplish mouse under one eye stood up. 'Yeah.'

Sergeant Long nodded and gave his name, rank, and why we were there.

'Yeah?' the guy said.

'Boy,' I said. 'This guy is sharp.'

'Who the hell are you?' he said. 'You a cop, too?'

'No,' I said. 'And neither are you. You couldn't even play one on TV. We're here for a wellness check.'

The fat lady stood up. She was about to sing. 'All visitation requests, even from law enforcement, have to go through our main office in Newton.'

'What if I told you I was a close and personal pal of Bobby Talos's,' I said. 'I'm into yachting.'

'No one said anything,' the fat lady said.

Long looked slightly amused. He gave the boy's name and said we wanted to see him.

'You got a warrant?' the man with the shiner said.

'No,' Long said. 'And don't need one. This property is leased from the city. That means I got every right. Go get the fucking kid.'

'Hey,' the fat lady said. She still had powder from the donut on her face.

'Now,' Sergeant Long said.

'He's out in the yard,' she said. 'Go get him yourself.'

I nodded at Long and we both brushed past the woman and the wiry guard with the military cut. The door had an electronic lock and by the time we reached it, the lock was buzzing. Long pushed it open hard and we were outside in a common rec area. The wiry guard followed us.

Out by an empty basketball court, I saw a kid sitting on a bench. He didn't look up as we approached. The empty recreation yard had other benches, ringed by a dirty snowbank pushed up off walkways leading from bunkhouses to a cafeteria and the offices. The wind seemed even stronger in that open place than it had in the harbor. It didn't whistle, it roared.

The kid was muscly and compact, with a shaved head. As I got closer, it appeared the boy had just gone twelve rounds with Mike Tyson. He had a lot of bruises on his face, neck, and arms. He had on a thin uniform that resembled hospital scrubs and was shaking. Someone had cuffed him to the bench.

I dropped down to a knee and said, 'I'm a friend of Dillon Yates's.'

The kid nodded. He was as pale as a bleached sheet, shaking, with dark circles under his eyes, his lips a bright shade of blue. He hugged his arms around his body, shivering without control.

'Give me the key,' I said to the guard.

The wiry guard stood next to me now, looking down at the kid. He had a smile on his face.

'He tried to escape,' the man said. 'He hid out and tried to kill me yesterday with my own weapon. You know how it goes. These kids. You can't give 'em an inch.'

'So this is punishment?' I said. 'Beating up a kid and then giving him hypothermia?'

'One less,' he said. 'Who gives a shit?'

I got to my feet, dusted off my knee, and punched the guard very hard in the stomach. He crumpled like a paper tiger. I reached down and felt into his pockets, pulling out a small ring of keys. I found three handcuff keys. The second worked.

I helped the kid to his feet. 'You took a weapon off this guy?' I said.

The boy nodded. We looked down at the man and the boy summoned enough energy to spit on him.

Long already had out his cell phone, punching up numbers and talking to someone in Boston. 'Gee,' Long said. 'What do you know? The reception is excellent.'

'What do you think?' I said.

'I think I've seen all I need to,' Long said. 'Kid gonna be okay?'

'He needs medical attention,' I said. 'And this place needs to be fumigated.'

Sergeant Long nodded at me. I took off my peacoat and helped the boy inside it. I put my arm around him and walked him toward the front office. The fat woman at the desk had seen everything that happened outside. She would not look me in the eye. Everyone in the front office tried in vain to look busy until the cops arrived and many reports were written.

54

By mid-May, the weather in Boston had improved greatly. Winter was all but a bad memory, and I'd switched out the flannel for a cotton button-down. I did wear a light sport coat, as I'd agreed to drive Dillon Yates to the federal courthouse that morning. Good to her word, Sheila had moved out of Blackburn to Framingham. She'd taken a job with a small law firm and Dillon had enrolled in the local high school. The Yates didn't need Blackburn anymore. Blackburn had come to them.

Dozens of angry parents had amassed on the brick plaza, holding hand-painted signs with some not-so-nice things to say about Joe Scali. Thanks to stories in *The Star*, they knew almost eighty percent of the kids in Scali's courtroom appeared without a lawyer. A juvenile justice group investigated further, finding parents had signed waivers outside courtroom doors. Never realizing they'd given away their kids' right to an attorney.

Scali was in the third day of his federal trial, the venue moving north to Massachusetts, where most of the crimes were committed. Gavin Callahan had already cut a deal and pled guilty to corruption and bribery. I was pretty sure that Jamal Whitehead was waiting for the right moment to connect Callahan to the DeMarcos. I wondered what would ever become of their boat.

The new digs of U.S. District Court were in a shiny new mirrored building just south over the Channel on Seaport Boulevard. As expected, there were news crews, onlookers, and weirdoes mixed in with the families. Making our way into the plaza, I spotted Jake Cotner and Ryan Bell. They walked over to Dillon and began to talk. Dillon was wearing a navy blazer and tie. He was expected to testify that morning.

My old friend Beth Golnick was nowhere to be seen. Jake and Ryan said she'd moved out of state.

'What do you think?' Sheila Yates said.

'I think Scali better watch out for flying tomatoes.'

'The prick.'

'And to think,' I said. 'This all started with a sandwich.'

'It was worth it.'

'It was a terrific sandwich.'

'I'll make good,' Sheila said. 'I'll pay you every last nickel for what you did. You and Miss Mullen.'

'Miss Mullen and I have agreed this one is on the house.'

'Are you kidding?'

'I would've paid you to take this on.'

Sheila Yates pulled me in and hugged me. She could squeeze very tight, and by now I'd grown accustomed to her perfume. As she held on, I spotted Iris Milford walking through the crowd and giving me a devilish smile. 'Am I interrupting something?' she said.

'Yes,' I said. 'We plan on doing this all day.'

Sheila Yates wiped her eyes and stepped away. She then turned to Iris and started hugging her. Iris was caught off guard. And then caught on to the spirit and patted Sheila's back a few times before Sheila joined Dillon and the two boys.

'All the news that's fit to print,' she said. 'And some of the shit left over for *The Star*.'

'How's the reaction in Blackburn?'

'Ran a story yesterday with Judge Price's wife and family,' she said. 'They still believe Scali killed him.'

'He did,' I said. 'In a way.'

'And there are some, although a minority, who believe he's been framed.'

'Thick heads.'

'Have you been to Blackburn?'

'Unfortunately.'

'People come from generations of millworkers,' she said. 'You do what the foreman says and ask no questions.'

Iris wore a stylish black wrap dress and carried a faux-cheetah purse. I guessed it to be faux, as I was pretty sure it was illegal to kill cheetahs these days. We walked over to a low brick wall and sat until

218

it was time for court to start. We both knew it'd be a long day, and we enjoyed the sunshine and nice breeze off the water. Way out in the harbor, the Feds had shut down the facility. The kids had been sent elsewhere. Parents, lawyers, and advocates wanted every kid tried by Scali to have their records expunged.

It was very likely to happen.

'You read where Bobby Talos is saying he's a victim?'

'I did.'

'He might get a wrist slapped.'

'The law isn't justice,' I said. 'It's a very imperfect mechanism.'

'You can say that again.'

'The law isn't—'

Iris held up her hand. We laughed and sat in silence for now, watching the boats out in the harbor. A woman passed us with a big sign that read BAD JUDGES BURN IN HELL. A teenager held up another reading GIVE ME BACK MY LIFE.

'*Mmm,*' Iris said.

'When they break, can I take you to lunch?'

'You can.'

'And we can discuss more imperfections of the world?'

'How much time do you have?'

'I'm here until the show is over.'

'What if he goes free?'

'It could happen,' I said. 'Both you and I know that.'

'But not likely.'

I shrugged. We watched the small sailboats catch a stiff spring breeze and skate across the calm harbor. The whole motion was smooth and effortless. I thought about the boy I'd met out on Fortune Island and I wondered what had become of him. He'd gone back to Blackburn and returned to school. There was talk of a lawsuit.

'More than a thousand kids,' she said. 'And nobody gave a shit.'

As I nodded, the crowd started to gather and yell. Scali walked in tow with his two lawyers as signs were raised and angry parents and kids pelted him with insults.

The judge wore a funeral black suit and tie, looking bemused and diminutive behind his purple-tinted glasses. The wind off the harbor knocking his comb-over up off his bald head. One woman screamed at him that he wasn't a god. An angry teenage girl called him a liar and a cheat. Behind him, the courthouse's mirrored windows shined in a giant reflection of the calm harbor.

As he walked inside, Scali was still smiling.

55

The night of Scali's sentencing, I took Susan to dinner at Grill 23.

It wasn't a celebration. Although he'd been found guilty of accepting bribes from Massachusetts Child Care, Scali skated on kids for cash. He told the court he never took a nickel to send a child to jail. The kickbacks, he and his attorney argued, were misconstrued finder's fees. The jury bought it.

'What a repulsive little man,' Susan said.

'Are you going to eat that?' I said, pointing to a scallop with my fork.

'Yes,' she said. 'But I'm taking my time. And how can you even eat after that verdict?'

I shrugged and cut into my medium-rare filet. I reached for my Eagle Rare on the rocks and took a sip.

'And Bobby Talos?' Susan said.

'After he's sentenced, he'll get to work on his tennis game in minimum security.'

'Ughh.'

'My sentiments exactly,' I said. 'But I did what I said. I got my client's son off the island and his records expunged. And I uncovered a nasty cottage industry in Blackburn.'

'And shut down Fortune Island.'

'For now,' I said. 'I'm sure it's to reopen under new management.'

'For-profit prisons,' she said. 'Their incentive is not to rehabilitate but rather to create a returning customer.'

'Therein lies the rub.'

I forwent dessert, as my target weight had been reached. I was back running on the Charles now that Z had returned from the West Coast. I paid and Susan and I walked out onto Berkeley. I'd parked a block away from my office building.

It was a lovely Boston night. Trees had leaves again. Tulips were sprouting in planters. We walked hand in hand down the sidewalk.

As we crossed over Providence, I noticed a car I'd spotted earlier that day. And the same car I'd spotted parked along Marlborough Street the night before. It was a recent-model Chevy Malibu painted an orangey brown. If you plan to tail someone, you should pick a more attractive color. Ugly always stands out.

It was parked on the corner where Providence runs to Berkeley. Right in front of the Souper Salad. Although I couldn't see their faces, and I didn't want them to notice me staring, I saw two men in the front seat.

'You walk on ahead,' I said.

'Excuse me?' Susan said.

'I want to say hello to someone,' I said. 'Here are my keys. Go up to my office. If I'm not up in five minutes, call Quirk.'

'There is a Dumpster in front of your building,' Susan said. 'Perhaps I could cower there while you fight the bad guys?'

'I only want to say hello.'

'I know how you say hello.'

'Five minutes.'

'Two,' Susan said.

I leaned in and kissed her on the cheek.

I strolled back in the direction of the Souper Salad. In all the years it had been next to my building, I'd had neither their soup nor their salad. Maybe you had to have both to make it Souper. Lots of options to consider.

I knocked on the glass of the Malibu.

A young guy in a black leather jacket was looking at his cell phone. The guy at the wheel looked nearly asleep. I had startled both of them.

I knocked on the glass again. The passenger window went down.

'Yeah,' the young guy said. He looked like a young James Caan without the looks. Or charisma.

'I'm Spenser.'

'So what?' the driver said. He had close-set eyes and no chin. His skin was pinkish, and he had the nose of a pig.

'I'm the guy Jackie DeMarco wanted to scare.'

'Who?'

'How can I fight pros at playing stupid?' I said.

'Hey,' said the younger guy.

'Fuck off,' said Pig Nose.

'You guys are even dumber than your predecessors,' I said. 'Things didn't go so great for them.'

Both men shuffled in their seats. The guy behind the wheel broke eye contact and scratched his cheek.

'You know where I live,' I said. 'You know where I work. And now where I eat.'

'Yeah,' the young guy said. 'We know everything.'

I leaned closer into the window. 'Brilliant,' I said. 'Just brilliant.'

'Watch your ass,' the driver said.

'Yeah,' the young guy said.

'Go home, get a drink, and for God's sake take a shower,' I said. 'If I hadn't seen you both, I would've smelled you. And tell Jackie I got the message. *We're not friends. He's angry.* Terrific.'

The driver looked at the younger guy. The younger guy thumbed his nose and told me to go fuck myself. The driver cranked the car and sped off with a lot of dramatics. C for effort.

I walked back along Berkeley. I pulled out my phone as I approached the Art Deco doors. Susan stood in shadow under the entrance.

'Do you ever take direction?' I said.

'Nice going,' she said. 'I bet they ruined a nice set of tires.'

'Second team,' I said.

222

'Because the first is dead?' she said.

I nodded toward the intersection where I'd left my Explorer. We walked over to it. And I opened her door and then moved around to the driver's side. I started the car and we drove along Boylston toward the Public Garden and my apartment.

'They'll come back for you,' Susan said.

'Of course.'

'All in the name of macho bullshit.'

'The new king must not be slighted.'

'Is that what he is?' Susan said. 'Jackie DeMarco?'

'I'm afraid so,' I said. 'My guys, the old guys, like Gino and even Tony Marcus, have gotten soft.'

'But not you.'

'Suze, I've had worn-out parts replaced and improved the older ones. Did I not mention I've achieved my fighting weight?'

'Better than ever.'

'Maybe not better,' I said. 'But still in the game.'

Susan placed her hand on my knee as I drove. 'I have no complaints on the consistency of quality,' she said. 'How about you?'

'Ah, no,' I said. My voice sounded a bit husky.

'Shall we have a nightcap at the Four Seasons?'

'Do you want one?'

'No.'

'Do you wish to test my enduring commitment to keeping in fighting shape?'

'Yes.'

I passed the Four Seasons, cut between the Public Garden and the Common on Charles, and headed back toward my apartment on Beacon. My SUV was very speedy.

She patted my thigh with her hand and leaned in to nuzzle my neck. 'Good boy.'

About Us

In addition to No Exit Press, Oldcastle Books has a number of other imprints, including Kamera Books, Creative Essentials, Pulp! The Classics, Pocket Essentials and High Stakes Publishing > oldcastlebooks.co.uk

For more information about Crime Books go to > crimetime. co.uk

Check out the kamera film salon for independent, arthouse and world cinema > kamera.co.uk

For more information, media enquiries and review copies please contact marketing@oldcastlebooks.com